M

MIMAR

RAVENDIABLO

Agent of Kali

Miko Montgomery

ISBN 979-8-9879334-4-2

M
Mimar/Montgomery
5235 Broadway St.
Indianapolis, IN. 46220

First Edition 2010
Second Revised Edition 2021
Third Edition 2025

Printed in the United States of America

For Marie-Noelle,
my personal superhero, now and forever.

Acknowledgments

I'd like to thank Clive Barker, Leo and Pat Behnke, Chris Bishop, Lel and Jenny Kihm, Marie-Noelle Olivier, David A. Ramsdale, MA, Mary Ninneman, Richard Klonfas, Stephanie Wilson, and Annie Vaccaro, for their active support.

Book cover concept/design by Miko Montgomery.

Contents

Introduction

In recent years, the comic book superhero has attained considerable respectability. This is due, of course, to the success of films like *The Dark Knight, The Avengers, Wonder Woman* and a host of others. Once upon a time, Hollywood dismissed superheroes as kid stuff. The film *Blade* was a game changing wakeup call. Dark and brutal, it was a long way from the Power Rangers. *Blade* was a surprise hit (R-rated, too) and the first box office success for Marvel. Hollywood suddenly realized there was serious money to be made, so the industry took superheroes more seriously. The rest, as they say, is history.

Superheroes deserve respect. The comic book superhero is a modern day incarnation of Gilgamesh, Beowulf, Hercules, the Arthurian Knights, and other heroic figures of myth and legend. When one examines the roots, it becomes clear that comic book superheroes are an integral part of world culture. They resonate for a reason.

Spoiler alert. The book you're holding is not a comic book (there are no pictures). Nor is the character, Ravendiablo, a modern-day incarnation of Gilgamesh, Beowulf, and the others. *Ravendiablo: Agent of Kali* is born of an obscure source, a 2000-year old form of Chinese literature called *wuxia* (pronounced "OOH-see-ya"), a term that roughly translates to "martial chivalry" and "martial hero". Though the plots vary greatly, *wuxia* focuses on the exploits of wandering warriors who fight for justice. *Wuxia* heroes are symbols of hope who restore harmony and balance to the world.

When one thinks of a hero's journey, one immediately thinks of the work of Joseph Campbell. But while Campbell's contributions are fascinating, his view is limited. According to Campbell, the hero's journey is strictly a male adventure. *Wuxia* is noteworthy because its heroes are as likely to be female as male.

Ravendiablo: Agent of Kali is a modern day *wuxia* fairy tale. In an age when the thug has risen to become the dominant iconic image of a generation, heroes are needed now more than ever.

Miko Montgomery
Las Vegas Nevada

1

Partners in Crime

Midnight.

In a wealthy suburban neighborhood, a teenage girl crouched down behind shrubbery, hidden by shadows. Her name was Sophia Drake. Dressed in black with her face covered in black makeup, she looked more like a commando on a mission than a teenager. Sophia watched another girl several yards away, Raven Chandler. Raven's eyes, meanwhile, were focused on a containment wall standing tall in the distance. In Raven's hands was a flexible, fiber-glass pole twelve feet long. Sophia flashed a small flashlight as a signal. Raven took a deep breath and took off running toward the wall. Sophia watched with both pride and amazement as Raven used the pole to effortlessly propel herself up and over the wall like a champion pole vaulter. She landed lightly on the other side and rolled to a crouched position. Several yards away sat a mansion, a huge structure that belonged to someone with wealth and means. Though the mansion was shrouded in darkness, one light shone from an upstairs window indicating that someone was home and possibly awake. Raven ran back to the wall and removed a rope from her backpack. She fastened one end to a nearby tree and tossed the rest of it over the wall. Moments later, Sophia came scrambling over the wall and when she joined Raven, they congratulated one another with triumphant hand slaps. The girls sprinted across the lawn to the mansion. On tiptoe, they made their way along the side of the building until they arrived at the rear. Raven spotted a circuit box near a basement window. She ran over to it, closely followed by Sophia. Crouched down, she opened a small door on the box. Inside was a chaotic-looking assortment of colored wires. Raven removed a small leather pouch from her pocket, opened it, and selected a small cutting tool. She glanced at Sophia and they both giggled mischievously.

In an upstairs bedroom of the mansion, a couple lay in a luxurious bed, gazing idly at a large flat-screen television mounted to the wall. On screen, a perky, dimwitted blonde reporter was doing her best to appear both intelligent and authoritative.

"Welcome back to Channel 9 Eyewitness News. I'm Denise Daniels. On tonight's 'In Focus', we focus on the rash of unsolved burglaries that have plagued the valley. For the last three years, a burglary ring has brazenly terrorized many of our more affluent neighborhoods with losses totaling in the millions of dollars. Is there no end in sight to these crimes? To help us answer that question, we've invited Metro Chief of Police Carter James to discuss the situation. Chief, thank you for being with us this evening. What can you tell us about these crimes and the ongoing investigation?"

Next to the perky reporter sat Chief James. He was sweating profusely and obviously uncomfortable in front of the television camera. Still, he tried his best to appear both intelligent and authoritative. "Thank you for having me, Denise," he began in great earnest. "It's a pleasure to be with you and to speak directly with the great people of this great city."

"People are very concerned about these crimes, chief."

"And so are we," he said defensively. "We're doing everything in our power to solve these crimes. These crimes are an outrage, but they will be solved. And the perpetrators will pay dearly for their actions."

"Chief, many of the victims have been somewhat critical of the investigation. They point out that while the crimes have gone on for nearly three years now, the investigation has produced absolutely nothing in the way of tangible evidence. Lately, it's even been suggested that Metro may indeed be bungling the case. Isn't that correct, chief?"

"Yes, that's cor ... no, that's *not* correct," he stammered, choking on his response. "Metro does not bungle cases. There may be people in the community who feel that way, and that's their right, but I can assure you, we're committed to solving these crimes. We're following every lead, and every scrap of informa ..."

"So there *are* leads?"

The chief cleared his throat as he gathered his thoughts. "Every crime scene has observable clues which ..."

"So there *are* clues?" The reporter could sense the chief's increasing unease, but she seemed to enjoy it. "This is the first we've heard of *any* clues in this investigation. Exactly what types of clues?"

"Denise, this is an ongoing investigation," the chief continued sternly. "So it's crucial that we not compromise the success of the investigation by revealing information that might be of ..."

As the chief struggled to maintain his dignity, Raven and Sophia weren't struggling at all. They had successfully entered the mansion. Raven sat on the kitchen floor playing with the German Shepherd watchdog. The dog lay on his back with legs in the air, allowing Raven total access to his stomach for tickling. Sophia searched the kitchen cabinets for snacks.

"Can we keep him?" asked Raven as she petted the dog lovingly. "Please? You know I'll take good care of him."

Sophia laughed as she continued her search for refreshments. In the refrigerator she found a variety of snacks to choose from. Raven stood up, but the dog was not ready to follow suit. He remained on his back, stubbornly refusing to move. Raven took a fresh steak bone from her backpack and the dog immediately leapt to its feet with a wildly wagging tail. Using the bone as a lure, Raven led the drooling dog out of the kitchen and into a nearby pantry. She kissed the dog's head, gave the animal the bone, then closed the pantry door. Then she joined Sophia back in the kitchen where sandwiches and drinks awaited. After a few bites of food, the girls examined various culinary items as they determined exactly what to steal. They argued playfully about a huge pasta pot. Sophia insisted that Raven didn't need another pot for pasta, but Raven vehemently disagreed. In her mind, one could never have enough cookware. After a few swigs of juice, the girls ventured out of the kitchen and into the large dining room adjacent. A long table that stretched the length of the room was set with expensive tableware. Raven carefully examined the china, silver, and crystal and nodded approvingly. Sophia made entries in a small notebook.

The girls left the dining room and entered the den. Artworks large and small covered the walls. Antique figurines were placed throughout the room. Ornate Oriental rugs decorated the floor. Raven closely examined many of the objects, commenting on the creator, the style, and the era. Sophia made more entries in the notebook.

The girls casually strolled into the living room where they found more expensive art objects and antique furniture. Raven caressed a chair, absorbed in the artistry and the design. As Sophia continued making notations in her notebook, Raven was drawn to a huge bookcase neatly stocked with books. She removed a book and examined it. She laughed and cynically commented that the book had never even been opened. The books were for decoration only. There were several books of interest to her and she pulled them out an inch or two.

Upstairs in the master bedroom, the couple snored soundly while the special news program continued. By now, the chief was particularly stressed since the program had begun featuring telephone calls from members of the community.

"Chief, we've got time for a couple more calls," said the reporter. "Caller, you're on the air."

"Am I on the air?" asked the befuddled-sounding caller, an elderly woman and apparently somewhat hard of hearing.

"Yes, you're on the ..."

"Hello? Hello? Am I on? Hello? Can you hear me? Can you ..."

"Caller, we can hear you perfectly. You're on the air," repeated the reporter, slightly agitated. "What's your question for Chief James?"

"Thank you very much for taking my call. Chief James, can you hear me? Can you ...?"

"Caller, Chief James can hear you perfectly!" said the reporter with evident agitation. "Please, what is your question?"

"I just have one question," the caller began sweetly. "I'd just like to ask how we, as a community, can feel safe in our homes when the ranks of our police force are filled with overpaid, underqualified, incompetents like yourself?"

"Ma'am," the chief began nervously, "you certainly have a right to your ..."

"There's a big problem with law enforcement here in the Valley," the caller continued. "The collective IQ of the Police Department has yet to reach double digits." The chief stammered and squirmed as the merciless onslaught continued. "If the perpetrators of these crimes had been doughnuts, I'm quite sure that Metro would have found them by now."

As the special news report continued, Raven and Sophia entered the master bedroom and set about rummaging through closets and drawers. They were so focused on their search that they paid no attention to the snoring couple or the special news report. Standing directly in front of the television screen and using it for light, Raven appraised pieces of jewelry as Sophia made entries in her notebook.

"Thank you for calling," said the reporter to the caller. The call ended, but Chief James remained visibly shaken and even more drenched with sweat. "Chief James, surely after three years, you must have some idea as to what type of individuals are committing these crimes."

"Yes, we most certainly do," answered the chief, relieved for the opportunity to reassert his intelligence and authority. "We've recently assembled a special task force to deal with this situation and they've been working diligently around the clock. They've come up with some fascinating conclusions. First of all, it's quite clear that we're dealing with an older, highly organized, extremely sophisticated, exceptionally intelligent breed of criminal here. Truly, an elite breed of criminal. We've never seen anything quite like it. I can assure you, these are *not* your ordinary thieves by any stretch of the imagination. In fact, our special task force has concluded that the perpetrators are most likely members of some well-funded, international crime syndicate. Probably Russian mafia. It's a frightening thought, but we're dealing with it. We're not about to let these crimes continue. We're going to bring this show to an end."

A large truck with the words Midnight Movers emblazoned on the side backed up to the front door of the mansion. Another teenage girl climbed out, calmly walked to the back of the truck and opened the rear door. She removed a small loading dolly, then continued up to the front door of the mansion. She was Shanice Jackson, the third member of the gang. The front door opened and Sophia stepped back to allow Shanice entrance to the house. The foyer was crammed with items selected for removal. Sophia took the dolly and handed Shanice a plate of food. As Shanice ate, she examined the booty admiringly and nodded her approval. Stacked in the foyer were furniture, paintings, rolled rugs, and numerous boxes filled with artwork and other expensive goods. Shanice smiled as she watched Raven across the room, carefully filling a box with books. Finishing her snack, she joined Sophia in loading the truck. The girls worked with calm efficiency as if they had all the time in the world. When the truck was filled from floor to ceiling with loot, the girls exited the mansion, climbed into the truck, and drove off into the night.

Upstairs in the master bedroom, there was complete silence save for the snoring of the couple. Eventually, the male half awoke. Bleary-eyed, he climbed out of bed to visit the toilet. As he stumbled toward the bathroom, he saw something that jarred him completely awake. The large flat-screen television was *gone*.

* * *

 RAVENDIABLO

The hideouts of thieves reveal much about the thieves themselves. They reveal, of course, their favorite flavors of loot ... art, antiques, jewels, electronics, or, sometimes, automobiles. But they reveal far more as well. A hideout reveals *mentality*.

The Raven gang was headquartered in a warehouse on Highland Avenue, a street just west of the Las Vegas Strip. Highland Avenue was the complete antithesis of the Strip—subdued, low key and devoid of neon and manic activity. The street was lined with nondescript businesses and blank-faced industrial buildings. Traffic consisted of delivery vans and semi trucks. Sophia's father was a wealthy executive and owned several warehouses in the area. When Sophia turned sixteen, she didn't ask for a car like most teenagers. She asked for a building, explaining that a warehouse would be her "treehouse" ... a place where she and her friends could hang out and stay out of trouble. It seemed both logical and harmless enough and Sophia was quite persuasive. Her father bought the line and gladly complied. As long as she kept her grades in good standing, it was her private, personal space and her father never snooped. Little did he know that this "treehouse" contained millions of dollars in stolen art, antiques, jewels, electronics, furniture, and other items.

The exterior of the hideout in no way called attention to itself. The structure sat several yards back from the street, tucked away from view and easy to miss. There was no wall or fence around the building, which hardly seemed to need such containment or protection. Only a keen eye would have noticed the elaborate security system the girls had installed themselves. Small, strategically placed hidden cameras provided a multitude of "eyes in the sky". Many motion detectors were scattered about and likewise well hidden. No one was getting into the building who didn't belong there. The sound of barking dogs inside the warehouse when any strangers approached discouraged the curious.

In stark contrast to the outside, the interior of the warehouse was anything but nondescript. The way the hideout was decorated, it would have been obvious to any outsider that the girls not only had expensive tastes, but also took pride in displaying their lavish goods. All the booty had been meticulously arranged with great style and flair. An interior decorator or film set designer would have been impressed. Every inch of floor space was covered with exquisitely ornate Oriental rugs. There was a wide variety of furniture, easily enough to fill a furniture store, albeit a very elite furniture store. Expensive couches, love seats, tables, chairs, lamps, and even statuary were carefully and artistically placed throughout the warehouse. There was also a long wooden table with high-back chairs that looked like something fit for royalty. Most of the wall space was covered from floor to ceiling with paintings of every conceivable size and style.

But there were other goodies as well. One area of the warehouse was clearly designated for homemaking pursuits and was filled with various household and kitchen items. There was a huge freezer, a couple of refrigerators, and an immense stove, all of which had been stolen from fine restaurants. Shelves were stocked with pots, pans,

 RAVENDIABLO

china, silver, and crystal. Cupboards were jampacked with food items. An opposite corner of the warehouse resembled a showroom for electronic gadgets. Several display cases were filled with expensive cameras and audio equipment. A large table was lined with laptop computers. Other display cases housed a wide assortment of watches and jewelry.

In the lounge area was a long couch facing a wall covered with flat screen televisions, including the one recently stolen from the mansion. Shanice sat at one end of the couch, Sophia at the other. Armed with a remote control unit in each hand, Shanice impatiently channel-surfed several television sets simultaneously. Sophia was engrossed in a video game. The noise in the lounge area was deafening.

In the farthest corner of the warehouse was Raven's personal space, her lair. She sat in a gargantuan, high-back leather chair that looked like a throne. The mammoth desk in front of her was equally imposing. Made of finely carved oak wood, the desk and chair had been stolen from the home of a multi-millionaire businessman. The desk was blanketed with open books. Beautiful floor-to-ceiling bookshelves lined the walls around her, laden with more books. Several feet away lay Raven's bed, a simple futon. The stark simplicity of the bed stood in direct contrast to everything else around her. Sleep was clearly of little importance to her. The futon's bedding, however, was fastidiously made with no trace of a wrinkle. Soft, exotic music played from an unseen stereo.

Sleeping peacefully at Raven's feet were several dogs of various breeds, or no breed. Some were strays she had taken in. Others were liberated from burglarized homes where there had been signs of obvious neglect on the part of the owner. A single black cat strolled along the edge of the desk, eyeing the dogs below suspiciously. Raven, however, was focused on a large book resting in her lap. Finally, she glanced at her watch and realized that it was time for dinner. She rose from her desk chair and carefully stepped over the dogs that stubbornly refused to move. The door on a large cabinet behind her was slightly ajar. Before closing it completely, she peeked inside. The cabinet was filled from top to bottom with rows and rows of cash, all neatly wrapped and separated by denomination. Closing the door, she made her way to the kitchen where she began preparing the evening meal.

Tonight's dish was spaghetti, boiled in the large pot stolen from the mansion, with salad and French bread. As the food simmered on the stove, Raven set the immense table with fine china, crystal glassware, and ornate silverware. Raven worked with calm efficiency in the same way as she burglarized homes and businesses. She didn't mind that Shanice and Sophia were too engrossed in television and games to offer assistance. The warehouse was both hideout and nest, and Raven relished her chosen role of mother hen. But like a true mother hen, she was forceful when she needed to be. Shanice and Sophia felt the vibe simultaneously, looking first at each other, then turning their heads to find Raven standing behind them with her hands on her hips.

"Dinner is served," she said sternly. "Now."

She wasn't kidding, either.

Shanice and Sophia knew never to keep Raven waiting for dinner, or anything else for that matter. They immediately rose and rushed off to the bathroom to wash for dinner.

* * *

Raven sat at her usual spot at the long table, dead center, with Shanice and Sophia sitting at opposite ends. Empty plates with scraps of food sat before both Raven and Sophia. Shanice was still very much actively involved in her meal. Licking her fingers, she rose and walked down to the center of the table for the Tabasco sauce. Noticing half a slice of bread on Raven's plate, she snatched it, returned to her seat, and resumed eating.

"I vote we liberate a smaller dinner table next time," Shanice said between bites. "I'm tired of crossing the street to get to the salt shaker. This is ridiculous. This isn't a table for normal people. This is a table is for the Last Supper."

Raven and Sophia laughed. Raven gathered up the plates and glasses and headed off to the kitchen. Sophia rose and joined her there. Shanice remained at the table and continued eating. She glanced at her watch then abruptly jumped up and sprinted over to the lounge area.

"What's for dessert?" Shanice asked as she picked up a remote unit, activated one of the televisions, and began surfing madly.

"You're like some junkie," said Raven from the kitchen with mock disgust. "You can't be away from that box for a minute. I think that flicker rate has got you hypnotized."

When Shanice located the weather channel, she immediately stopped surfing and plopped down on the couch, intently focused on the screen. A young, handsome weatherman stood before an animated map of the world describing the weather conditions for the coming week.

"The only thing that's got me hypnotized is Poindexter here," said Shanice with a sly grin. "He's as square as a box, but that's the way I like 'em."

The weather forecast ended far too soon for Shanice and she sighed with obvious disappointment. A local commercial came on advertising an upcoming special event.

"Stop dreaming about being a millionaire," said the animated announcer. "Now learn the skills to become a millionaire. Let Legs Diamond show you how."

"Come here quick!" Shanice called out.

Raven and Sophia hurried over and joined Shanice. When Raven saw the screen, her displeasure was obvious and she made no attempt to disguise her feelings. The man onscreen was the world famous tycoon, Legs Diamond, renowned for his wealth, his ego, and his oddly, inexplicable hair style, dyed blond and swept in several directions at once.

"Legs Diamond will be appearing this Friday night at The Phoenix Hotel and he's bringing a lifetime of money-making secrets with him," continued the announcer. "Good seats are still available. You won't want to miss this once-in-a-lifetime opportunity."

"You called me over here for this?" Raven said with a sneer. "You know how much I hate this prick. If he's so rich, why can't he pay somebody to fix that hair of his? He's a joke."

Shanice and Sophia giggled.

"That hair may be a joke, but his bank account is absolutely for real," said Sophia. "My father knows people who work for him. Diamond's a joke but he definitely ain't broke. He's so loaded it's ridiculous. And he never travels with less than a half mil in play money. *Cash* play money. He's a big freak and loves to party."

Shanice turned off the television. The warehouse was plunged into silence, but the mutual epiphany was loud and clear. These three partners in crime were *of one mind* and they instantly understood the implications of Sophia's words. They smiled simultaneously.

* * *

Dressed in the white uniform of a kitchen worker, Shanice pushed a service cart down a hotel hallway. The cart was completely covered with a large linen cloth. On top of the cart was a bouquet of flowers, a bottle of champagne and a huge basket filled with cheeses, chocolates, and other goodies. Shanice stopped at a door and knocked. A slender, sandy-haired man opened the door—Legs Diamond's personal assistant.

"May I help you?" he asked, confused by Shanice's presence. "We didn't order room service."

"I'm really sorry to bother you," said Shanice. "This is a gift from hotel management for Mr. Diamond. Tickets for the show have been selling really well and hotel attendance is way up, too. This is just our way of ..."

"Okay, just wheel it in, okay?"

Shanice wheeled the cart into the large suite and the assistant closed the door behind her. He briefly glanced at the various items on the cart, but his mind was elsewhere. His cell phone rang and he answered it.

"Yeah, it's me," he said. "I'm leaving right now. I'll be meeting with Mr. Diamond in the showroom in about twenty minutes so get there as soon as you can. We've got some last-minute details to go over before the seminar tonight. There were some glitches in the rehearsal this morning and we don't want any more problems. Everything has got to be smooth for tonight, do you understand me? We're being broadcast live all over the world."

Shanice scrutinized the lavish suite. It looked like an old school, retro bachelor pad from the Rat Pack era. A door leading into the bedroom drew her attention.

"I don't care what you have to do to get it right," continued the assistant, "just get it right. I'll see you later. And don't be late."

He ended his conversation and stepped over to a mirror to adjust his tie and brush his hair. In the mirror he saw Shanice standing awkwardly, waiting for a tip. He put on his sport coat and an insincere smile, then took Shanice by the arm and escorted her to the door.

"Thanks again for bringing this up. Mr. Diamond will be very pleased," he said as he opened the suite door. On a nearby table was a stack of pamphlets. He snatched one up and handed it to Shanice.

"And please ... take this," he said. "Mr. Diamond would want you to have it. It's the most valuable tip he could ever give you."

Shanice looked at the pamphlet which was called *My Tips For Wealth*. She faked a smile of her own. The assistant ushered Shanice out of the suite and followed close behind. At the exact moment he closed the door, Raven and Sophia scrambled from beneath the tablecloth covering the cart. After a quick survey of the living room portion of the suite, they rushed into the bedroom. Several suitcases rested on a dresser beside the circular, king-sized bed and Sophia rummaged through each of them. Raven opened a closet and found several expensive suits hanging from a rack. Lined up on the floor were numerous pairs of shoes. There was something else as well. A box labeled "Books" caught Raven's curious eye. She stared at it suspiciously. Sophia and Shanice always said Raven had an extra sense which they called "Raven radar". Raven grabbed the box and carried it over to the bed. When she opened it, she saw what appeared to be numerous copies of Diamond's latest book, *Wealth By Stealth*. Raven removed a book and saw that the box actually contained neatly wrapped bundles of cash. Raven haphazardly tossed Diamond's book onto the bed and it landed on top of a television remote, activating it. On a wall across the room, a large flat-screen television suddenly sprung to life and the room was filled with the sounds of whipping and moaning. On the screen, Legs Diamond was seen dressed

as a schoolgirl. He was strapped face down to a crude torture apparatus. An extremely obese black man dressed as
a dominatrix towered over him wielding a whip.

"You've been bad again, haven't you, Gwendolyn?"
asked the dominatrix sternly between strokes. "Don't lie
to me!"

"Yes, *mistress*, I've been bad. I've been so bad," wept
Diamond. "I'm a bad girl. I just can't help myself."

The dominatrix then unleashed a violent series of
blows that made Diamond squeal with pleasure.

"Then bark like a dog!" the domme ordered.

Diamond made a series of strange animal noises, none
of which seemed particularly canine.

"I said like a dog, you dumb bitch!" The dominatrix
flogged Diamond mercilessly, much to his orgasmic delight.

Raven and Sophia fell on the bed howling with laughter. Then they quickly refocused on the task at hand and
hurried out of the bedroom with the box of money. Still
giggling, the girls changed into kitchen clothes that, like
themselves, had been conveniently hidden beneath the
tablecloth. They placed the box of money under the cart
and were preparing to leave when Raven's radar picked up
something of interest. On a table beside a stack of pamphlets, she spotted a red DVD case marked "Seminar Presentation". She looked back toward the bedroom door.

And she smiled *diabolically*.

* * *

With the afternoon sun high above, Shanice sat behind the wheel of a sedan on the roof of the hotel parking structure. Nervously awaiting the arrival of her friends, she chain-smoked while watching people come and go. Finally, Raven and Sophia emerged from an elevator several yards away. Shanice immediately brightened and started the engine. Raven and Sophia had changed out of their kitchen uniforms and were now dressed in their own clothing. Carrying an innocent-looking shopping bag, they calmly approached the waiting vehicle and climbed into the backseat. Shanice drove off unhurriedly and made her way down through the winding corridors of the parking structure. She exited the structure and drove away like a little old lady. Soon the car was cruising on the Vegas Strip, far from the scene of the crime. Shanice handed Raven and Sophia bottles of juice and they all settled back with sighs of relief. Shanice focused on the road and her driving. Sophia played with a hand-held game device. Raven absentmindedly stared out the window, her thoughts elsewhere.

"I need something to eat," said Shanice.

"So what else is new?" answered Raven and Sophia simultaneously.

"I want some pancakes to start with," Shanice continued. "Then let's cruise out to Red Rock later and watch the sun go down. It's a perfect night for it. It's going to be cool this evening. Cool with a high of 87 and a low of 78. Chance of intermittent showers later, followed by ..."

The girls erupted in laughter.

"Hey, weather is important," insisted Shanice defensively. "There's nothing wrong with being on top of the weather. I'd like to be *more* on top of the weather ... if you know what I mean."

"Pancakes it is," said Sophia. "I could eat something, too."

Soon the girls were far from the bustle of the Strip and cruising through a quiet residential neighborhood. As the car idled at an intersection waiting for the red light to change, Raven noticed a small public park several yards in the distance. She smiled as she watched the carefree children playing happily. Then Raven's radar picked up something strange ... and troubling. A well-dressed middle-aged man walked hand in hand with a young girl perhaps eight years old. His stride was purposeful as he led her away from the play area and toward parked cars. The little girl seemed confused. Though the man tried to appear normal and nonchalant, there was something suspicious in his body language. He constantly gazed around him, as if to make sure he wasn't being watched. Only he *was* being watched. Raven watched in mounting dread as the man led the child to an expensive sedan. He opened the rear passenger door, seized the child, and literally threw her onto the back seat. He calmly closed the door, walked around to the driver side, and climbed in. As he leisurely drove away, Raven shrieked as if she had been stabbed, completely startling her friends. The abductor was now heading off in the opposite direction, unseen by anyone but Raven.

"What's wrong with you?" yelled Shanice angrily, totally shaken by the sudden outburst. Sophia's wide-eyed shock echoed her sentiments.

Raven jerked Shanice to one side and scrambled from the back seat and into the driver's seat. She violently turned the steering wheel, floored the accelerator, and sped off after the abductor. Shanice and Sophia screamed in unison as Raven narrowly missed a collision with an oncoming car. Raven barely flinched. She turned onto the street that the abductor had taken and spotted his sedan in the distance. There was no time to explain to her confused friends what she had witnessed—she had driving to do. Raven's face reflected her crazed determination as she pursued the sedan. She steadily increased her speed, weaving in and out of traffic with controlled abandon. Soon, the abductor was only two car lengths ahead of her.

Unaware he was being followed, the abductor crossed an intersection and cruised through a yellow light. When the light turned red, Raven should have stopped. Instead, she stomped the accelerator and ran the red light, narrowly avoiding the crossing traffic and causing her friends to scream once more. Shanice and Sophia were witnessing a side of Raven that they had never seen before. Raven was *possessed*. The abductor was still ahead by two car lengths, and Raven could now see the kidnapped little girl frantically looking out the back window and crying hysterically. The sight of the frightened child ignited a fuse inside of Raven. She floored the accelerator enabling her to quickly move from behind to beside the sedan.

Now the abductor knew he had been identified and he increased his own speed. As the cars raced alongside one another, Raven glared over at him with eyes ablaze. She jerked the steering wheel and slammed her car into the side of the sedan. The frightened man tried to move ahead, but Raven wasn't about to let him get away. She slammed into the car again, only this time with more force. Shanice and Sophia continued screaming as the dangerous drama unfolded, but Raven was calm. She didn't appear to be frightened at all. Approaching police sirens could be heard somewhere in the distance.

Raven slammed into the sedan once more, only this time the abductor lost control of the vehicle and crashed into the side of a parked car. Though momentarily stunned by the impact, he quickly collected himself, leapt from the car, and took off running down the street. Watching him run in the distance, Raven nodded and smiled. He wasn't going anywhere. She floored the accelerator and burned rubber, turning her vehicle into a missile. The car hurtled into the man and the force of the impact literally sent him flying. He spun several times in midair before slamming to the ground in a bloodied, broken heap. He managed to struggle to his knees and Raven was happy for another opportunity to strike. Again, she floored the accelerator and this time, she ran the man over completely. Then she shifted the car into reverse and backed over the man for good measure. Raven shifted the car back into drive and prepared to run him over yet again, but both Shanice and Sophia physically restrained her. By now, the cops had arrived on the scene with weapons drawn. Shanice and Sophia cried hysterically, but Raven sat without emotion, staring straight ahead. She was in another world completely.

2

Oakwood Garden

Grim-faced and sullen, Raven sat beside her court-appointed attorney in a packed courtroom. Her attorney looked both inexperienced and petrified as he listened to the prosecutor deliver his closing remarks to the jury. Raven's eyes reflected the helpless rage that burned inside of her. Sitting beside her attorney's open briefcase was a large, leather bound edition of Black's Law Dictionary. She glanced over at her attorney to witness him sweating nervously and occasionally chewing his nails. Raven rolled her eyes in dismay.

Looking down from her bench, Judge Durgan watched the proceedings closely. She was a mature judge with stern, yet caring, eyes. She kept her eyes focused on Raven as the prosecutor presented his case. Judge Durgan was enthralled by the fierce young girl sitting before her. The rest of the courtroom was mesmerized by the oratorical skill of the prosecutor—none more so than the prosecutor himself, an arrogant windbag who clearly loved being on stage and the center of attention.

"Ladies and gentlemen of this jury, you have heard the terrifying testimony," he began slowly and deliberately, "and like me, you were chilled to the marrow of your bones. Because, ladies and gentlemen, we have been *violated*. You and I and this wonderful city of Las Vegas. We have all been repeatedly violated in the most crude and unspeakable ways. And the perpetrator of this heinous violation is seated before you right now. And her name ... is Raven Chandler."

The jury was primarily comprised of elderly people and they looked at Raven with a combination of disgust and terror. They seemed particularly susceptible to the prosecutor's rhetoric and he was well aware of it. It only encouraged his excruciating overacting.

"Do not be fooled by her gender or her youth," he continued. As he spoke, he looked at Raven as if she were a serial killer. "Because seated before you now is not an innocent young girl, but a dangerous and hardened criminal. And she must be dealt with accordingly."

The prosecutor's vocal delivery suddenly segued into a more southern-fried, evangelical tone. Judge Durgan finally looked away from Raven and stared at the pompous prosecutor in disbelief.

"For three years," he continued with a southern drawl, "Raven Chandler and her gang of vicious criminals have conducted a reign of terror on our good, decent, God-fearing community. They broke into our homes, stripped us of our dignity, and left us naked ... and violated. And the perpetrator of these vile acts is seated before you now."

The prosecutor paused a moment, as if he were emotionally overcome by the power of his own words. He took a deep breath and forced himself to continue. Judge Durgan rolled her eyes.

"Ladies and gentlemen of the jury, look at her. What you see before you now ... is a *failure!*"

Raven suddenly looked up at the prosecutor as if he had plunged a knife in her heart. The wily prosecutor somehow instinctively knew that the word "failure" would wound her deeply. And it did. It was the one word that Raven could *never* bear. She gritted her teeth as she fought back tears. Judge Durgan focused her eyes back upon Raven, struggling to maintain her illusion of impartiality in the case.

"That's right," the prosecutor continued. "A complete failure. Failure on the part of her parents to instill goodness and righteousness in her. Failure on the part of our society to make up for the failure of her parents. But most of all, what you see before you now is failure on the part of Raven Chandler herself, failure to control the evil impulses that permeate her wicked young flesh."

Raven could barely control the rage welling up inside of her.

"But you, ladies and gentlemen of the jury, you will not fail. Because you have heard the terrifying testimony and you were chilled to the marrow of your bones. So you cannot and you must not fail. You must send a message loud and clear. A message to our God-fearing, peaceful, law-abiding community that we will not tolerate lawlessness and criminality in any form. But most of all, you must send a message to this ... this ... Raven Chandler. You must tell her that in Sin City, sin will not go unpunished! She must pay, and pay dearly, for all of her damnable deeds!"

Judge Durgan looked at the jury, aware of how hopelessly influenced they were by the prosecutor's performance. The prosecutor knew it as well. He could hardly contain the sense of pride he felt for grinding Raven into hamburger.

"So do your duty this day, ladies and gentlemen of the jury. You must convict Raven Chandler. This incorrigible liar, this irredeemable thief, and this attempted *murderer*!"

Raven erupted and screamed in fury. She leaped up from her chair and grabbed her attorney's law dictionary. When he attempted to subdue her, she clubbed him with the book and knocked him to the floor. She charged at the prosecutor who stood frozen with genuine fear. Holding the dictionary in one hand, she snatched the prosecutor by the tie and slung him to the floor. Raven straddled him and pummeled his head with the dictionary. Pounding her gavel angrily, Judge Durgan demanded order in the court as several police officers rushed out to restrain Raven. It wasn't easy. Raven managed to beat down several officers before she was finally restrained. It took four officers to carry her out of the courtroom kicking and screaming.

* * *

Judge Durgan sat at her desk, engrossed in the file folder spread out before her. It was Raven's file. The Judge picked up a photo of Raven and stared at it closely. There was a knock at the door.

"Come in," she said.

Two officers entered the office and Raven was with them. She was literally draped in chains. Judge Durgan looked at her and immediately rose to her feet in fury.

"Take that shit off of her right now!" she ordered.

The officers were clearly shocked by both her request and the intensity of her anger. Somewhat confused, they dutifully complied and removed Raven's shackles.

"Now leave us alone," the Judge said with eyes still blazing. "And if I think I need some assistance, I'll let you know!"

The officers turned and exited the office, carefully closing the door behind them. Judge Durgan sat back down. Raven stood perfectly still, trying to hide her emotions. She was visibly shaken. She stared at Judge Durgan, not quite sure what to expect next. Judge Durgan tried to hide her emotions as well. Her heart was breaking for the young girl standing before her. It was all she could do to keep from rushing over and comforting her. She forced herself to continue playing the part of judge.

"As for you young lady ... sit down!" she ordered sternly.

Raven slowly walked over to a chair in front of Judge Durgan's desk. She sat down and stared at the floor. Judge Durgan stared at Raven in sadness and admiration.

"So what am I supposed to do with you?" Judge Durgan asked with convincing gruffness. "In my twenty-five years on the bench, I have never had an outburst like the one I witnessed in my courtroom this morning. I'm ready to kick your ass out of the world, cat burglar!"

Raven didn't answer, but continued staring at the floor.

"I don't think you understand what's going on here. So let me explain it to you. And I'll go nice and slow to make sure you get it. You're in deep *shit*, girlfriend. I can't even see the top of your head!"

Raven took a deep breath as she prepared herself for more.

"You and your girls have done a lot of damage over the last few years. Three million in stolen goods. That's a record, by the way, in case you're interested. Worse than that, you've made Metro look like idiots. So they want to nail your little half-slick ass to the wall. They want to make an example out of you and save whatever face they think they've got left. Do you understand what I'm saying?"

Raven was silent. Suddenly Judge Durgan exploded in genuine anger.

"Am I talking to the wall in here or what?" she yelled. "Do you hear me talking to you?"

Raven nodded sadly. "Yes," she answered softly. "Yes, ma'am."

Raven's emotional armor was slowly disintegrating and Judge Durgan knew it. The judge tried to hide her pity, determined to play her role right to the end. It was difficult.

"You're not as lucky as your girls. As you know, they come from money. *Big* money. Their families can afford *real* lawyers, not like that court-appointed knucklehead you've got. Their families have already bought their freedom. Your foster parents haven't even shown up yet." Judge Durgan sat back in her chair and sighed wearily. "Somebody has got to go down for this nonsense. And I'll give you one guess as to who that somebody is. You're looking at some serious time, cat burglar. Ten years."

Raven could restrain herself no longer. She buried her face in her hands and sobbed violently. Judge Durgan gripped her desk to keep herself from running over to Raven. Clenched, she waited as the girl wept. After having drained herself of tears, Raven sat in silence once again, staring at the floor. Finally, to break the heavy mood, Judge Durgan picked up a remote and activated a television set across the room. A news report came on, detailing the bizarre happenings at the recent Legs Diamond seminar.

"Legendary millionaire entrepreneur Legs Diamond is an international laughingstock following the bizarre turn of events at a recent seminar that took place in Las Vegas. It seems as though the wrong DVD was presented, and people were treated to a side of Mr. Diamond they had never seen before."

As Judge Durgan watched the screen, the office was filled with the sounds of Legs Diamond's freaky encounter.

"Bark like a dog ... I said, like a dog, you dumb bitch!"

The judge watched and listened in amazement for a few moments, then turned off the television. She looked over at Raven with mock bewilderment. Then she burst out laughing. Raven didn't laugh but smiled diabolically.

The judge sighed, then became serious again. She cared about Raven and there was little need to hide it any longer.

"That little girl *was* being abducted."

Raven looked up at Judge Durgan and their eyes locked.

"Your instincts were right," continued the Judge, no longer hiding her admiration. "I don't know how you knew, but you knew. If you hadn't stepped in the way you had, who knows what would've happened. Her parents are obviously grateful. More than grateful and, luckily for you, they just happen to be influential people. *Very* influential. They're the kind of people you need to know in this town. They've got jack ... and juice."

Judge Durgan settled back in her chair and looked deeply into Raven's eyes. "I've got juice, too. I've been on the bench for over twenty-five years and that means something in this town. Metro may want you to go down, but I've got other ideas. Technically, you're still a minor. So I'm in a position to work some deals behind the scenes. Vegas is all about favors and a lot of people in this town owe me big time." Then Judge Durgan's eyes blazed with a mother's love and she made no attempt to conceal the depth of her feelings. "No one is going to lay a hand on you," she said with supreme confidence. "I'll make sure of that."

Raven looked up at Judge Durgan hopefully.

"There are all kinds of ways to pay your debt to society. Instead of some jive-ass juvenile facility, you're going someplace else," said the judge with a devious smile. "Someplace that's going to do you some good. I suppose you could call it ... a rest home. As wired as you seem to be, you could use a little rest."

Raven looked confused. She also looked relieved. Judge Durgan looked triumphant.

* * *

With the merciless afternoon sun beaming high above, a small passenger van cruised along a dirt country road. Raven was the only passenger. She stared blankly out the window at the desert landscape, her mind elsewhere. The van driver was a middle-aged man with a perpetual grin. He glanced in the rearview mirror from time to time, both curious and concerned. It was obvious that Raven was troubled. He decided to try and pull her out of her shell.

"You know, I've read all about you," he said watching her closely for some kind of reaction. "You're pretty famous. Or, well, infamous. I'm originally from Buffalo. Nice place, too. They have four seasons there: almost winter, winter, still winter, and construction. I moved to Las Vegas years ago to make a brand-new start. Overnight, I became a desert rat. I love it here. The desert, I mean. I don't much care for Las Vegas, but the land it's built on, that's different. A lot different."

Raven remained silent, staring out the window, absorbed in thought.

"Most people don't know it, but the desert is a very special place. A spiritual place. Strange place to build a city of sin, that's for sure. People have always gone into the desert to find themselves, to search for truth. And wisdom. It's an ancient tradition. Sin is for distraction, but desert is for … well … direction. And sometimes, redemption."

Raven didn't respond. She didn't even seem to hear him.

"You're going to like Oakwood," he continued. "It's a for-real oasis in the middle of the desert. Laid back, relaxed. And the people there, they're very … well … *different*. You'll see."

The van passed a small sign that read Oakwood Garden and entered the courtyard of a sprawling compound. There were many buildings, each with its own highly distinctive style of architecture. There was an English manor house, a western-style ranch house complete with stables, a Swiss chalet, and even a small Greek temple. And on it went. As a result, Oakwood Garden both looked and felt *surreal* ... like the backlot of a bizarre movie studio in an alternate dimension. It wasn't frightening, but it was eerie.

There was a large fountain in the middle of the courtyard, which appeared to be the hub of the compound and the center of activity. Some of the residents milled about on canes and walkers and in wheelchairs. Others needed no assistance at all. Animals ran freely. Everyone was watched over by a smiling staff wearing brightly colored Hawaiian shirts. The driver parked the van near a tall building that looked like a Victorian hotel. He climbed out and hurried over to open the door for Raven. She climbed out of the van and forced herself back to reality. The driver removed Raven's suitcase from the van and set it down beside her. He looked at her as if he wanted to say something reassuring to her, as if he wanted to make some kind of positive connection before they parted. Finally, he found the right words.

"You'll be a very different person when you leave here," he said. And for once, he wasn't smiling.

Raven finally looked at him. His eyes were serious. He placed his hand on her shoulder warmly, as if for good luck, then turned and climbed back into the van. He drove off leaving Raven in a huge cloud of dust. When the dust settled, Raven found herself standing beside a distinguished, well-dressed man of middle age. He seemed pleased to see her.

"Hello, Raven," he said, beaming. "Welcome to Oakwood Garden. I'm Mr. Freeman."

He extended his hand and Raven shook it. His smile was kind and inviting, and he looked at Raven as if she were someone special.

"We're so glad to have you join us," he said. "Please, follow me."

Raven picked up her bag and walked beside Mr. Freeman as he led her toward the Victorian building. The residents and staff watched Raven closely as she passed them, almost as if she were some kind of celebrity. Mr. Freeman led Raven up a stone walkway to a gargantuan oak door that looked like something out of a fairy tale, like the door to an enchanted castle. He turned the huge knob and opened the door, revealing a stunning interior that, much like the outside, was *otherworldly*. Raven followed him into what appeared to be the lobby of a grand hotel from another era. The huge chandelier hanging high above looked as if it belonged in a royal palace. The couches, chairs, and other furniture were unusually large and outlandishly ornate. Gigantic, colorful paintings decorated the walls. There were several marble statues and a suit of armor. Brightly colored rugs covered the floor. Sweet, angelic music filled the air, courtesy of a woman playing the harp. The lobby was filled with residents and a few staff, and they all stared at Raven curiously as she passed by.

An old black woman crowned with a mane of outrageously unkempt hair sat in a wheelchair. She was dressed in flamboyant colors and wore a red medallion around her neck. As Raven passed her, the old woman suddenly extended her cane in Raven's path and caused her to trip and fall. The woman laughed maniacally at the outcome. Mr. Freeman was both shocked and angered by the act.

"How dare you do such a thing!" he scolded. "You should be ashamed of yourself! This is our guest!"

Raven angrily jumped back to her feet and turned to face the old woman. The woman glared right back at her, then stuck out her long, red tongue at Raven tauntingly. This only angered Raven more and she seemed seconds away from lashing out. The old woman spun her wheelchair around and rolled away cackling with glee.

"I'm really sorry about that, Raven," said Mr. Freeman with genuine embarrassment. "I don't know why she did that. I don't know what got into her. I'm so sorry."

Raven took a deep breath and regained her composure. Mr. Freeman put his arm around her and led her up a marble staircase and down a long hallway. He stopped at room number 9.

"Welcome to your new home," he said with a smile.

Mr. Freeman opened the door and led Raven inside. Her displeasure was instantaneous. The room was Spartan in the extreme. There was a bed, a dresser, and a chair ... and nothing else. Even the floor was bare. Mr. Freeman noticed Raven's disapproval.

"I know it's a far cry from the way you've been accustomed to living, but hopefully, you'll get used to it. You're certainly free to decorate it in any way you please. You can do anything you want with it. We very much want you to feel at home here at Oakwood. This is your home now. Please try and give it a chance. Okay?"

Raven was too choked up to answer and nodded instead.

"You might want to get some rest before dinner," Mr. Freeman said as he prepared to leave. "I'll come back for you later."

Mr. Freeman turned and left the room, closing the door behind him. Raven continued staring at the room in disbelief. Finally, she put down her suitcase, fell on the bed, and sobbed uncontrollably.

* * *

The Oakwood dining room was teeming with energy. Sitting at tables, residents laughed and talked amongst themselves. Staff members assisted other residents to their seats. As Mr. Freeman and Raven entered, all chatter immediately died down. Raven once again became the center of attention with all eyes looking in her direction. Mr. Freeman led Raven to an empty table and they seated themselves. Raven was more than aware of the stares, and she was clearly uneasy. Mr. Freeman sensed her discomfort and took her by the hand as he reassured her.

"You didn't know you were a celebrity, did you?" he asked with a smile. "They don't mean to stare, they'll get used to you soon enough." Mr. Freeman thought for a moment, then laughed. "They'll have plenty of time!"

Raven didn't laugh. For a moment, Mr. Freeman seemed embarrassed by his joke, aware that perhaps he might have hurt Raven's feelings. He then quickly turned to other matters.

"Raven, I do need to explain a few things so that we're on the same page. You were sent to Oakwood for a reason. This is your new home and we very much want you to feel at home here. But it's also your new job. You'll be assigned a variety of duties and responsibilities, and you'll be expected to perform to the best of your abilities. Do you understand?"

Raven looked directly at Mr. Freeman and her demeanor was every bit as serious as his.

"Yes, sir, I understand," she answered.

Mr. Freeman beamed at her response and her attitude. "Good."

The staff began serving the evening meal. A Chinese woman dressed in white kitchen clothes put a plate of food before Raven. She looked at Raven with large eyes.

"Raven, I'd like to introduce you to someone very special here at Oakwood," said Mr. Freeman proudly. "She runs the kitchen here, among other things. Her name is Mao Ying."

Mao Ying wiped her hand on her apron before extending it out to Raven. When they shook hands, Raven immediately noticed the power in her grip.

"Pleased to meet you," said Raven.

"Nice to meet you, too," responded Mao Ying sweetly, "I hope we can be friends."

"Oh, I'm sure you will be," Mr. Freeman interjected. "I was just explaining to Raven that she's going to be a busy young lady from now on." Mr. Freeman looked at Raven with a sly smile. "Mao Ying is in need of some good, hard-working kitchen help. And you've just been drafted. Understood?"

"No problem," answered Raven.

"And if I'm not mistaken," Mr. Freeman continued, "tonight's meal is very special. Mao Ying prepared it in your honor, Raven."

Raven looked up at Mao Ying who continued watching her closely. Mao Ying was obviously waiting for Raven to try the food. Raven took a bite and was pleasantly surprised.

"This is great," said Raven.

Mao Ying looked relieved. "Thank you so much," she said, genuinely touched by the positive response. "I'm glad you like it. There's more if you want it."

Mao Ying turned and hurried off to other duties as Mr. Freeman smiled at Raven proudly. Finally, he stood and held up his water glass to make a toast.

"Ladies and gentlemen," he began, "as many of you know, a new resident has come to join us here at Oakwood. You'll be seeing a lot of her. So I want you all to make her feel at home. She's now a part of our family. Please join me in welcoming Miss Raven Chandler."

The room erupted in applause, and Raven was both surprised and humbled by the warm response. Mr. Freeman encouraged her to stand and she complied somewhat shyly. Suddenly, a piece of food came flying across the room and struck Raven squarely on her forehead. Raven scraped it off and angrily looked to find the culprit. Several feet away sat the wild-haired, black woman who had tripped her earlier. The woman smiled mischievously at Raven, then stuck out her long, red tongue tauntingly. Raven glared at her angrily.

* * *

Early the next morning, Raven entered the Oakwood kitchen ready for work and it showed in her temperament. No longer grim and sullen, Raven was resigned to her fate. Besides, her fate could have been worse. Though she no longer lived in freedom and splendor with her girls, she wasn't in the juvenile detention center either. Oakwood was her home now, and Raven was determined to make the best of it.

The kitchen was deserted, giving the curious Raven an opportunity to examine the place freely. The kitchen was beyond immaculate. Everything shone. The stove, the refrigerators, the freezers, the sinks, the cabinets, and even the floor sparkled and glistened. It was radiantly clear that Mao Ying took great pride in her work environment. She was fastidious in the extreme, a trait that certainly appealed to Raven. On the walls were a variety of pictures, most of them relating to food and nutrition. The only exception was a single poster of Bruce Lee. Raven smiled when she saw it, correct in her assumption that even the shy Mao Ying was capable of a crush.

Noises coming from outside caught Raven's attention, and she went over to an open window to investigate. In a spacious area behind the kitchen, Raven saw Mao Ying actively engaged in the elaborate movements of some martial arts form. Mao Ying was clearly an advanced practitioner, and Raven was instantly enthralled. Mao Ying's martial arts were in curious contrast to her sweet personality. The style she practiced wasn't soft and gentle like a Tai Chi form. It was fierce with aggressive kicks and punches, and it was the ferocity that mesmerized Raven. As she studied Mao Ying, Raven even tried to mimic some of the movements herself. Finally, Mao Ying finished her practice and made her way to the kitchen. Raven moved away from the window and hurried over to the dishwashing machine. She pretended to be examining it when Mao Ying finally entered.

"Good morning, Raven," Mao Ying said happily. "Would you like a little snack first?"

"No, thank you," answered Raven. She tried not to stare at Mao Ying, but it was difficult. Mao Ying was so sweet, yet so lethal. She was a mild-mannered murder machine, a strange combination that fascinated Raven.

"Then let's get started. Follow me and I'll show you around."

As Raven followed after Mao Ying, she stared at the woman intensely. And respectfully.

* * *

Though it was a facility for the elderly, most of the residents of Oakwood Garden seemed to be unusually robust and full of life. While some of them chose to relax in the shade in comfortable lounge chairs beneath huge umbrellas, most were involved in physical activity of some kind. Frisbee was the sport of choice for many. Others were engaged in the more traditional horseshoe tossing. Several residents performed Tai Chi led by one of the staff members. Other residents paced around a special walking track that surrounded the perimeter of the courtyard. The courtyard pulsed with vitality and was clearly both the hub and heart of Oakwood.

One afternoon, Raven was making a delivery to the stables. She pushed a large cart stacked with bales of hay. As she walked, she exchanged greetings with the residents and staff she encountered along the way. Then Raven noticed someone else. Sitting in her wheelchair beside the fountain was the wild-haired, black woman. When the woman spotted Raven, she again poked out her long tongue tauntingly. Raven glared back at the woman. Several dogs rushed over to greet Raven and she petted them all before continuing on her way. The stables were adjacent to a corral filled with horses, and a man stood at the fence watching them closely. Even from a distance, he cut a striking figure. He had long, thick grey hair that he wore in a ponytail that hung down past his waist. His buckskin leggings and moccasins were an odd contrast to the ankle-length, brightly-colored Japanese robe he wore. A horse trotted over to greet him and the the two of them exchanged secrets, the horse whinnying softly as the man murmured in her long, velvety ear. Raven parked the cart and approached him. When he turned to face her, the first thing Raven noticed was the Bob Marley T-shirt visible under his robe. Then she looked at him. He was dark and exotic, of some ethnicity Raven couldn't immediately identify, with soft eyes and a welcoming smile. He looked as though he belonged on an island.

"Hello, there, Raven," he said sweetly. The sound of his voice was soft and soothing, and by now Raven was used to denizens of Oakwood knowing her name before they had been introduced. "It's about time we met. I'm Red Knife. Welcome to Oakwood. You finding your way around okay?"

Raven moved closer to the fence, reached out and allowed Red Knife's horse friend to smell her hand. She pretended to focus on the animal, but it was the man beside her who had her full attention. Raven was always in control, particularly when it came to her emotions, but now, standing near Red Knife, the tables had turned.

"So far, so good," answered Raven. "I like your friend here."

"She seems to like you, too. Her name is Sleeps With One Eye Open."

"Good name," laughed Raven as she petted the horse. "Very practical."

"You like animals?"

"I prefer them to people, actually."

"I agree. You pretty much always know where you stand with a beast. With a human, you're never quite sure. Nice to meet you."

The two shook hands and Raven felt a hot jolt of electricity surge through her body.

"I've heard quite a bit about you."

"As long as you didn't hear it on television, it might even be true."

"I've never owned a television."

"I like you already."

The horse snuggled closer to Raven; the natural bonding between the two was obvious.

"Looks like you've been adopted," said Red Knife.

"Maybe I'll have better luck this time," said Raven sardonically. "I've never been around horses before."

Red Knife was shocked. "Is that a fact?" he asked in disbelief. "Sure doesn't look that way. Maybe it's time I got you broken in."

Red Knife climbed inside the corral and motioned for Raven to follow. He gently took hold of Sleeps With One Eye Open's reins and lead her closer to Raven. He then grasped Raven around the waist and effortlessly hoisted her up onto the horse. Raven wasn't fearful at all—she was excited. She took hold of the reins and guided the horse around the corral with ease. Red Knife watched her closely. Straddling the horse, Raven looked both confident and majestic.

"Natural born horsewoman, I'd say," said Red Knife, beaming.

"She's doing all the driving. I'm just in the passenger seat."

"You're doing fine. Just be one with the beast. As long as you remember that, you'll be okay."

After a few minutes of circling the corral, Raven guided the horse back over to Red Knife. He helped her down from the horse and took the reins. Raven hugged the animal lovingly, like an old friend.

"That was very good for your first time," Red Knife said with a smile.

"There's a first time for everything."

"I like you, Raven. You've got a lot of potential ... for a human being," laughed Red Knife. "There may be hope for this world yet."

"You'll be seeing a lot of me," Raven said as she walked over to the fence. "In the meantime, that's enough of a break. I've got a delivery for you."

Red Knife and Raven stepped out of the corral and headed over to the cart piled with bales of hay. Red Knife took control of the cart and guided it toward the stable, with Raven following close behind. She stared at his long braid and wondered what it felt like to touch.

"Coming to the show tonight?" he asked.

"What show?"

"There's a variety show tonight. You should come, there's a lot of talent at Oakwood. You'd be surprised at the kind of people you meet here."

"I'm starting to see that," Raven answered.

* * *

One of the most unusual buildings in the Oakwood compound was the theater. The exterior was grandiose, like a cross between a French opera house and an old-fashioned

New Orleans bordello. The inside was equally lavish, with luxurious carpeting, fabric-covered walls, and ornate lighting fixtures. Despite the elaborate decor, however, it was a very intimate theater, with only three hundred seats, all filled with enthusiastic residents and staff waiting for the show to begin. There was an unmistakable electric current of anticipation in the air, and Raven could feel it as she sat in the back row beside Red Knife.

The lights slowly dimmed, the red curtain rose, and music filled the theater. Raven sat back and was quickly swept away. She was soon treated to a wide array of entertainment. There were musicians, singers, dancers, jugglers, and even acrobats. They were all of advanced age, yet all very talented and proud to present themselves before the appreciative audience. Raven was genuinely dazzled by the show.

Suddenly, the entire theater was plunged into total darkness and silence. A gong was struck three times and purple mist slowly filled the stage. A tall man dressed in black stepped out of the mist. Even from the back of the theater, Raven could feel the power of his gaze.

"Who is this?" she asked Red Knife urgently.

"Guy Dupont. The greatest magician in the world."

Dupont's voice was soothingly hypnotic, but he rarely spoke. He chose to let his amazing magical skills speak for him. He conjured up objects and even small animals from the most unlikely of places, only to make them disappear again. He caused inanimate items large and small to be filled with life; trousers walked, furniture danced, and musical instruments floated in midair and played themselves.

Dupont seemed to take the greatest delight in card manipulations, and he controlled them with virtuosic skill. After performing a series of dazzling tricks, he flung cards to the floor in rapid succession, causing them to bounce and then fly all over the theater. Enthusiastic audience members scrambled excitedly to catch the cards. Raven caught one as well—the Queen of Spades. When Dupont announced his last trick for the evening, he informed the audience that he would require an assistant. He asked that whoever held the Queen of Spades come to the stage. Raven immediately stood, both nervous and excited. Dupont gestured for her to come forward and she quickly made her way to the front of the theater. Dupont helped her up onto the stage and eyed her closely. Then he took Raven by the hand and escorted her over to a table on which sat a large birdcage. The cage was tightly wrapped in chains and secured with a huge padlock. Inside the cage was a large black bird that seemed particularly agitated, stamping with its yellow-clawed feet, shaking its wings, tossing its head nervously, and gazing around with bright black eyes. Dupont asked Raven to inspect the cage and she complied. The chains and lock were very real. Raven looked as confused as the bird trapped inside the cage. Dupont covered the cage with a yellow cloth.

"Come forth!" he ordered as he focused his powerful gaze upon the covered cage.

Dupont held his arms outstretched with the palms facing upward.

"Rise, and come forth!" he commanded with more force. "Now is your time."

Suddenly, the yellow cloth began to slowly rise, propelled upward by manic movement from underneath. Dupont snatched away the cloth, revealing the black bird flapping its wings wildly. The empty cage remained secured by the chains and lock. The audience applauded enthusiastically but Raven stood motionless. She knew she had just witnessed *real* magic and instinctively understood the magical message being conveyed. Dupont extended his arm and the bird obediently flew over and landed on his hand. Then he turned to Raven and offered her the bird. As Raven reached out to receive the black gift, she looked at Dupont and their eyes locked.

"No chains will ever hold you," he said.

* * *

One morning, Raven entered the Resident Lounge carrying a mop, a pail, and a box of cleaning products. There had been a birthday party the night before and the lounge was still littered with decorations and trash. Raven set down her gear as she surveyed the work awaiting her.

Just then a slender, gray-haired woman dressed in red entered, walking with the poise and grace of an aristocrat. She walked right past Raven and over to a grand piano in the far corner. She seated herself and warmed up by playing a few scale patterns. Then she played a song, a mid-tempo waltz, and the sweet music filled the lounge. Raven loved waltzes. There was a dance floor near the piano, and Raven rushed over to it and began to dance. The pianist looked up from the piano as if noticing Raven for the first time. Raven was greatly moved by the music, and it showed in her dancing. She was obviously untrained in dance, but her passion and confidence compensated for her lack of technical skills. Raven danced fearlessly and the pianist was impressed, though she pretended not to be, maintaining an icy exterior. When the pianist completed the song, Raven burst into applause.

"I love that song," said Raven excitedly.

"It is beautiful, isn't it?" the woman replied without emotion. Her accent was thick and lovely.

"My name is Raven."

"I am Loona Shumenko. And where did Raven learn to move in such a manner?"

"I don't really know how to dance," Raven answered, slightly embarrassed.

"I can see that," Loona said fighting a smile. "Well, you should learn and learn properly. It might help correct that hideous posture of yours. Straighten your back."

Raven immediately straightened her back.

"Are you in some kind of pain?" Loona asked.

"No, ma'am."

"Well, you certainly stand as if you are. Hold back your shoulders."

Raven complied. Eyeing Raven up and down, Loona frowned a bit and shook her head with mock disappointment.

"You do seem to have some natural ability, but it's going to take a lot of work. You have a lifetime of bad habits that need to be corrected."

Loona reached in her small bag for a pen and paper.

She jotted down a book title, abruptly stood from the piano and headed for the door. As she passed Raven, she handed her the piece of paper. "That's a good place to begin," said Loona.

"*Proper Body Mechanics*," said Raven, carefully reading the words on the paper. "It sounds interesting."

"It *is* interesting," snapped Loona. "I wrote it. Thirty years ago, but the information is as applicable today as it was then. Read it, and then come see me."

Raven carefully folded the piece of paper and slipped it into her pocket as she watched Loona leave the lounge. She danced once again, without music but with much better posture.

* * *

With the sun shining high above and the compound far behind her, Raven explored on horseback with the confidence of an experienced rider. As the horse galloped at breakneck speed, Raven rode fearlessly. She stopped momentarily to give the horse a rest and to bask in the beauty of the nature around her.

The sudden, echoing sound of gunshots startled her. In the distance, she saw a man doing target practice in a meadow beside a river. Curious, she rode toward him for a closer inspection. Raven brought the horse to a stop several yards from the man, then dismounted. She gave the horse a kiss and tethered the animal to a nearby willow.

The shooter was a black man flamboyantly dressed in a style that was a combination of cowboy, pirate, and gypsy. His name was Blake Swanigan. Beside him was a table with an assortment of handguns and rifles. In front of him several yards away was a fence lined with bottles and cans. Raven smiled and seated herself on a large rock. She knew she was about to see something special.

Swanigan was well aware that he was being watched, and he went out of his way to put on a dazzling show. He quickly drew a large revolver from his side holster, dropped to one knee and fired off three shots in rapid succession. Three bottles exploded. He holstered the revolver and drew a modern semi-automatic pistol from a shoulder holster. He fired off a string of shots and struck all the remaining targets on the fence save one, a shot glass. Swanigan coolly stood and spun the pistol several times before returning it to the holster. Suddenly, he snapped his arm down and a derringer pistol slid from out of his sleeve and into his hand. He aimed, fired, and struck the shot glass. Raven was deeply impressed. Unable to contain her excitement any longer, she applauded enthusiastically. Swanigan pretended he had never known she was watching.

"Well, hello there, sweet young thing," he said with a sparkling smile. "How long you been there?"

Raven climbed down from the rock and hurried over to Swanigan. She extended her hand and he shook it warmly.

"Long enough. My name is Raven."

"I'm Blake Swanigan," he answered. He eyed her up and down and smiled slyly. "Oh, yeah, our newest resident. The youngblood. I've heard a lot about you, Miss Lady."

"I hear that a lot. My reputation precedes me."

"That it does!" laughed Swanigan. "It's nice to have a pretty new face around the place."

"Glad you like it. You'll be seeing a lot of it, for the next few years at least. By the way, you shoot fabulously."

"Thank you very much," Swanigan replied, genuinely touched by her praise.

"I mean it. I really like your style," insisted Raven. "A lot of people shoot *straight*, but you're different. You've got a style all your own."

"I never thought of it that way, but I suppose that's true. Do you shoot?"

"Nope, but I wouldn't mind learning, though. I bet with the right instruction, I could be fabulous, too."

Swanigan took an immediate liking to Raven. "I might be able to help."

"Oh, I know you can!" Raven said eagerly. "Let's talk about it sometime. Right now, I've got to get back to work."

As Raven headed back to her horse, Swanigan watched her closely and curiously. She mounted her horse, turned in the saddle to wave goodbye, then rode away. Swanigan continued to watch her until she was far in the distance.

* * *

Raven walked down a long hallway carrying a tray of food. She stopped at a door and knocked. She waited, but there was no response. She knocked again, but with more persistence. Finally, a man answered. From the tone in his voice, it was obvious he was being disturbed.

"Yes, who is it?" he answered angrily.

"I've got your dinner here," said Raven.

"Well, take it away. I don't have time to …"

Raven was in no mood to argue. "Let me in there," she said sternly, "I've brought your dinner. What you do with it is up to you."

There was a long pause. "Oh, all right," the occupant said in exasperation. "Bring it in."

Raven was curious to meet the irritable owner of the voice, whose name Mao Ying had told her was Warrington Beasley. Raven had giggled. "He sounds lke an English lord or something," she had said.

Mao Ying had smiled. "Not far off," she had answered. "But be careful. He's not very sociable."

Now Raven entered what appeared to be a laboratory. There were several tables throughout the room. One was covered with microscopes, Bunsen burners, test tubes, beakers, and other scientific gear used in experiments. Another was littered with a variety of odd electronic gadgets and devices. Still another table was strewn with books and papers. Virtually every inch of wall space was covered by floor-to-ceiling bookshelves bulging with books. The sound of orchestral music filled the air.

In the far corner of the room, Beasley sat at a table tinkering with a gadget. Close beside him was a steaming cup of tea that filled the entire room with an unusually pungent odor. A cigarette holder protruded from his mouth, but the cigarette was unlit. Raven approached and rested the tray beside him. Taking a seat directly across from him, she was careful to make as little noise as possible. Beasley never looked up from his work.

"You didn't come down to dinner, so Mao Ying had me bring dinner up to you."

Beasley didn't answer. He took a few sips of tea, never taking his gaze off of the gadget he worked on. Raven watched him, far more interested in the man than the gadget. He didn't look like a scientist at all. He looked like a male model from another century, nattily dressed in a finely tailored, old-fashioned pinstripe suit. He must have been quite handsome in his youth, because the wrinkles of age only complimented his sculpted face. His white hair was neatly combed back into a small ponytail. While his laboratory was hardly fastidious, the man himself was the epitome of order. His impeccable suit, gold cuff links, silk handkerchief, pink carnation, silver watch chain, and even the cigarette holder worked in carefully constructed harmony. He evidently took great pride in his appearance and arranged his wardrobe like a piece of music. His choice of footwear completed the ensemble in a surprisingly modern way. The shoes were made of blue suede. The elegant scientist remained oblivious to her.

"Re-inventing the lightbulb?" Raven asked sarcastically. Her words inadvertently struck a major chord.

"Lightbulb?" Beasley spat angrily. "Edison … that hack! He stole everything. He was a second-rate scientist but a first-class thief."

Raven's curiosity immediately heightened. Beasley's intensity was somehow endearing. It was the intensity of someone gifted and opinionated, yet hopelessly doomed. A doomed dreamer.

"People don't understand," he continued. "Science is as much an art as music, poetry, and dance. There's no difference, none whatsoever. Originality, style, uniqueness ... Edison had none of these. Yet what happens? The history books make him out to be some kind of Mozart!" Beasley shook his head in disgust. "It's a conspiracy," he said sadly. "That's what it is. Edison was a hack, but he was a crafty hack. He knew how to ally himself with the money interest. That was his *real* talent. They served him well, didn't they? They put him on a pedestal while the great ones went forgotten. They always forget the great ones."

Beasley placed the gadget he had been working with off to the side. Overwhelmed by the sad truth of his own words, he sighed heavily and took another sip of tea. Raven wanted to soothe him in some way and she searched her mind for the right words.

"Tesla would have kicked Edison's sorry ass," she said emphatically.

Beasley looked up into Raven's eyes, focusing on her for the very first time since she entered his room. He was both surprised and impressed by her response.

"And you wanna know something else?" Raven continued. "Tesla *did* kick Edison's sorry ass. It's just that no one knows about it. And you know why? It's a conspiracy!"

Still focused intently on Raven, the dapper old scientist nodded his head in total agreement. "But what can we do about it?" he asked with a kind of childlike inquisitiveness.

"Well, the first thing we've got to do is eat," Raven answered, sliding the food tray closer to him. "First things first."

Beasley considered her words. He positioned the food tray in front of himself and took a bite of the food. It was delicious, and more bites followed. Then he stopped eating and looked up into Raven's eyes.

"I don't normally allow guests in my lab," he said softly and apologetically. "Sometimes ... I'm a little abrupt."

"I've got an idea," Raven said in almost a whisper. "You and me, we understand what's really going on. We'll start our own secret society. Besides, I'm not your guest anyway, I'm your friend."

Beasley nodded his head in agreement. Staring at Raven, he instinctively realized that he had just made his greatest discovery.

* * *

The Oakwood library was Raven's favorite building. The exterior had been constructed to look like an ancient Greek temple. The interior was an endless maze of shelves that stretched as far as the eye could see on several floors. There were comfortable, mismatched couches and chairs along with the more traditional and austere wooden tables and benches. The library never closed which made it the favored destination for insomniacs. Raven could usually be found there in the wee hours of most nights, hunched over a table filled with books. Late one night, Raven sat reading Loona's book, *Proper Body Mechanics*. She closed the book, glanced at her watch, and rubbed her eyes wearily. Sitting back in her chair, she reflected on her new home and the unusual residents who lived there.

"Who *are* these people?" she wondered.

3

Mao Ying

Raven had noticed early on that there were two distinct flavors to Mao Ying—sweet and sour. The Oakwood residents certainly responded to her sweetness. Everyone looked forward to mealtimes, but the reasons why involved more than just the delicious food. Though Mao Ying was an accomplished cook in several styles, the most delightful item she served was herself. She knew each resident by name, their particular dietary requirements, and their favorite foods. During the course of each meal, Mao Ying would emerge from the kitchen and dutifully move from table to table like a concerned honeybee, making sure that everyone was enjoying both themselves and their food. One elderly resident who had lived in China had a secret crush on Mao Ying and referred to her by the name Madam Tang. Tang is a Chinese candy, and the nickname was appropriate, indeed. Mao Ying's facial features were certainly sweet, particularly her eyes. Her eyes were her most prominent feature, and were so entrancing that one never really noticed anything else. Mao Ying's eyes *were* her face. Because their gaze was warm, welcoming and somehow *healing*, she didn't really need to smile. She rarely did.

Mao Ying very much enjoyed her own cooking. She was a bit plump, but she moved with graceful steps, perfect posture, and head held high. She never wore traditional Chinese clothing except on special occasions and holidays. Instead, she favored colorful, modern running suits and sports shoes. She was rarely seen without a special cap that she treasured, a cap with an embroidered image of her favorite cartoon character, the Tasmanian Devil. She wore the cap with the brim facing backward.

Raven enjoyed working in the kitchen with Mao Ying and always looked forward to being there. Mao Ying delegated tasks sweetly, instructing Raven with the calm concern of a patient mother hen. Raven was hopelessly intrigued by Mao Ying, stealing glances at her whenever possible, searching for clues that might reveal more about her. Mao Ying never volunteered information about herself. It was obvious that she loved elderly people, no doubt a reflection of her old-world Chinese heritage. It was also obvious that she was disciplined and organized. Her kitchen was the epitome of order.

For Raven, the most fascinating part of Mao Ying was her martial arts skill. Her fighting prowess exuded a barbarity that seemed totally at odds with her sweet nature. This ultraviolent intensity mesmerized Raven. Every morning at dawn, Mao Ying practiced outside, oblivious, perhaps, to Raven who watched from the kitchen. Mao Ying the martial artist was clearly an entirely different person from Mao Ying the cook. Mao Ying fought like a *bitch*. Raven was determined to know more about this bitch and to learn from her as well. Early one morning, Mao Ying was outside, stretching in preparation for her workout. She turned to find Raven standing a few feet away, looking at her with hopeful eyes. Mao Ying stared back at Raven sternly before speaking. When she did speak, the tone in her voice was very different from usual. There was no trace of sweetness in her voice or in her eyes. Her demeanor was cold. She well understood what Raven wanted.

"I learned Gung Fu from my mother," she began. "And my mother learned from her mother. What I know has been passed down from many generations, directly from the Shaolin Temple. I've never taken a student or wanted to ... until now."

Raven felt a rush of excitement at Mao Ying's words. She wanted to smile, but she fought the temptation.

Mao Ying placed her hands on her hips. "Come here," she ordered.

Raven rushed over to Mao Ying. By now, Raven had been working in the kitchen for quite some time, yet Mao Ying eyed her up and down as if they had only just met. Mao Ying slowly circled her, scrutinizing her carefully. Suddenly, Mao Ying pushed Raven slightly with one hand. The force was incredibly strong, knocking Raven down and sending her rolling back several feet.

Astonished, Raven struggled to catch her breath as she climbed back to her feet. Confused, she walked back over to Mao Ying.

"In return for my instruction, I require two things," Mao Ying said without emotion. "Persistence and determination."

"Deal," answered Raven without hesitation.

"Good. Let's get started."

Mao Ying stood a few feet in front of Raven and assumed a fighting stance. Raven quickly assumed the same stance. Mao Ying moved through different postures and Raven did her best to mimic and shadow her. It was difficult, but Raven was persistent and determined. By the time Mao Ying pressed her palms together and bowed, indicating that the session was over, Raven was damp with sweat and beginning to ache in some of her muscles. Mao Ying wanted to smile, but she didn't.

* * *

Late one night, Raven was in the library studying when Mr. Freeman entered and joined her at her table.

"I'm learning Gung Fu!" Raven exclaimed excitedly.

Mr. Freeman smiled. "I'm not exactly surprised. It was only a matter of time," he said. "As you've already no doubt surmised, Mao Ying is a highly complex individual. A delicate orchid with the fury of a dragon."

"Sweet and sour," said Raven.

"Sweet and sour, indeed! Well said. Due no doubt to her unusual background. Mao Ying was born in Foshan, a city in Guangdong Province, China. Have you heard of it?"

"No. I'm a little weak on my Chinese geography."

"It's many centuries old and well known for its porcelain industry. It's also famous for having produced many renowned martial artists. Like Mao Ying's mother who was descended from a long and illustrious line of them. Mao Ying's father was a brilliant doctor, well-known, and highly respected for his compassion as well as his medical skill. When the Japanese invaded, committing terrible atrocities against the Chinese people, China was plunged into chaos. Two armies mobilized against the Japanese invaders: the Communists led by Mao Zedong, and the Nationalist Guomindang led by General Jiang Gaishek. The two forces formed a tactical alliance to drive out the Japanese. But while they succeeded in defeating the Japanese, they failed in maintaining their alliance. Civil war broke out between them. Mao Ying's father was a wise man who trusted neither side. When he dared to speak out against the injustice and brutality that swept across the country he loved, he was killed."

Raven listened closely as Mr. Freeman continued his briefing on Mao Ying.

"Years later, during the so-called Cultural Revolution, the Communists sought to eradicate what they called the Four Olds. Old customs, old culture, old habits, and old ideas. As you can imagine, Mao Ying's family was steeped in tradition and her mother and grandmother were among the many casualties. They, too, were killed. Mao Ying might have lost her life, as well, but with the help of friends, she managed to escape the persecution and fled to the West. But she lost absolutely everything. Everything."

Raven could now well understand the source of Mao Ying's sour side. It was a tragic tale, and as Raven reflected on Mr. Freeman's words, she wondered how many tears had fallen from Mao Ying's eyes. No wonder she never smiled. Mr. Freeman could tell that Raven had been deeply impacted by Mao Ying's story and that perhaps she needed to be alone with her thoughts. He stood, said goodnight, and left the reading room.

"Sweet and sour," whispered Raven to herself.

* * *

One morning, after breakfast had been served, Raven was in the kitchen washing dishes. Her sunrise workout with Mao Ying had been particularly intense, leaving her sore and barely able to move. She rested against the sink momentarily.

"Are you injured?"

Raven turned to find Mao Ying standing beside her. Mao Ying's eyes were filled with concern.

"I don't know," answered Raven.

Mao Ying slipped her arm around Raven's waist and led her away from the sink and down a hallway. They walked down a staircase to an area Raven had never seen before, Mao Ying's private quarters. It was a modest apartment, sparsely furnished but characteristically immaculate. Mao Ying helped Raven onto a massage table, then hurried off to another room. As Raven waited for Mao Ying to return, she looked around the apartment curiously. There were many shelves filled with books, mostly Chinese. There were English books, as well, the majority seeming to be medical. Much of the wall space was covered with human anatomy diagrams.

Mao Ying returned and placed a tray on a table beside Raven. On the tray were containers of various salves and ointments. There was also an ornate wooden box. Mao

Ying opened the box, revealing acupuncture needles of varying sizes. She turned on a stereo and the apartment was filled with soft, soothing Chinese music. Mao Ying began with a massage, lovingly kneading Raven's aching flesh. Within minutes, Raven drifted off to a deep, blissful sleep, complete with snoring. Mao Ying continued the treatment with the careful insertion of needles into strategic points.

When Raven finally awoke, Mao Ying was gone. Raven sat up and looked at her watch. She was surprised by the amount of time that had passed. She climbed down from the table and was prepared to leave when a small, framed picture on the wall caught her attention. It was a photo of a young Chinese girl standing with a group of adults who appeared to be her parents and grandmother. While the father smiled cheerfully, the two women were subdued and even a bit grim. The four of them stood close together, indicative of the bond they shared. Raven stared at the picture for a long time, then hurried out of the apartment.

Upstairs, in the kitchen, Mao Ying was preparing a special juice concoction in a blender. When she saw Raven, she greeted her anxiously. "Feeling better?" she asked with concern.

"Yes, a lot better."

"We'll go more slowly tomorrow morning," Mao Ying said apologetically. "I pushed too hard."

"No, it's okay, I'm fine. Really."

"No, more slowly," insisted Mao Ying. "I don't have to hurt you to teach you."

Mao Ying led Raven over to a table and seated her. She poured the juice into a glass and handed it to Raven. "This will make you feel better," Mao Ying promised. "Drink."

Raven drained the glass and smiled approvingly. She prepared to stand, ready to return to work, but Mao Ying wouldn't allow it.

"No," said Mao Ying sternly, "you sit and rest. I'll make a snack for you."

Mao Ying hurried off to another part of the kitchen while muttering to herself. "Too hard," she repeated softly. "Too hard."

Part orchid, part dragon, and all heart.

* * *

Mao Ying practiced a form of martial arts called Wing Chun Gung Fu. She spoke very little during morning practice sessions, usually only to explain particular techniques and their application or to correct Raven in some way. Outside of practice, Mao Ying never discussed martial arts at all. Raven was endlessly curious about anything that interested her, and she loved martial arts. She was convinced that there was more to learn about it *intellectually*. One afternoon, as they peeled potatoes for the evening meal, Raven asked Mao Ying to talk about Wing Chun Gung Fu. Mao Ying thought for a moment. She stopped peeling and seemed to drift away. Raven watched her closely, awaiting her response. For minutes, Mao Ying said nothing, and the kitchen was strangely silent. Finally, she spoke.

"In my country, women are not considered special. Far from it. But my father was different. He didn't think that way at all." Suddenly Mao Ying giggled like a child. "My father always said that women were *better* than men!"

"That's different all right," agreed Raven, transfixed by the very different Mao Ying who glowed as she remembered her father.

Mao Ying's glow burned brighter as she continued. "One day, when my father was out for a walk, he saw my mother practicing her Gung Fu in the park and he fell in love."

"He fell in love with her Gung Fu?"

"In a way. He fell in love with what it represented. My mother was a very talented martial artist. Her family was famous for their Gung Fu, and her skills were extraordinary, superior to the skills of most men. Yet she was often ridiculed for it."

"A woman's place is in the home, not the dojo," Raven said with a sardonic smile.

"Many people do feel that way. But my father was different. To him, Gung Fu made my mother very special, *unique.* In his eyes, my mother was a unicorn."

"And unicorns are good luck."

Mao Ying nodded excitedly, barely able to control her giggling. "And that's exactly how he felt! He said his luck changed the moment her saw her."

"I've heard of love at first sight, but love at first Gung Fu, now that's really romantic."

"Yes, I suppose it is."

Raven watched Mao Ying. It was strange to see her smiling and to hear her childlike laughter. It was obvious that her childhood was the happiest time of her life. Her beloved father had made a profound and lasting impact on her.

"He must have been proud to see you follow in your mother's footsteps," Raven said.

"Yes," Mao Ying said softly. "Very proud."

Mao Ying's mood abruptly changed. She fell silent, focusing on the images in her mind, images clearly dark and disturbing. Raven had never seen Mao Ying look so wounded. Raven's radar could easily sense the emotional downward spiral, so she immediately shifted the direction of the conversation.

"Tell me about Wing Chun Gung Fu," said Raven, watching Mao Ying closely.

It took Mao Ying a few moments to process Raven's request. But slowly, Mao Ying shifted her thoughts away from her past and pondered Wing Chun. To Raven's surprise, Mao Ying suddenly seemed quite ready and willing to discuss her art.

Mao Ying focused her gaze on Raven as she spoke. "There are many styles of martial arts, but Wing Chun is unique, perhaps the most unique of them all."

"Why is that?"

"Because Wing Chun was invented by a woman. A Chinese woman."

Raven was shocked by this information. It made her interest in Wing Chun increase exponentially. "You've gotta be kidding," she said in disbelief. "There's actually a martial art invented by a woman? Does everybody know this?"

"It does seem like a secret, doesn't it?"

Raven pulled her chair closer to Mao Ying, eager to hear more.

"Well, the exact origins are somewhat mysterious," continued Mao Ying. "There are many variations to the story. This is the version taught to me by my mother, who was taught by her mother. Many years ago, over three hundred years ago, there was a Buddhist nun named Ng Nui from the Shaolin Temple. The Shaolin Temple was famous for being the birthplace of many styles of martial arts. Ng Nui was a master of various styles and she combined many of them into a new streamlined system, incorporating the best aspects that each had to offer. Her goal was to create the most effective and efficient martial art, particularly for a woman. The style she created relied on biomechanics rather than brute force. It emphasized close-range combat. Angular deflections with simultaneous attacks. Low kicking. Her new style stressed simplicity, economy of movement, and economy of energy."

Raven listened closely as Mao Ying finally opened up about Wing Chun Gung Fu.

"The ruling government of that time, the Manchus, was evil and repressive. Martial arts training was strictly forbidden. The Shaolin Temple was eventually attacked and burned to the ground, but there were survivors who managed to escape, and Ng Nui was one of them. She passed her skills on to a young girl she had befriended named Yim Wing Chun. Yim Wing Chun was very eager to learn martial arts. She practiced hard and became highly proficient. The system is named after her. It means 'beautiful springtime'."

Raven smiled. "I like that story."

"So do I."

"So tell it again, but go a little slower this time."

Raven and Mao Ying laughed in harmony, and Mao Ying happily retold the tale.

* * *

Early morning Gung Fu practice continued and Raven proved to be an eager and dedicated student. Mao Ying maintained her stern teaching demeanor and Raven blossomed radiantly under the intense tutelage. In time, Raven developed into a young martial artist of extraordinary skill. Mao Ying was obviously pleased with Raven's progress and never failed to give praise and encouragement. She loved Raven's innate fierceness, a fierceness that increased with her growing prowess. Mao Ying particularly loved introducing Raven to advanced fighting techniques that were more vicious. It was thrilling to have a student who was both naturally gifted and naturally ruthless. Raven enjoyed the beautiful brutality of Gung Fu which delighted Mao Ying; she enjoyed it, too. In addition to empty-hand combat, Mao Ying taught Raven various weapons as well. Once Raven had reached a certain level of development, the two women engaged in wild battles that would have been frightening to the uninformed observer. These violent confrontations sharpened Raven's growing skills even more. Mao Ying was as proud of Raven as her mother and grandmother had been of her.

While Raven and Mao Ying certainly shared the blood lust, violence was only one aspect that bonded them. In addition to her deadly fighting skills, Mao Ying was also an accomplished healer, well trained in herbal medicine and acupuncture. Many evenings after the dinner meal had been served and the dishes washed, Raven would go to Mao Ying's apartment to study. Mao Ying loved Raven's insatiable hunger for knowledge, martial and otherwise. Raven proved to be as fascinated by the medical arts as she was the martial arts.

Even dragons have weaknesses and Mao Ying had hers. She was particularly fond of chocolate chip cookies which just happened to be a Raven specialty. Sometimes Raven would prepare the delicacy, and the two of them would retreat to Mao Ying's apartment to watch classic Gung Fu films. Mao Ying's film collection was enormous, and Bruce Lee's films were naturally her favorite.

4

Red Knife

Raven loved horses. Between her various daily tasks, Raven would often steal away to the stable or the corral just to be near the horses. Red Knife was as fascinated by Raven as she was fascinated by the horses. He was intrigued by her intimate relationship with the animals. In addition to all the horses that had grown to adore her, there were the many Oakwood dogs that eagerly followed after her whenever they saw her. Red Knife knew animals very well, well enough to know that they usually chose correctly. The Oakwood animals had unanimously given Raven their seal of approval.

One afternoon, Red Knife found Raven sitting on the corral fence watching the horses. He approached and stood beside her, but she was so absorbed in the animals that she was oblivious to him. Red Knife removed a pocket knife and a small piece of wood from his robe, and began to carve. Raven turned to find him standing beside her and she smiled.

Raven turned back to watch the horses. "Being near horses is like being near water," she said.

Red Knife nodded. "Horses are therapeutic. That's why it feels so good when you hug them. They've got a special energy all their own. A healing energy." Red Knife moved closer to Raven. "I've noticed something interesting lately," he continued. "Sleeps With One Eye Open has been sleeping with both eyes closed. She's a lot more relaxed than she used to be. You've got a special healing energy, too."

Raven didn't respond and felt herself blushing.

Red Knife could see that Raven was blushing, so he redirected the conversation. "You must miss your old life. It's only natural."

Raven contemplated the question. "I miss my girls. I think about them all the time." A cloud passed over her. "But I don't miss Las Vegas."

As Red Knife carved, he stole glances at Raven while she watched the horses. She was so familiar. Perhaps because Red Knife was born on an island and remained an islander in his heart, he was instinctively drawn to water. Raven *was* water; calming, soothing, raging, and healing. Like an island, he felt surrounded by her. Whenever he was near her, he felt as though he were drowning. Red Knife spoke to calm himself.

"You're a young girl, Raven. Don't you feel stuck here at Oakwood, surrounded by all these old people? You were running wild and free. Now you're stuck."

Raven remained focused on the horses as she spoke. "I like being around older people. I'm starting to think I prefer it. Besides, it pays off."

Red Knife glanced at Raven curiously. "How so?" he asked.

     RAVENDIABLO

"Older people know a lot more than I do about all kinds of things. So when I'm around them, I tap what they know. Like going to the bank and making withdrawals."

Red Knife laughed. "I suppose that's one way to look at it."

"Didn't know you were a bank, did you?" she asked playfully.

"Didn't know I was old either," he laughed again.

"Older," she corrected with a grin.

"Oh, I don't mind being old. Old age is youth in full bloom, at least I like to think so."

Red Knife handed Raven the carving he had been working on. It was an intricately carved horse's head that fit neatly in the palm of her hand. Raven stared at the piece in amazement. She thanked him with her eyes.

"You make *deposits*, too," he said. "Works both ways."

Raven climbed down from where she was perched and hugged Red Knife tightly. "I don't feel stuck," she said. She turned and walked away, heading for the library.

As Red Knife watched her walk away, he wondered when he might be surrounded by her again. He hoped it would be very soon. Then Raven turned around and flashed him a smile with a sly twinkle in her eye.

"Not yet!" she called out. She turned and raced toward the Greek temple.

Red Knife leaned against the fence to brace himself, convinced he was drowning.

* * *

Mr. Freeman sat at his desk, huddled over a stack of papers when a knock at his office door jarred his attention.

"Come in," he said.

Raven entered with a tray of food.

"I noticed you didn't make it down to lunch," Raven said cheerfully as she placed the tray on his desk.

Mr. Freeman's eyes went wide with excitement. He immediately moved the stack of papers aside, positioned the tray in front of him and began to eat. Raven had never been in his office before and was instantly drawn to his well stocked bookshelf.

"May I?" she asked.

"Please," he said with a mouthful of food.

"I always ask permission first. A person's books are private, like a window to their mind. You can tell a lot about a person from what they read." Raven laughed. "You might not want me to have a window to your mind."

"Oh, I'm not sure you'd find very much there of interest. And just so you know, if you want to start a personal library of your own in your room, it's perfectly all right. I know you're quite a bookworm."

"I don't mind going to the library." answered Raven. "I like it there."

"I'm sure you do, but I just want you to feel at home. I know your old home was filled with books. I bet Red Knife could whip up a nice shelf for you in no time."

Raven was happy to hear Mr. Freeman mention Red Knife. His timing was perfect.

"He's so peaceful. I always feel more relaxed after being with him."

Mr. Freeman smiled. "Yes, Red Knife is a man of peace. Which is quite amazing, considering his past."

Raven pretended to be unconcerned when in fact, she was curious. Mr. Freeman was about to reveal insights into Red Knife and Raven's blood grew hot at the prospect. She wanted to know more about the most beautiful man she had ever seen.

"Red Knife has a very colorful background. And I don't mean his ethnic background which is Hawaiian and Native American by the way. Red Knife was once a soldier." Mr. Freeman paused for a moment to carefully choose his words. "Red Knife was ... an *assassin*. A most accomplished assassin. Our peaceful friend is actually one of the most dangerous men on the planet."

Raven turned to look at Mr. Freeman incredulously. Red Knife hardly had the demeanor of a soldier, let alone that of an accomplished killer. It was a shocking revelation. Raven dropped the pretense of unconcern, reshelved the book she had been pretending to read, and took a seat beside Mr. Freeman's desk.

"Red Knife was a man of war," he continued. "Well-trained in the arts of war: hand-to-hand combat, weapons, explosives, surveillance—you name it, he had mastered it. He was the leader of a covert group of super soldiers called the Ghost Warriors. The group did highly secretive work for military intelligence, and their specialty was assassinations. They were legendary for their skill. It's amazing to think that such a peaceful man could have so much blood on his hands, but it's true. Red Knife was a killer. But something happened to change all that, and he's never been the same."

"What happened," asked Raven.

"Red Knife killed the wrong man."

"What do you mean?"

"Working as a soldier for the government is a tricky thing. Sometimes, a soldier is ordered to do things for God and country that have nothing to do with God or country. This is particularly true in the shadowy world of military intelligence where people are routinely killed for a wide variety of reasons. Red Knife discovered that one of his victims had been targeted for termination because he had opposed the human trafficking taking place in his country. Red Knife may have been an assassin, but he was an assassin with a strict code of honor. When he realized that he was responsible for the death of an honorable man, a righteous man, he immediately lost faith in his superiors, his country, and himself. He was so traumatized by what he'd done, he ultimately lost his mind. So he set out to find it, and he walked away from everything."

"I don't imagine anyone can just walk away from military intelligence," said Raven perceptively. "That must be like trying to walk away from the Mob."

Mr. Freeman smiled at the depth of Raven's insight. "That's quite true. Yes, he certainly encountered opposition to his decision to walk away. Considerable opposition, as a matter of fact. Of course, Red Knife was well trained to deal with opposition and he never encountered a situation he couldn't handle. So he traveled the world for many years, living in the shadows, working menial jobs, studying various religions and philosophies, searching for truth and some kind of redemption for the life he had led.

In time he rebuilt himself, and perhaps even redeemed himself. He swore he'd never take another life and he never did. Never."

Raven smiled as she thought of Red Knife. At that very moment, he was probably puttering in his beloved garden behind the stable, talking sweetly to the many flowers he had planted there, ever careful not to accidentally step on a bug as butterflies hovered about him. If ever a man were truly in touch with his feminine side, it was Red Knife. And yet, this sweet, peaceful soul had been a highly trained professional killer. A Ghost Warrior. The very notion boggled Raven's mind, and aroused her even more. By now, Mr. Freeman had finished eating. Raven rose from her chair, took his tray, and prepared to leave.

"Was I of any help?" he asked.

Raven smiled. "Always. Oakwood is quite a puzzle."

Mr. Freeman smiled as he brushed crumbs from his lips. "You're exactly right. But not to worry. You've got plenty of time to solve it, and solve it you will. Once you do, everything will make total sense. I guarantee it."

Raven exited the office, closing the door behind her.

* * *

Red Knife lived in a trailer behind the stable. The interior was Spartan-simple and devoid of all but the absolute necessities. There was a queen size futon and a round, low-to-the-ground wooden table surrounded by pillows. A small shelf was stocked with a handful of books, mostly poetry. In one corner sat a mysterious trunk. One afternoon, Red Knife was sitting on the futon reading when he heard noises from outside. He walked over to the open window, peered out, and discovered Raven actively involved in an unusual activity. She had attached a life-sized dummy to the limb of a tree and it hung suspended, inches from the ground. Red Knife smiled at the handiwork of the dummy. It was close to six feet tall, a creatively haphazard mix of burlap sack cloth, flannel shirt, and overalls. It was stuffed with rags to make it as full and life-like as possible.

While the construction of the dummy itself was somewhat crude, the marking of vital nerve points on the figure revealed a high degree of anatomical knowledge. Raven was obviously aware of the various points throughout the body, points that when struck would inflict maximum damage. Small red pieces of fabric were sewn onto the dummy at these strategic points. Red Knife was amazed by what he saw.

Raven practiced a variety of punches and kicks, making sure to strike the various nerve centers. Red Knife leaned against the window in astonishment as he watched her. He had been unaware of her martial arts abilities and found her level of skill to be surprisingly high. Red Knife was fascinated by Raven's temperament. He had only seen the sweet side of her, the side that revealed itself when she interacted with animals or with him. But now, as she practiced with the dummy, she displayed the deadly demeanor of a warrior, a particularly *fierce* warrior. Red Knife was riveted by the sight and he smiled in admiration.

Raven delivered a well-placed kick to the dummy's chest causing it to break loose from the tree and land several feet away. Raven walked over to retrieve the dummy, and when she reached down to pick up the fallen figure, she was surprised to find Red Knife beside her, smiling.

"Let me give you a hand," he said.

Raven saw the opportunity of a lifetime presenting itself. Looking deep into his eyes, she got right to the point. "You wanna really give me a hand?" she asked. "Then be my *bank*. Teach me ... to be a *ghost*."

Red Knife the old warrior was hopelessly seduced by Raven's young warrior spirit, a spirit that made her irresistible. The wily Raven was perceptive enough to know that Red Knife the pacifist wanted to refuse her request, but Red Knife the warrior could not and would not. The student had the teacher by the throat and he was helpless.

Raven smiled *diabolically*.

When Red Knife saw that cruel smile, he realized that he was doomed to teach her every deadly skill he knew.

* * *

Several times a week, Raven met with Red Knife behind his trailer for lessons. He was trained in a variety of fighting styles but maintained that the love of his life was the style called Kenpo. He had learned the style from his grandfather in his native Hawaii. Red Knife had a different teaching style than Mao Ying. Where Mao Ying spoke very little during practice, Red Knife spoke a lot. While he was certainly firm in his instruction, his demeanor was considerably warmer than Mao Ying's. Red Knife was impressed with what Raven had learned from Mao Ying. He had studied some Wing Chun as well and held it in high regard. He was convinced that Raven would be well served by studying both Wing Chun and Kenpo and that each style complemented the other perfectly.

Red Knife had instructed many warriors throughout his life, but he had never encountered a more naturally gifted martial artist than Raven. In addition to her physical gifts, she also possessed an intellectual understanding of martial arts far beyond her young years. Red Knife explained that punches, kicks, slaps, and blocks were like the individual letters of an alphabet. Various combinations of these lethal letters formed words, sentences, and paragraphs of motion; an entire *vocabulary of motion*.

Raven grasped the concept completely. "You're teaching me a language," she said. "The more words I know, the more sentences I can create. The more sentences I create, the more paragraphs I can invent. The bigger my vocabulary, the more literate I'll be." She giggled at the lethal possibilities. "And the more *badass*."

Red Knife nodded as he fought a smile.

* * *

Late one evening, Red Knife lay on his futon reading poetry but unable to concentrate. Exotic music played in the background and the smell of incense filled the air. There was a soft knock at the door. Red Knife wasn't expecting anyone but he well knew who was knocking. His heartbeat quickened as he slipped on a robe.

"Come in," he said.

Raven entered carrying a tray. On the tray was a pot of tea, two cups and a small plate of biscuits. Instead of her usual jeans and Gung Fu shoes, she wore a colorful, loose-fitting peasant dress and sandals. There was an orchid in her hair. Her eyes were anxious and apprehensive.

"I know it's late," she said softly. "I hope I'm not interrupting you."

Red Knife was always happy to see Raven but he had never been more happy to see her than tonight. "*Nani*," he purred sweetly.

Red Knife always wore his long hair pulled back in a ponytail except at night. Now, the thick, grey mane hung loosely about his shoulders making him look like a beast. Red Knife stood and walked over to Raven who lingered by the door.

"It's okay," he warmly reassured her as he took the tray from her. "You're always welcome. I'm glad you came."

"Really?" she asked.

Red Knife didn't answer with words but convinced her with his eyes. The more she looked into them, the less nervous she felt. Red Knife placed the tray on the low round table and seated himself on one of the pillows.

"This smells good," he said approvingly. He poured tea into each of the cups.

Raven remained standing. She had never been in Red Knife's quarters before and she looked around curiously. "You don't have to worry about bumping into furniture, do you?" she said.

Red Knife laughed. "Feel free to give yourself a tour." He sampled the tea. "Excellent."

Raven's curious eyes immediately focused on the trunk in the far corner. She looked at Red Knife inquisitively. He rolled his eyes, sighed and shook his head in mock exasperation. He took another sip of tea, then stood and walked over to the trunk. He motioned for Raven to join him and she happily complied. They both knelt simultaneously, and Red Knife slowly opened the lid of the trunk. One by one, he removed a variety of weapons. There were several handguns of various calibers and exotic knives of different shapes and sizes. There were nunchucku, batons, throwing stars, darts, whips, chains, and brass knuckles. The weapons made a dramatic impact on Raven. She stared at them as if they were holy relics bathed in a heavenly glow. Red Knife went back to his pillow, leaving Raven to linger over his deadly arsenal.

As he sipped his tea, he watched as Raven intimately interacted with the weapons with glazed eyes. She seemed to be in a mild state of ecstasy and Red Knife was slightly amused by her reaction. After Raven had scrutinized each and every weapon, she reverently placed them all back into the trunk. Then she looked over at Red Knife and smiled *diabolically*, that cruel smile that both excited Red Knife and chilled him. Red Knife was certainly attracted to Raven, but he had long been troubled by her as well. Tonight, he finally understood why: Raven was a natural-born killer. She closed the trunk and joined Red Knife, sitting beside him on one of the floor pillows. There were large beads of sweat on her brow, her breathing was labored, and her eyes remained glazed. Her arousal was obvious. She drank the cup of tea Red Knife had prepared for her, then quickly poured another and drained that as well.

Red Knife watched her closely. "Are you okay?" he asked playfully.

Raven nodded as she wiped her brow.

Red Knife noticed that Raven was still wearing her sandals.

"Are you in a hurry?" he asked as he motioned toward her shoes.

Raven slipped off the sandals and tossed them aside. Red Knife picked up the plate of biscuits and offered it to Raven. She took a biscuit.

"Got any butter?" she asked.

Red Knife smiled with calm assurance. "Tonight, I make jelly."

5

Warrington Beasley

The Oakwood residents and staff had little contact with Warrington Beasley, and that's the way he wanted it. The human race depressed him, and he preferred to be separated from it, safely hidden away in his lab, surrounded by his gadgets, books, films, and tea. To him, people weren't people, they were *sheeple*; grazing together, collectively ignorant and ultimately destined for the slaughter.

Beasley rarely came down to the dining room for meals. As a result, he and Raven were able to devise the perfect ploy. She would arrive with a tray of food and knock on Beasley's door. He would angrily order her to go away, Raven would insist to be let in, and back and forth they would argue until he finally relented and allowed her entrance. But once she was inside, they dropped all pretense. Unbeknownst to Oakwood, Beasley and Raven had formed their own secret society.

Raven loved her secret sessions with Beasley. There was something forbidden about them that excited her, and the charade of bringing his meals only added to the thrill. Sometimes the sessions took the form of formal classes where Beasley taught traditional school subjects. Always impeccably dressed in a dapper tailor-made suit,

Beasley stood at his blackboard and used his cigarette holder as a pointer. Whether explaining complicated mathematical equations or dense philosophical theories, Beasley had a gift for making the most difficult ideas clear, concise, and understandable. He was a wonderful teacher, ever patient and endlessly encouraging.

Other times, instead of formal classes, Raven and Beasley simply hung out like two friends. As he tinkered away on some gadget, she sat beside him, absorbed in one of the books from his library. Beasley was proud of his library and felt honored that Raven loved it, too. Because she was so well read on such a variety of subjects, Raven thought and spoke with a knowledge far beyond her years. She enjoyed debate and wasn't afraid to challenge Beasley's ideas, and, naturally, he adored her for it. Beasley found Raven's youth and wisdom intoxicating and he became addicted to her presence. Raven was a fascinating specimen, unlike any human Beasley had ever known. The scientist in him felt compelled to study her.

One day after finishing lunch, Beasley began an informal scientific inquiry into the mystery of Raven. "You must have been an exceptional student. Did you like school?" he asked nonchalantly as he tinkered with a piece of equipment.

Raven was sitting on the floor beside one of the bookshelves, absorbed in a book on Indian mythology. The question caught her off guard, and she seemed a bit disturbed. Beasley noticed her mood darken.

"I never spent that much time in school," she answered.

"That's quite a surprise." Beasley poured himself a cup of tea and the room was filled with that strange fragrance. Raven remained a bit dour and Beasley was concerned that perhaps he had unearthed some unpleasant memories with his question. There was a long, awkward silence.

"You're by far the most intelligent young person I've ever met," he said cheerfully, taking a sip of tea. "What's your secret?"

Raven thought for a moment. "My secret? I don't know ... half a brain and a library card I guess."

Beasley laughed. "So you're a dropout! I'm not surprised one bit. And it's nothing to be ashamed of, by the way. Modern education very much needs to be abandoned. I applaud your decision. Smart girl."

Raven carefully re-shelved the book she had been reading and joined Beasley at his table.

"The modern concept of education is considerably different from the traditional definition ... the correct definition," Beasley continued. "The word 'education' is derived from the Latin word *educare* which means 'to bring up, to train, to raise, and to support'. Ideally, education is supposed to bring out the best in someone. Modern education does no such thing."

"But you're an educated man," Raven said.

"Indeed, so, I speak with authority." Beasley laughed. "Modern education teaches students to *answer the questions*. But in order to be one's best, one must *question the answers*."

Raven considered Beasley's words.

"You're not like most people. I could tell that from the first time I met you," Beasley said confidently.

 RAVENDIABLO

"What makes you so sure?"

"Because you stick out like a unicorn in a barnyard."

Raven laughed. Beasley could tell he was making an impression on her and it excited him. Though he spoke disdainfully of education, he was nevertheless a supremely gifted teacher. Nothing thrilled him more than illuminating a young mind, particularly a mind as ravenous as Raven's.

"Modern education serves the king," said Beasley. "It teaches all the king's subjects to believe the same fairy tales, especially the biggest fairy tale of all ... the one called civilization."

"You don't believe in civilization?" asked Raven.

"Of course not," he answered, as if surprised by the question. "Do you?"

"Well, I ..." Raven hesitated before saying more and committing herself to a position. "What's wrong with civilization? I thought that was the whole point, to have a civilized society. Isn't that the master plan?"

"Precisely!" Beasley answered. "A civilized society *is* the master plan. It's the plan of every society, and has been since civilization began, thousands of years ago. And do you know why? Because civilization destroys imagination."

"But why would a civilized society want to destroy imagination?"

"Because imagination is a pair of wings."

Raven contemplated Beasley's words.

"Civilization is the *wheel*," Beasley continued, "and the wheel need spokes. In the civilized society, the spokes are the citizens, and their wings have been clipped. Spokes certainly don't need wings."

"You speak blasphemy, Mr. Beasley," Raven said.

"Fluently."

"But you're a *product* of a civilized society."

"That's quite correct. I spent most of my life as a spoke in the wheel. So again, I speak with authority. Civilization is an amazing system, a set of connected parts that form a complex whole. Government makes laws to maintain the system. Banking and business make money from the system. Education molds minds to embrace the system. Religion preaches transcendence beyond the system. And mass media reinforces the belief that the system is totally real. When, in fact, it's nothing but a *mirage*."

"A mirage? The world we live in is just a mirage?"

"Yes, that's quite right," Beasley answered as he took a sip of tea.

"So if it's all just an illusion, then what's the truth?"

"The truth?" he responded. "Well, it's quite simple. We're all slaves."

Raven laughed.

"Traditionally, the word 'slave' is used to describe the worst of all possible existences," said Beasley. "And yet, literally speaking, a slave is merely someone who serves a master. Depending on the work, the wages, and the master, slaves can live lives of complete fulfillment. And most of them do, because civilization itself is the master and the citizen is the slave."

"That's quite a worldview you've got there."

"When I referred to you as a unicorn in a barnyard, that was just a silly way of saying that, unlike most of the subjects in the kingdom, you are an *individual*. You're no sheeple by any stretch of the imagination. And your imagination appears to be perfectly intact."

Raven smiled. "I've still got my wings, if that's what you mean."

"Indeed you do, which makes you more than just an unusual individual. It makes you an *outlaw*."

* * *

Late one evening, after leaving Beasley's quarters, Raven returned to the kitchen with a food tray. Mao Ying had long since gone to bed. Raven had placed the dirty dishes in the sink when she was startled by a sound behind her. She turned and found Mr. Freeman. He was searching in one of the refrigerators for a snack.

"Is there any more of that apple pie from lunch?" he asked sheepishly.

"I'll get it for you," Raven answered. "Have a seat."

Mr. Freeman closed the refrigerator and seated himself at a table. Raven washed her hands, then headed off to another part of the kitchen. She returned moments later with a large slice of pie in a bowl, topped with ice cream. Mr. Freeman's eyes went wide with excitement.

"You've got to be kidding?" he asked as Raven placed the bowl before him. Then he smiled impishly. "Actually, you read my mind."

Raven smiled. "I do that sometimes."

"I know it's late, but will you join me?" Mr. Freeman asked as he pondered which part of the dessert to attack first.

Raven sat beside him and watched him eat.

"It's nice that Beasley has finally found a friend," he said. "He could certainly use one."

Raven was surprised at Mr. Freeman's words. She thought that her secret relationship with Beasley was just that, a secret.

"I suppose you could say we've connected. Though I really don't know much about him."

"He's a mystery to be sure."

Mr. Freeman glanced over at Raven, well aware that she was waiting for him to fill in the missing blanks.

Raven poked a finger into his ice cream. She licked the finger and settled back in her chair. "Go for it."

"In a just world, the name Warrington Beasley would be both widely known and highly respected. It's quite unfortunate that a man of such immense and varied gifts could make the contributions to society that he's made, yet end up completely unknown ... and discarded."

Raven took a deep breath as she prepared herself for what would inevitably be a grim tale.

"As you've probably guessed from his accent, he's English. Born and raised in the town of Dudley, his roots are working class, though you'd never know it from his wardrobe. His father worked for British Railways and his mother was a teacher. Right from the beginning, his parents, particularly his mother, could tell that he was unusually bright. She nurtured his enormous intellect in every way she could—determined to make sure he had every opportunity to succeed. Beasley was an excellent student and enjoyed school very much, the subjects more than his fellow classmates."

"No doubt," laughed Raven.

"Beasley does have one well-known claim to fame. He's still the youngest student ever allowed admission to Cambridge University. He stayed there many years, basically collecting degrees. Chemical engineering, biotechnology, mathematics ... the list goes on and it's quite remarkable. He's surprisingly humble about his academic achievements. He's probably never even mentioned them to you. Beasley loved school *passionately*. It was his refuge, both as a child and as an adult. The academic life was his safe haven. But ... like many brilliant scholars, Beasley was ultimately recruited into, shall we say, government service."

"Intelligence?"

Mr. Freeman smiled. "Yes, that's quite correct. His various areas of expertise were well suited to an organization like MI6."

"MI6 ... that's CIA Brit style, isn't it? James Bond?"

"Bond, James Bond. That's quite correct".

Raven yawned, unimpressed. "James Bond, he's a company man."

"Well, Beasley viewed working for MI6 as his patriotic duty, a duty he took very seriously. He saw himself as a scientist in the service of the Queen. And his service was exemplary. Beasley was instrumental in the development of many important technologies used in the world of espionage. Many of his inventions are still used to this day by intelligence organizations all over the world ... MI6, CIA, Mossad, and others. He's anonymous to the general population but within certain circles, he's a living legend. In time, he became disillusioned with the world of intelligence."

"Let me guess, he found out James Bond was just a fairy tale?"

"Yes, that's right. The real James Bond doesn't save the world from egomaniacal lunatics bent on world domination. Intelligence is often as much a tool of big business as it is government. The *real* James Bond is more often than not a mercenary working for the highest bidder. Beasley took a long time to realize that, and when he finally did, it was quite a revelation for him. Though it was a far more difficult revelation to find out that his groundbreaking work was, shall we say ... " Mr. Freeman paused to find his words.

"Not his, but the Queen's?"

"That's correct. All of his original ideas, discoveries and inventions were ultimately taken from him. Stolen. In addition, a great many scientists went on to considerable fame and fortune building on Beasley's work. And there was nothing he could do about it, except walk away."

"Considering who he worked for, he's lucky he was able to do *that*."

"He returned home to Dudley a bitter man. Ultimately, he returned to what he did best and loved most. He became a schoolteacher."

Mr. Freeman finished his dessert with a smile. "That was quite delicious. Thank you."

"You want some more?"

Mr. Freeman smiled. "No, do you?"

Raven stood. "No, I've had enough ... for now."

Raven said goodnight and headed off to the library to learn more about MI6.

* * *

Beasley, the reclusive dapper genius, had a surprising secret, which Raven discovered by accident. One evening, Raven arrived at Beasley's laboratory carrying a covered food tray. Their secret sessions were always scheduled in advance, but no plans had been made for tonight. Raven showed up without invitation. Beasley was a movie fanatic with a collection befitting a university film school, and Raven shared his passion. It was love of film that moved Raven to do something she had never done—to show up unexpectedly. Beasley and Raven loved classic horror films, and Beasley's favorite was the British film, *Horror of Dracula*. Naturally, he owned the film, but only on videocassette. Knowing this, Raven ordered the film on DVD and decided to bring it to him, gift wrapped and unannounced, along with a tray of her famous chocolate chip cookies.

Raven knocked at Beasley's door but there was no response. She waited, then knocked again, with the same result. Beasley almost never left his lab; he had to be there. Raven knocked once more, but still no answer. Maybe he was in the bathroom and had been running water when Raven knocked. Surely that was it, and with that thought in mind, Raven turned the doorknob and happily found the door unlocked. She opened the door slightly, poked her head inside, and called out to Beasley in a voice loud enough to have been heard. Raven waited for a response, but there was none. The lab was dark except for a light that shone from a room at the end of a hallway, the one

Beasley had converted into a screening room. It was there he conducted his personal film festivals, and where Raven had learned about *film noir*, David Lean, and Hammer Films. Raven could hear sounds coming from the room and she called out again, almost shouting now, but still there was no answer.

Raven knew that Beasley was home, but for whatever reason had not heard her. Now, having convinced herself that something was indeed wrong, and that Beasley might even be in some genuine need, Raven entered Beasley's laboratory. It was nothing less than a home invasion.

Raven slowly made her way through the darkness and down the hallway, fighting her dwindling guilt with mental images of Beasley lying unconscious. Surely, it would have been wrong for her *not* to enter Beasley's lab. When she reached the screening room, she paused in the doorway and peered inside. The air was thick with the pungent aroma of one of Beasley's special tea blends. On the far wall, a large, flat screen monitor displayed the lush, black and white images of David Lean's classic film, *Great Expectations*. Beasley sat facing the screen in his favorite rocking chair with his back to Raven. She didn't call out to him as she should have done, but instead walked over to him, careful to make sure her steps were not heard. Beasley hadn't moved a muscle since Raven entered the room.

On a table beside him sat his favorite teapot. Beside it was an ornate wooden box that Raven had never seen before. Raven reached Beasley and found him just as she had imagined, unconscious. His favorite teacup rested empty in his lap. He was dressed, or rather, partly dressed,

 RAVENDIABLO

in a bathrobe and nothing else. It was an amazing sight, because Beasley was *always* dressed, and fastidiously so. His normally neat and slicked back hair hung loosely at his shoulders. His eyes were glazed and drool ran from his open mouth.

Raven rested the tray of cookies she had been carrying on the table beside the teapot. She picked up the wooden box and opened it. Inside were several small containers, all filled with different tea blends. Raven knew that Beasley had a passion for tea, a passion she had never pondered, nor questioned. It was hardly out of the ordinary for a Brit to love tea. Still, the aroma of Beasley's tea *was* out of the ordinary and unlike any traditional tea Raven had known. Raven had grown accustomed to the strange, exotic scents of his favorite blends. The aroma of Beasley's tea was an integral part of his apartment, like the orchestral sound-track music that he always played.

Raven sat on the floor beside the rocker with the wooden box resting in her lap. It was the size of a shoe box and intricately carved. It could easily have been the coffin for a bird. Beasley slowly awakened. When his eyesight focused, he found Raven sitting beside him cradling his tea box. He was momentarily startled by the sight of her but expressed no anger at her intrusion. Even his embarrassment at being discovered in such a disheveled state was short-lived, replaced by *relief*. Beasley no longer had to keep secrets from his one true friend. He sighed wearily and directed his gaze away from Raven and to the images of *Great Expectations*. Raven picked up a remote laying on the floor nearby and turned down the volume of the film.

"Disappointed?" Beasley asked. He desperately wanted to look at Raven and gauge her reaction, but he kept his eyes fixed on the screen.

Raven, in turn, didn't look at Beasley but kept her focus on the wooden box in her lap. "Beasley's a junkie," she said flatly, without emotion.

"Raven, I'm no junkie," said Beasley with a trace of sadness in his voice.

Raven laughed. "Well, you sure look like one to me!"

"I am not a junkie!" Beasley insisted defensively. "I'm an explorer ... in the further regions of experience. I do what I do to open doors."

"There are things known and things unknown, and in between are the doors, is that it?" Raven asked sardonically.

"That's quite correct. I've spent a lifetime expanding my consciousness. An expanded consciousness is a *creative* consciousness. I'm not a junkie, I'm a scientist."

Raven sneered. "Feeding your head, huh?"

"Something like that."

"Are you sure you're feeding it and not just living in it?"

"For what it's worth, I don't condone what I do for others."

"Don't even worry about it," snapped Raven. "I'm a control freak." Her tone was arrogant. She caressed the box. "I can just imagine what you've got in here. This little box must hold the sum total drug knowledge of the last few thousand years." Raven sighed as she considered the possibilities. "You've probably invented the greatest drug of all time."

Beasley looked away from *Great Expectations* and to Raven.

"I have!" he exclaimed with an almost childlike enthusiasm. "I truly have! There's never been anything like it!"

Beasley's excited response was hilarious and Raven wanted to laugh, but she steadfastly maintained her somewhat icy demeanor. She had decided that she *was* disappointed in Beasley after all and she wanted him to know it. "Dressed or undressed, you're still a junkie," she said dryly. "Wardrobe, or lack thereof, has got nothing to do with it."

"I've just opened a door unlike any other."

"But where is it taking you? Cause from what I can see, you're not going anywhere."

Raven stood and placed the wooden box back on the table. She leaned over close enough to whisper in Beasley's ear. "Maybe civilization didn't clip your wings. Maybe you clipped your own wings," she said. Raven lovingly kissed Beasley on the cheek. "But you're still the bee's knees."

Raven walked away from Beasley and out of the screening room.

"The bee's knees," he repeated with a wistful smile. The words transported him to another time and place. "I do love that child."

6

Blake Swanigan

Blake Swanigan looked like a movie star. He wore red boots, black leather pants, large buckle belts, pirate shirts with billowing sleeves open to the waist, brightly colored scarves, and an enormous wide-brimmed hat strategically tipped to one side. Swanigan dressed as if he had just swung in on a rope from a movie set. Though he was magnificent in physical appearance and style, Swanigan was genuinely lacking in arrogance or egotism, which of course made him all the more attractive. He was a real beauty, particularly his widescreen, Technicolor smile.

Raven adored Swanigan. Initially, it was his extraordinary firearms skill that had mesmerized her. She had never seen anything like it, even in the movies. He could hit any target at any distance with any type of firearm. With his style and skill, he personified the term *sharpshooter*. He had obviously spent a considerable amount of time practicing to achieve such prowess, but he always made his shooting skill seem completely effortless. Swanigan was proud of his private shooting range in the meadow, a shooting range unlike any other. He stood on a wooden dancefloor ten feet in diameter that allowed him to slip, slide, and spin with ease. A portable stereo played his favorite flamenco music.

Beside him was a table lined with various weapons. Several feet away, scattered around him in all directions was an assortment of targets placed on fences, tree stumps, boxes, and crates. Swanigan turned his target practice into an elaborate extravaganza. He would fire off several rounds in rapid succession, spinning and firing simultaneously for maximum dramatic effect. Raven had never seen anything like it.

Swanigan loved performing and Raven was his dream audience. She greeted each Blake Swanigan show with the enthusiasm of a child. Sitting safely off to the side, she wildly applauded his performances. Swanigan was more than just a flamboyant showman; he was a legitimate firearms expert and took weaponry very seriously. When it was apparent that Raven was destined to be his pupil and protege, he first gave her a thorough grounding in gun safety. He also taught her how to properly clean and main-tain the firearms. Swanigan was impressed with Raven's attentiveness and dedication. He was also impressed that she wanted to learn all aspects of firearms, not just shoot-ing targets. Raven loved guns and proved to have a high degree of natural ability. With Swanigan's careful instruc-tion and her own diligent practice, Raven became profi-cient quickly.

It was obvious to Swanigan that Raven was a born shootist. He felt it was imperative that she also under-stand firearms *intellectually*. Swanigan had a unique firearms philosophy and the time soon came to share it with Raven.

One afternoon, standing beside one another on the dancefloor, Swanigan and Raven focused on targets in the distance. Perched on a fence post several yards away sat an empty wine bottle. Resting on the mouth of the wine bottle was a shot glass filled with water. Raven wore her favorite holster and pistol. Music played softly in the background.

"You're born to the gun, youngblood," Swanigan said. "I've never seen anything like it."

"Born to the gun," Raven repeated with a smile.

"Guns get a lot of bad press. But a gun is like anything, it's got rules," he insisted. "And as long as you follow those rules, you're okay. Don't wear it if you don't know how to use it. Don't pull it unless you *intend* to use it."

"And when I do use it ... *shoot to kill*. Right?"

Swanigan looked over at his prized pupil and smiled. "Yeah, that's right. That thing strapped to your leg is made of steel. But don't let it fool you; it's *alive*, like a wild beast."

Raven listened closely as she concentrated on the target in front of her.

"A wild beast is filled with great power and capable of great things. But a beast is absolutely nothing without *control*. Control focuses power. Control maximizes power. Control makes all things possible. Control the beast and you'll hit the target. Understand?"

"Yes, sir."

Swanigan stepped back. Still focused on the target in front of her, Raven took a deep breath, drew her pistol and fired. She missed the shot glass and shattered the wine bottle instead. Raven shook her head in disappointment. Swanigan wasn't disappointed at all.

"Hey, that's what practice is for," he said reassuringly with his widescreen, Technicolor smile.

* * *

Raven later realized that Swanigan's skills went beyond shooting and dancing. One morning, Raven received a message that Swanigan wished to see her in his quarters. She had never been with Swanigan anywhere but the meadow shooting range. She was ecstatic at the opportunity to meet him in his private, natural habitat. When she arrived, Swanigan greeted her, dressed in his typical flamboyant attire. The hat was missing, though he wore a long purple headscarf and a huge, hoop earring. Raven entered the apartment and surveyed Swanigan's surroundings, an unusual blend of rustic, western style furniture, Asian artwork and Persian rugs. Flamenco music played in the background.

"Make yourself at home," he said. "I'll be right back."

Swanigan walked away, giving Raven the opportunity to get a closer look at the private Blake Swanigan. She spotted a bookshelf across the room and hurried over to it. Raven was surprised to find that there were no books on firearms. Most of the shelf space was devoted to books on psychology, criminology, and forensics. But it was a movie poster hanging beside the bookshelf that aroused Raven's curiosity the most. The poster appeared to be very old, and it was for a western film called *The Flamenco Kid*. The illustration of the dashing cowboy holding a gun and a whip looked somewhat familiar. The name at the bottom confirmed the identity.

"It's you!" yelled Raven excitedly.

Swanigan returned with a glass of orange juice which he handed to Raven.

"Hollywood movie star! I knew it!" she exclaimed. "You better give me your autograph! You've been holding out."

Swanigan laughed shyly, genuinely touched by Raven's excitement. "Yeah, well, that was many moons ago. And not exactly Hollywood, either."

Raven studied the poster carefully as if it were a rare piece of artwork hanging in a museum. "What do you mean?"

"Hollywood was never ready for a black cowboy star. Certainly not in those days, that's for sure. When I was young, I did a few pictures specifically for the black movie theater circuit. Because of the dancing, they ended up being pretty popular south of the border. More popular, actually."

"The Flamenco Kid ... I love it." Raven continued to stare at the poster in awe.

Swanigan stood beside her and gazed at the poster with a bittersweet smile. "Yeah, he was my baby. A dancing black Zorro!" Swanigan laughed. "It was fun while it lasted, but it ended and I moved on."

Raven took a sip of juice, looked over at Swanigan and winked. "I think we need to have a movie night real soon, don't you?"

Swanigan blushed. "One day, one day, I promise. But I had you come over to talk to you about something else. I need some help, and I want to make you an offer. Follow me."

Swanigan led Raven down a hall and into another room and she was unprepared for what she found there. It was a sewing room. There were two large tables covered with fabrics. Each table had its own elaborate sewing machine. Beside each table was a life-size mannequin. There was another table covered with a variety of sketches, mostly of clothes. Swanigan took a seat at the drawing table and searched through the pile of pictures. Looking around the room, Raven felt as if she had just stepped into the workroom of a fashion designer.

"So here's what's up, Blood," he said as he searched. "I'm making some new drapes for the joint. I suppose I could do it by myself, but it would go a lot faster with some good help. Not only that, I'll pay you. This is different from that other stuff they've got you doing. This is extracurricular."

Raven sat on a stool beside Swanigan, still amazed by the sights surrounding her. She glanced over at Swanigan and carefully eyed him up and down. "So you make your own clothes, huh?" she asked with a smile.

"Of course, I do," he said, still searching. "I love fashion, but there's something you've got to remember, something really important. The word fashion is also a *verb*. If I let someone else force me into *their style*, they're forcing me to play by *their rules*, I make my own rules, so I make my own clothes. You feel me?"

"I feel you." Raven laughed. "Fashion is a verb."

"And don't forget it, either. So ... do you sew?"

"A little, but with the right instruction, I could be fabulous."

Swanigan finally found the picture he had been searching for. "Bullseye!" he said happily.

He handed the picture to Raven. It was an intricately drawn, finely detailed picture of her. It was a remarkable likeness, though with a few creative touches. She had wildly flowing hair and her face was a horrifying mask of fury, complete with a long, protruding tongue. Instead of two arms, she had four; one held a sword and the others held bloody body parts. Swanigan drew Raven as a terrifying monster, and as she stared at the picture in amazement, it was clear that Raven felt deeply honored by the depiction. She couldn't stop staring at it.

Among his other talents, Swanigan was a gifted artist. He was also an uncannily accurate judge of character. In drawing Raven as a monster, Swanigan had indeed captured the *real* Raven. Swanigan often thought of the first day he met her, when she blazed into his life on horseback. Swanigan immediately knew that he was in the presence of a child of destiny. His grandmother used to call them "beacons" because they shone so bright. Raven was such a light, a child of destiny to be sure. But in spite of her glorious light, she remained an exceedingly *dark* child, and therein lay her paradox. Because Raven had the heart of an angel, but the spirit of a *hellraiser*. Raven was a criminal mastermind, or perhaps, hopefully, just a gifted young mind with criminal inclinations, but in need of loving guidance.

Fortunately, Raven's criminal inclinations had completely disappeared after she came to Oakwood. Swanigan was pleased to discover that she was a mature and serious

   RAVENDIABLO

student, always eager to learn new skills. However, it was the skills of death that thrilled her the most. Her insatiable passion for guns, knives, and other weapons reflected a dark truth that Swanigan both recognized and understood. Raven was a natural born hunter, but cunning enough to hide behind a carefully manufactured mask of civility. To the many residents and staff, she was Raven Chandler, a former juvenile delinquent with a heart of gold, a lost child who found her way at Oakwood. Her mask was not a lie, but merely a *front*, for Raven certainly did have a heart of gold. Swanigan's radar recognized the goodness and decency in Raven, and he loved her for it. But Swanigan saw something else when he looked into her eyes, something disturbing. He saw his own reflection. Raven and Swanigan were of like mind. He recognized her darkness because it was his darkness as well. Blake Swanigan was a natural born hunter, too. His mask was his widescreen, Technicolor smile.

Raven continued to stare at Swanigan's frightening sketch. "That's me!" she said with gushing pride.

"Yeah, I know," sighed Swanigan. "I just draw what I see."

* * *

Late one night, Raven grew weary of waiting for Swanigan's often promised movie night to materialize. She finally took the matter into her own capable hands and searched the video shelves in the audio/visual room of the Oakwood library until she found the Holy Grail. The DVD was titled *The Flamenco Kid's Revenge*. Raven seated herself at one of the special viewing tables equipped with a player and a video monitor. Soon, the room was filled with the sound of gunfire, flamboyant dance steps, and Raven's own squeals of delight as she beheld the sight of a young Swanigan as the Flamenco Kid, righting wrongs in between elaborate dance numbers. When the film ended, she was ready to play the disk a second time.

"He's quite spectacular, isn't he?"

Raven turned to find Mr. Freeman standing beside her. He was holding a large, leather-bound book.

"He sure is," Raven said turning back to the screen. "He's fabulous. Pull up a seat. Where's the popcorn?"

Mr. Freeman smiled as he seated himself beside Raven. "Yes, Blake Swanigan is quite fabulous, though I have a hunch you still don't know to what extent. Here, have a look at this."

The book Mr. Freeman was holding was called *Legends of the Texas Rangers*. He opened the book to a specific page and handed it to Raven. Raven was shocked to see Swanigan's picture taking up an entire page. He was a bit older than the Swanigan on the television screen, but considerably younger than the Swanigan Raven knew. He was still very dashing, but his face was stern and serious, devoid of the widescreen smile.

"That's no Hollywood coffee table book you're holding," said Mr. Freeman. "Allow me to introduce Blake Swanigan, legendary lawman. Surprised?"

"Nothing much surprises me anymore, not around here." Raven sat back in her chair with her eyes glued to Swanigan's picture.

"Blake Swanigan was a legend among legends. He was one of the first to integrate the all-white Texas Rangers. Moreover, he proved himself to be one of the greatest Rangers to ever wear the badge. He was cited for extraordinary bravery on several occasions. The most famous involved a notorious gang of bikers called the Bad Bunch. One night they crashed a quiet little diner, hungry for trouble. They found it all right because Swanigan just happened to be dining there. He finished his meal, then he finished them. All ten of them ... single-handedly. As a Ranger, he routinely tangled with the roughest and the toughest."

"I bet he always got his man," said Raven. Raven moved her eyes from the book and back to the television screen where the Flamenco Kid was doing a spectacular dance routine.

Mr. Freeman smiled. "He's a strange bird, far too humble to sing his own praises or blow his own horn. Blake Swanigan is of the old school with values from another age entirely. The age of chivalry; the age of King Arthur and the Round Table."

"Swannie would've been the Black Knight."

Raven and Mr. Freeman laughed.

"Swanigan was always a black sheep, even as a child," Mr. Freeman continued. "Never able to fit in with his peers, always an outsider looking in. Fortunately, he was raised by a wise and loving grandmother who understood just how unique he really was. She nurtured him very carefully. She instilled him with old world values, and taught him a variety of skills. Swanigan's not like other men. He's a rainbow."

"He sure shines like one, that's for sure."

"Yes, that he does".

"So he went from movie star to Texas Ranger? That's a strange segue, isn't it?"

Mr. Freeman laughed. "Perhaps, but not really. Not for a black knight. Swanigan always possessed a strong sense of justice, just like his character, the Flamenco Kid. I would imagine that his beloved grandmother taught him that righting wrongs is the most important and rewarding of all endeavors."

Raven looked at the photograph in the book once again. "Can I hold onto this for awhile?" she asked.

"Be my guest. Goodnight, Raven."

Mr. Freeman stood and exited the room leaving Raven to her thoughts. Finally, she closed the book and held it close to her breast as she pressed PLAY for another viewing of the *Flamenco Kid's Revenge.*

* * *

One afternoon, Raven decided to put on a special show of her own for Swanigan. She stood in the meadow on the dance floor, dressed in boots, jeans, and a leather vest she had made herself. With her hands on her hips, Raven scrutinized the various targets with which she had surrounded herself. Bottles, cans, and shot glasses were carefully and strategically placed. Raven smiled at her handiwork.

Sitting on a stool several feet away, Swanigan smiled, too. He knew he was in for a special treat. Raven turned on the boombox and the meadow was filled with the sounds of flamenco music. Raven strapped on two holsters. One was a traditional holster that hung at her side. The other holster hung in front of her, crossing over her thigh at an angle. She glanced over at Swanigan who could barely contain his growing excitement. Raven coolly moved to the center of the dance floor and closed her eyes in concentration. She took a deep breath, opened her eyes and quickly drew the pistol strapped at her side. Effortlessly, she fired shots in rapid succession, striking several of the targets. Swanigan wanted to applaud, but he restrained himself.

Raven spun the gun back into its holster gunslinger style, a move that caused Swanigan to spasm in unexpected delight. She glanced at the remaining targets, six shot glasses resting on six wine bottles. She drew her second pistol, dramatically dropped to one knee and fired off several more shots. Every shot glass exploded and Swanigan leaped to his feet cheering.

Raven was saving the best for last. She slowly stood as she holstered the smoking gun. The music swelled as if on cue. Then Raven burst into a mad flurry of complicated dance steps, expertly imitating the fancy flamenco footwork she had studied from the Flamenco Kid DVDs. Swanigan was awestruck. He had yet to screen his films for Raven, and had never taught her any of his dance moves. Raven had clearly done her dance homework and moved skillfully and confidently, sometimes adding dramatic moves of her own invention. When the music finally ended, Raven stopped dancing and glanced over at Swanigan. His eyes were filled with pride and tears. The widescreen, Technicolor smile was plastered across his face.

"I feel you, Blood!" he yelled. "I feel you!"

"That's what practice is for." Raven winked at him and pretended to be nonchalant, but inside, she was dancing.

7

Loona Shumenko

Most of the Oakwood residents and staff were deathly afraid of Loona Shumenko, and with good reason. She was a fearsome creature. Her ferocious temper and propensity for extreme physical violence were legendary. Over the years, she had been involved in several incidents, the most notorious involving a male attendant who had entered her quarters one morning without knocking. She broke both his jaw and his arm and hurled him out of her fourth-story window. Oakwood lawyers managed to settle the case out of court. Though she stood barely over five feet tall, she was unusually strong and agile, particularly for her age. Once her anger had been aroused, it generally took several people to subdue her. She routinely carried a blade in her boot and was considered armed and dangerous. Loona had the personality of a hellion, and the face of an angel— a stunningly beautiful angel. It was this strange paradox that made her so compelling, particularly to Raven. She was the most beautiful woman Raven had ever seen.

Loona's head was crowned with long silver hair that she wore in a thick, single braid wrapped around her head, so it actually looked like a crown. She usually dressed in red: red scarf, red vest, red baggy silk pants, and red boots.

Her shirts were always white with intricate red embroidery on the collar and cuffs. Loona took great pride in her appearance and never emerged from her quarters until she deemed herself impeccable. Though she was small in stature, her presence was colossal and unsettling. Like a tornado or a tidal wave, Loona Shumenko was a formidable force of nature. Of course, she wasn't always a raging hellion. Typically, she was cold and aloof. Her demeanor was a suit of armor and she wore it at all times. It kept people at arms length, which, of course, was the idea. Loona had no use for people.

However, there were two exceptions.

Whenever Loona came down to the dining room for meals, she entered like a red dragon and anyone in her way quickly stepped aside. She always dined alone since no one ever dared sit with her. In fact, residents tended to sit as far away from her as possible. She preferred it that way. Loona didn't attend every meal, but she never missed breakfast. That's because Mao Ying always prepared a special dish solely for Loona, a Ukrainian pancake called a "blini". Blinis can be filled with a variety of items from butter and jam to meat or caviar. Every morning, Loona's special breakfast blini would be filled with a different item. Whenever Mao Ying came out to greet the residents during meals, she always made a point of reaching Loona's table last. Loona was well educated and spoke several languages. Though she wasn't fluent in Mandarin or Cantonese, she spoke them reasonably well, well enough to converse with a delighted Mao Ying. Loona was a perfectionist and always encouraged Mao Ying to correct any pronunciation mistakes she might make. Mao Ying never did. She was enchanted by Loona's accent and saw no need for correction. To Raven, the chemistry between Loona and Mao Ying was obvious, probably the result of each one viewing the other as a strange, exotic creature. Whenever the two of them were together, they were oblivious to the world around them.

Raven forever endeared herself to Loona accidentally. She had read Loona's book, but Loona's frigid, aloof demeanor had dissuaded her from approaching the legendary fierce little woman with the crown of silver hair—and besides, she was learning so much from her other mentors.

One evening, many of the residents were gathered in the Oakwood lounge. The lounge was a hub of activity and a popular area for residents, particularly in the evening hours. Some residents sat at tables playing cards, chess, and other games. Other residents sat in front of a large television watching an international variety program. The program featured a assortment of entertainment from singers and dancers to magicians and animal acts. When the program host introduced an eastern European dance troupe, the screen was filled with athletic men doing squatting kicks and acrobatic leaps accompanied by lively folk music. Raven was in charge of refreshments, and floated about the room serving treats and refilling glasses. She looked up from a particular task and was shocked to see that Loona had wandered in. Loona *never* came to the lounge if there were people, but she had heard the music while walking the hallway and had come in to investigate.

She stood motionless, transfixed by the activity on the screen. As she watched, her normally blazing eyes were noticeably soft and filled with longing.

Several residents sat at a table nearby watching the program while playing poker. One of them, a somewhat arrogant woman, offhandedly commented that if she had to watch Russian dance, she much preferred ballet to the Cossack chaos on the screen. Raven heard the comment and corrected the woman, explaining that the dancing was actually Ukrainian and *not* Russian. Raven's comment stunned Loona. She glanced over at Raven and eyed her with intense curiosity, recognizing her as the girl who, many months ago, had danced to the waltz she had played on the piano.

The dancing on the television, the Cossack chaos, was called Hopak. Hopak is universally but erroneously labeled as being Russian. While the dance is Cossack in origin, only a highly knowledgeable person would know the Ukrainian connection. For a young person to be aware of the connection was unfathomable. Raven's wise words had a profound effect on Loona. She immediately realized that Raven was no ordinary young girl. The arrogant woman then made an unfortunate comment.

"Well, what's the difference between a Ukrainian and a Russian, anyway?"

Loona exploded with rage. She rushed to the table and kicked it, sending it flying far across the room and into a wall. Everyone who had been sitting at the table frantically scrambled in all directions, attempting to escape the Ukrainian tornado that had been unleashed. Shrieking in anger, Loona turned her sights on the arrogant woman, but several quick-thinking staff members subdued her before she could attack. It was still a struggle. Loona was small and advanced in years, but she had the strength of someone younger and larger. The staff members had a difficult time restraining her and the more they tried, the more combative she became. Raven quickly hurried over to assist. She looked into Loona's eyes reassuringly and caressed her cheek. Raven's tender intervention diffused Loona's anger, and she calmed down and stopped struggling. The staff members reluctantly released their grip. Raven tenderly slid her arm around Loona's waist and led her out of the lounge. As they exited, the lounge exploded in loud boos and catcalls directed at the fearsome Loona.

* * *

The roof of the Oakwood library was the perfect place to watch the sunset. It was Loona's favorite spot, and most evenings she could be found there. She was pleased when Raven began to join her. Raven's presence filled Loona with joy and made her lonely life at Oakwood more bearable. Raven melted Loona's armor and brought out the sweetness she kept hidden from the world. Before long, the two of them would often sit on the roof at a table and play chess by candlelight as the sun went down. Of course, Loona was a chess master.

Occasionally, while waiting for a stymied Raven to make a move, Loona would stare out into the orange distance with sad eyes. She looked more like a lost child than the tornado of Oakwood. The only time Loona ever appeared to be truly happy was when she spoke of her childhood. Born in the city of Kyiv, the largest city in Ukraine, she was raised by a loving and eccentric grandfather whom she called Dido.

"When I was a little girl, I wasn't like other little girls," Loona said as she casually moved a chess piece.

"No doubt," said Raven who found herself perplexed by the move.

"I hated girl's clothes and housework and anything else girls were supposed to be and supposed to do." Loona laughed wickedly. "I preferred knives to dolls. This made my Dido proud!"

"He never tried to force you to be ... traditional?"

"No, never!" answered Loona excitedly as she remembered days gone by. "He said it was good for me to rebel. He said it showed I had the spirit of a Cossack. My Dido was a real Cossack who descended from a long line of Cossacks."

"What does 'Cossack' mean anyway?" asked Raven, as she pondered her chess predicament.

Loona smiled with even more pride. "Free person."

"That's a good thing to be."

"It's the best thing to be! It's not easy to be free. Freedom requires self discipline and imposes great responsibilities. And it doesn't make you safe, either." Loona sneered. "Slavery is easy. Society's chains are designed to be comfortable. But to be free, to live free, that's hard to do. Because to be free, you must fight. From the day you're born to the day you die. A free person is a rebel."

"But I thought rebel was a bad word," Raven said sarcastically.

"It *is* a bad word ... to whomever you're rebelling against! Cossacks are born rebels. We had to be. Ukraine has long been a Garden of Eden surrounded by predators who tried to take what was ours and make us slaves!"

"Bad idea."

"Yes! Very bad idea!" exclaimed Loona. "Mongols, Tartars, Turks, Poles, and Russians! They all came and they all fell. We Cossacks destroyed them! Chains don't become us and we refuse to wear them!"

"And you're great dancers, too."

Loona laughed heartily. "Yes, we're great dancers, too! We do dance fiercely, do we not? You like Hopak, no?"

"I love it." Raven smiled mischievously. "If someone taught me, I could learn to move like that. I bet you could teach me ... if you wanted to. I've read your book, by the way. Twice." Raven's tone was sly and playful and it brought a warm smile to Loona's face.

"You knew Hopak was Ukrainian ... not Russian. How did you know this?" Loona asked curiously.

"I don't know, I just knew. I probably read it somewhere."

Loona nonchalantly performed a checkmate that effectively ended the game, leaving Raven thoroughly stunned.

"Did you also know Hopak was actually a martial art, disguised as a dance?"

Raven looked up from the chessboard. She was surprised to hear that information. "No, I didn't know that."

Loona smiled like a shark and her dark eyes sparkled. "I could teach you."

* * *

Loona and Raven met in the gymnasium for Hopak practice. Loona never established a fixed, predetermined time for practice sessions. She preferred to meet informally whenever the mood struck or whenever each party happened to be available. Loona said it was important for Hopak to remain flexible, not fixed. Because of her continuing studies with Mao Ying and Red Knife, Raven was certainly no stranger to martial arts. Hopak was very different from Wing Chun and Kenpo. Loona was extremely proud of her Cossack heritage and made a special point of differentiating Hopak from other styles of martial arts.

"Hopak is based on the natural movement of the body, not fighting stances and predictable, prearranged patterns of movement. Hopak teaches practical responses to realistic situations. It's a system of tactics, not a collection of techniques. Techniques create a box and limit the ability to problem-solve. On the contrary, tactics are determined by the uniqueness of a particular situation. Hopak is not a fixed pattern, it's a spontaneous, improvised process. And Cossacks don't meditate themselves into a state of hypnotic unconsciousness. We are always aware. And battle ready."

"Battle ready" was a favorite term and Loona used it often.

"In a violent world, one must be prepared for the possibility of violence at all times. The Cossacks understood this because we lived surrounded by enemies. But our circumstances made us stronger and our enemies feared us. They knew we were battle born and battle ready."

Loona was trained in ballet, modern dance, and gymnastics, but her heart was clearly Hopak. Music was an integral part of Hopak practice and Loona always brought a small portable stereo and several CDs of traditional Ukrainian music. Sessions began with elaborate stretching and breathing exercises. Loona insisted that flexibility and relaxation were crucial for learning Hopak. To Raven, it often seemed that Loona taught very little actual dancing, instead concentrating on the fundamental elements of martial arts like kicking, punching and grappling. Loona was a patient and encouraging teacher. She could see that Raven had extraordinary natural ability and was destined to be a formidable warrior. Loona saw Raven as more than her student. Raven was her natural heir.

One afternoon after a particularly grueling session, Raven sat on the gymnasium floor. She was exhausted by the session and somewhat disappointed in her performance. Loona sensed her sadness and sat beside her.

"My little *bebik*," Loona said sweetly. "Why so sad?"

"My game was a little off today. I'll do better next time."

"Hopak is teaching your body to think, and that takes time. You're learning far more than a fighting system. The true purpose of Hopak is self-understanding. Discovering your strengths and weaknesses, gaining insight into that unique mechanism called your mind. These things can be difficult and sometimes painful." Loona laughed warmly. "Self understanding is a form of sculpting, an artistic process. With each session, you slowly chip away at yourself. The more layers you remove, the closer you get to the masterpiece."

"I guess that makes me a work in progress."

Loona hugged Raven and didn't release her. "I'm old but my eyes are well trained. I can see the masterpiece already. My *bebik* is a Cossack. Battle born."

Raven's spirits were somewhat lifted. "And battle ready."

* * *

Raven had been assigned the task of repainting the quarters of several residents. She loved painting, turning it into a form of moving meditation, a term she learned from Red Knife. Painting allowed her to zone out while remaining totally aware and focused on the job at hand. One morning she prepared one resident's apartment, painstakingly covering furniture with plastic protective covering.

"You're very thorough."

Raven turned to find Mr. Freeman had entered the apartment. Mr. Freeman smiled as he scrutinized the meticulous way in which Raven had prepared the room for painting. "You're better than the hired help," he said admiringly.

"Anything worth doing is worth doing right."

"By the way, I wanted to mention something. I've

noticed a marked difference in Loona. After her last outburst, I was very concerned about her. We don't allow
such behavior here at Oakwood. Lately, she seems to be
much more at peace."

"Is that right?" Raven hurried over to where several
cans of paint awaited her. She knelt down and examined
the writing on one of the cans.

"We've tried to make Oakwood as comfortable and
pleasurable as possible," Mr. Freeman continued. "Most of
our residents are able to find some happiness here, but
never Loona. She's always been the walking wounded of
Oakwood. I don't know what magic you've worked, but
you've definitely healed her."

Raven kept her back to Mr. Freeman as she carefully
stirred one of the cans of paint. "So who wounded her? It
can't be easy to wound a Cossack."

"As you've already discovered, Oakwood is home to
many unusual residents. I would place Loona at the top of
that list. As a young girl in the Soviet Union, it was clear
that she was gifted in a wide range of areas. Athletic, intellectual, artistic. A senior Communist Party member in the
Ministry of Culture who knew her grandfather from pre-
revolutionary days saw to it that her natural gifts were
lovingly nurtured. He arranged for her admission to an
elite school for girls in Moscow. It was a great opportunity
for her, but she was miserable there. She desperately
missed the life she left behind in Ukraine. Like a true Cossack, though, she persevered, remained in Russia, and
continued her long education. Loona could have had an
illustrious career in any number of fields—music, lan-

guage, science. She chose dance and started her own company. The Culture Ministry recognized the propaganda potential of her troupe and supportd her efforts. Loona and her company performed to great acclaim all over the world. Unfortunately, the Nazi invasion put an end to her artistic career. But it was something else which changed the direction of her life forever."

"Did it involve Dido, her grandfather?"

"Yes, as a matter of fact, it did. After the war and the Nazi surrender, her grandfather and several other men, mostly dissident Party leaders, were involved in a conspiracy. They plotted to assassinate the Soviet General Secretary, Joseph Stalin, the dictator who had ruled Ukraine as part of the Soviet Union for many brutal years. They vowed to end Stalin's reign of terror and they almost succeeded. But they were betrayed, discovered, and executed after torture. Though Loona had no knowledge of the plot, the authorities arrested her just the same. Members of her dance troupe dramatically rescued her from captivity, but they, too, were killed in the process, including the love of her life. From that point on, Loona spiraled out of control, eventually becoming somewhat of an underground legend."

"An underground legend? What do you mean?"

"As you know, Cossacks are natural-born outlaws. Loona continued that Cossack tradition in her own unique way and became ... well, a kind of roving executioner. She targeted Party members, government officials, and anyone else she blamed for the tragedy in her life. She was both renowned and feared for her cunning, her ruthlessness, her incredible skills at disguise, and her extreme violence. Her colorful exploits generally went unreported, or *misreported*, but people well knew the name Sister Sabre.

Raven smiled. Dido would have been very proud indeed.

8

Guy Dupont

Raven was greatly influenced by all her mentors at Oakwood, but it was Guy Dupont who made the most profound impact. What she ultimately learned from him consolidated and maximized the knowledge she gained from the others. Initially, it was his mastery of performance magic that had spellbound her. Whether doing close-up magic with coins and cards or complex illusions with large props, Dupont was a magical virtuoso. Watching him work not only thrilled her, but inspired her as well. Dupont's magic almost literally spoke to Raven, informing her that if she worked hard and focused her powers, she, too, could perform the miraculous and do magic in her own life. Being in his presence left her feeling positively charged. But there was something else. Raven instinctively knew that Dupont was destined to play some pivotal role in her life. In fact, he already had. That first time he called her up on stage to assist him, he changed her life forever.

That's when Raven realized that she was born to magic. She had found her calling, and it was entirely due to Dupont. In time, she became an integral part of Dupont's magic act.

One evening, following a performance, Dupont and

Raven were backstage loading props into trunks and cases. As Dupont worked, he watched Raven from the corner of his eye. He was impressed by the care and reverence with which she handled the many items. She treated the tools of the profession like priceless artifacts, and it made him admire her all the more. Dupont loved being with her, both on and off the stage. Her presence was electric and left him positively charged. It was clear to Dupont's keen eye that Raven possessed the necessary skills to become a magician herself. She was intelligent and motivated. She remained cool and collected under pressure. She was an excellent judge of people. But most importantly, she always seemed to be in a state of heightened awareness. Dupont saw Raven as more than a talented protegee. Raven was going to be his greatest creation ... his magical masterpiece. Her mysterious arrival at Oakwood seemed to confirm something that a wise old Gypsy fortune-teller had told him many years ago. The Gypsy had said that Dupont's ultimate creation would be made of flesh and blood.

"You did well tonight, my child," Dupont said as he loaded items into a trunk. "Your digital dexterity is nothing short of amazing. You've been blessed with an astounding pair of hands. They'll serve you well, I assure you."

Raven laughed. "How do you think I ended up here?"

"I'll teach you everything you need to know. I promise."

"Can you teach me the Chinese Water Torture Escape? And the Milk Can Escape?"

Dupont rolled his eyes in exasperation. "Yes, I can teach you those tricks, I know them well. But tell me, why the focus on the great Houdini?" When Dupont said "the great Houdini", his tone was clearly dismissive.

"Isn't Houdini the greatest magician of all time?"

Dupont laughed sarcastically. "I'm sure in *his* mind, he probably was. But no, he was hardly the greatest magician of all time. Far from it. I would say that honor goes to the man from whom Houdini took his name, Jean Robert-Houdin. Houdini was a skilled entertainer and a master showman, but his skills at self-promotion far exceeded his skills in magic."

"But isn't hype a kind of performance magic, an illusion? Isn't the whole point of hype to create belief?"

Dupont smiled at the wisdom of Raven's words. "Yes, you're quite correct. Hype most certainly is a kind of magic, and the great Houdini was a master of it, that's for sure. But when one believes one's own hype as Houdini did, the effect can be quite disastrous."

"Like believing in a mirage?"

"*Exactement.* Houdini, the master escape artist, was hopelessly trapped inside an illusion of his own making. There's a substantial difference between self-confidence and self-adoration, a difference the great Houdini remained blissfully unaware of. His ego was the real straitjacket, the one from which he could never hope to escape."

Raven stopped working, pulled up a stool and seated herself. She wanted to give her full attention to Dupont. He continued working as he spoke.

"The ordinary person is incapable of achieving greatness because greatness is a lofty mountaintop, and the road to that mountaintop is long, rocky, and filled with fire-breathing dragons. To ascend that mountaintop, the ordinary person must do the impossible and transform themselves into the *extraordinary* person. Unfortunately, many people end up creating monsters in the process."

"Was Houdini a monster?"

"He was certainly possessed by a monster, a demon that possesses many talented people. A demon called ego. It's a hideous demon, both foul and disgusting. There's a curious phenomenon that I've seen often throughout my long life. A person works hard to summon the fortitude necessary for self-transformation. They overcome the obstacles, setbacks, and other dragons that present them- selves. Then they successfully reach the mountaintop, only to end up defeated by a demon of their own creation. The demon called ego."

"Crushed by the weight of their own big heads."

Dupont laughed. "By the way, one of my teachers once witnessed a performance by the great Houdini. He said Houdini couldn't dip his hands in the park without rustling the leaves. Yet, when it came to blowing his own horn, Houdini was a virtuoso par excellence."

"You seem to have some serious Houdini issues."

"The great Houdini was an egomaniac to be sure, but that's not why I detest him so. I loathe him because he did something completely unforgivable. He wrote a vile, dis- gusting book entitled *The Unmasking of Robert-Houdin*. He used that book to mercilessly attack not only a great artist, but a great man. And there was no need for it, aside from Houdini's obsessive, infantile need to exalt himself above the true greats. It was a book written by a demon."

"Ego."

"That's correct. In spite of his fame, fortune, and accomplishments, the great Houdini remained an ordinary man. Ironic, is it not?"

"Is this what they call a cautionary tale?"

"Raven, you're filled with infinite possibilities and destined for greatness. But be warned, success is far more difficult to deal with than failure. The mountaintop is a dangerous place to be. You can easily lose your balance, your focus, and even your mind. Success has made failures out of many people."

"I'll remember that."

Dupont walked over to Raven, kissed her head, and hugged her warmly. "My dear Raven, you're the most extraordinary human being I've ever encountered. Divine Providence has blessed you with abundant gifts, yet you remain as humble as a blade of grass ... and just as beautiful."

Raven blushed.

"You're doomed, my dear; doomed to ascend to the mountaintop ... to many mountaintops. But promise me one thing."

"Anything."

"Promise me that if the demon ego ever rears its ugly head in your life, you'll cut it off."

Raven smiled. "With one blow."

* * *

The Oakwood dining room was empty except for Raven. She sat at a table in the far corner of the room, shuffling and reshuffling a deck of cards. All the residents and most of the staff had left the compound and gone into the city on a casino expedition. Raven stayed behind. The compound seemed deserted and Raven enjoyed the solitude. She was eager to practice her card manipulations. Dupont had recently shown her several particularly difficult techniques and she was determined to master them.

"Don't you ever relax?"

Raven looked up from the cards and saw Mr. Freeman peeking in the dining room.

"I *am* relaxed, it's the cards that are agitated. I'll get 'em under control. Come on in."

Mr. Freeman entered and made his way over to Raven's table. As he seated himself, he watched Raven expertly handle the cards. He smiled, impressed by her skill. Afraid to break her concentration, he sat silently and continued to watch.

"You can talk if you want to," she said. "You're not bothering me."

"I'm surprised to find you here. Why didn't you go with the others?"

"They'll be all right without me."

"By the way, I particularly enjoyed last week's performance. I've noticed that lately, you've become a bigger part of Dupont's show."

"There's only one star on that stage. I'm sorry, do you want a snack? I can get you something, if you like. Mao Ying's got a tray of brownies sitting back there waiting for some attention."

Mr. Freeman laughed. "Well, they won't get any attention from me ... at least not until later perhaps. For now, I think I'll pass. Speaking of Dupont, I've noticed that, like most of the residents around here, he's taken quite a liking to you."

"I'm irresistible."

"Well, you're certainly that, but I have a sneaking suspicion that you're being ... groomed."

"I could use some grooming. Still a little rough around the edges."

"You seem to be quite at home onstage. You look like you belong there. Is magic something you'd like to pursue?"

"I think magic is pursuing me. Actually, the pursuit part is over. Mr. Dupont has taught me a lot."

"If magic is, indeed, your destiny, as I suspect it is, you could have no better teacher than Guy Dupont. He's probably the world's greatest living magician. The term 'living legend' is quite applicable to him."

Raven continued working with the cards. The manipulations were becoming easier, but she was struggling with her thoughts. She weighed her words carefully before she spoke.

"A while back, when I first started working with Mr. Dupont, I spent a lot of time in the library studying up on magic and magicians. I went through a lot of books, but I never once saw the name Dupont in any of them. Not one single time. What's up with that?"

"What do you mean?"

"Well, he's obviously an accomplished magician, and

with a lot of miles on him. There should be some kind of record of him somewhere, but there isn't. There's no mention of a Guy Dupont anywhere. It's like he never existed. It's a little mysterious. Actually, it's a *lot* mysterious."

"That his name is not included among all the others?"

"Yes. How come there's no record of him anywhere? It's a legitimate question."

"Yes, it is. And while I'll attempt to answer it, I can't promise you that I'll be able to solve the mystery. You see, Guy Dupont is an example of what might be called an anonymous living legend. He's extremely well known within the magic community and has been for much of his life. But he's totally unknown by the general public. The world has never heard of Guy Dupont."

Raven shuffled the deck one last time, then rested the cards on the table. She looked directly at Mr. Freeman. "Why?"

"In the field of magic, there are several visible components. The magicians, the assistants, the tricks and props. But Dupont represents the single most important component ... the invisible component. Guy Dupont was the man who actually *created* the illusions. Much like in the field of music where many great musicians don't compose their own songs or symphonies, many great magicians don't create their own illusions."

"Really?"

"That's correct. And Guy Dupont was the man who most magicians turned to—the magician's magician. He's solely responsible for creating many of the greatest, most famous illusions in the world of magic. But he chose to work his magic in the shadows and as a result, no one knows the name Guy Dupont."

"It doesn't seem right."

"Perhaps, but that's the way Dupont wanted it."

"Now, that *is* a mystery."

"In the self-centered, ego-driven world of show business, Dupont represents a man of inverted ambitions. He never aspired to fame or fortune. And as a result, he achieved neither."

"Let me guess, all he really cared about was developing the art form of magic. In his mind, fame and fortune would have polluted the purity of the art. Is that it? No wonder he was a legend among his peers—a magician's magician. I bet they loved him all right. Everybody loves a sucker, especially a magician!" Raven burst into a fit of sarcastic laughter.

Mr. Freeman didn't laugh. He also didn't attempt to debate Raven's wise words either. "France has long been a mecca for the art of magic. Dupont comes from a family of prestigious magicians, a family who took the art of magic very seriously, like a religion. His family was instrumental in bringing magic out of the streets and into the theaters where it shared the stage with all the other performance arts. The Dupont family helped to make magic legitimate and respectable. They were driven by the love of their art form, not the love of money or celebrity. Is that so terrible?"

"No, not at all. I bet they all died broke, too."

"They ... struggled."

"No doubt ... starving artists always do." Raven sneered and shook her head in disgust.

"Raven, please, don't be so judgmental. Dupont is a great artist and a good man."

"I'm not disputing his greatness as an artist or his goodness a man. I do happen to care about him. Very much. I've learned a lot from him, and I'll learn a lot more. But I've learned something else tonight, something very important."

"What's that?"

"Even a magician can be fooled. There's *absolutely* nothing wrong with fame and fortune; as long as you control *them*, and not the other way around."

Raven remembered Dupont's intense hostility toward Houdini. She realized that while Houdini's enormous ego placed him far in one extreme, Dupont's distorted notions of art and celebrity placed him far in the opposite extreme. Raven vowed to place herself somewhere in the middle.

* * *

Late one evening, close to the midnight hour, Raven sat at a table in one of the library reading rooms. She was focused on the book that Houdini had written, *The Unmasking of Robert-Houdin*. She heard someone enter the library. The approaching footsteps were unmistakable to her and she smiled in anticipation. Dupont entered the reading room. When he saw Raven, he, too, smiled. He kissed her on the cheek and seated himself directly across from her. Raven closed her book and slid it off to the side.

Dupont took a deck of cards out of his pocket and shuffled them. "I knew I'd find you here."

Raven quickly snatched the cards away from him. "Gimme those," she said playfully.

Dupont sat back and watched Raven shuffle the cards in a variety of outrageous ways. She was clearly out to impress him. And she did.

"I can't keep up with you," Dupont said.

"You've been doing all right so far ... for an old dude. Can I ask you something?"

"Of course."

Raven carefully considered the question she was about to ask. "Do you believe in magic?" she asked.

Dupont didn't answer right away. He quietly continued to watch Raven. Her focus was still on the cards, but after a few moments, she looked up into his eyes. Raven stopped shuffling and slid the deck of cards back toward Dupont.

"I would imagine you're referring to *real* magic as opposed to ... performance magic. Is that correct?" Dupont asked.

"You know what I'm talking about."

Dupont smiled as he recalled a sweet memory. "Do you remember the first night you stepped on stage with me so long ago?"

"Yeah, that was *real* magic. I'll never forget it." Raven looked at Dupont sweetly.

"Nor I." Dupont picked up the deck of cards and shuffled them very slowly ... lovingly ... as if he were caressing them.

"Since the beginning of time, the world has been hopelessly fascinated by magic. Understandably so. It's a powerful concept, one that conjures up an infinite variety of notions and emotions. Throughout history, magicians, those mysterious practitioners of the art, have been both worshipped as gods and burned alive. So, clearly, magic produces strong feelings."

Raven sat back in her chair and listened closely as she watched Dupont manipulate the cards.

"Do I believe in real magic? Of course, I do. Because I am a man of science, and magic *is* science. The science of the metaphysical. Magic is the use of will, to manipulate energy in order to cause change. But in order to perform magic, *real* magic, the magician must possess the one attribute that all *ordinary* people lack."

"Self-control."

Dupont smiled at Raven. "That's quite correct."

Raven smiled. "So the *will* is the *wand*."

"Well said, my child. The will is, indeed, the wand. It's the instrument that makes the miraculous possible and attainable. Your natural understanding of that fact is what makes you a *born* magician. The ordinary person is hopelessly adrift in the sea of life, tossed about by the waves of chance, unable to navigate themselves. Most of them simply drown. It's a fact. Society is a beach littered with the lifeless bodies of the ordinary. I personally believe that everyone is born with the wand but they lack the persistence and determination necessary to develop it. Hence the world's fascination with magic and the magician. Because the magician is seen, and rightly so, as an *extraordinary* person, a miracle worker. Magic is about *transformation*. And self-transformation is the most difficult, the most extraordinary and the most magical act of all. Self-conquest is the greatest of all victories, but it's a difficult battle indeed. Only an extraordinary warrior can emerge triumphant. As a result, the ordinary person could never hope to do magic. Because, as you so wisely said, the will is the wand."

"You can't control a deck of cards or the forces of nature if you can't control yourself."

"*Exactement*! And the stronger the wand, the more powerful the magic."

 RAVENDIABLO

9

The Black One

Raven's life at Oakwood was a joyful one. From the day she arrived, residents and staff warmly embraced her as a welcome addition to the compound. She was always quick to make herself available when needed. She went about her daily chores without complaint. She maintained a sunny disposition that charmed everyone who came in contact with her. And, of course, the former stray had been taken in by six loving mentors. Oakwood had collectively responded to her in a positive way. But there was one glaring, literally glaring exception—the old woman with the wild hair and protruding tongue, the black one. From the day of Raven's arrival at Oakwood, she had appointed herself Raven's personal tormentor. As a result, Raven was routinely tripped, struck, scratched, spat upon, pelted with food, and much worse. The black one had an uncanny knack for emerging without warning, seemingly from nowhere, and attacking Raven with glee. Indeed, she was the only negative in an otherwise idyllic, enchanted environment. And Raven was terrified of her.

One fateful afternoon, the courtyard was bursting with excitement, the result of the annual Oakwood carnival. Residents, staff, and visiting family members merrily mingled with clowns, mimes, jugglers, dancers, and strolling musicians. The courtyard was decorated to look like a medieval marketplace. The air was alive with music and laughter. Raven was dressed in an outfit she had taken great care in assembling. Her wide brim white hat was accented with a huge purple feather. The form-fitting black leather vest was a stylish contrast to the purple pirate shirt with billowing sleeves and upturned collar. The baggy black leather pants and bright red sash were pure Cossack. Black moccasin boots with dangling, beaded fringe completed the dashing ensemble. Admiring eyes followed Raven as she gracefully moved about the courtyard with tray in hand, serving refreshments to guests. Raven was clearly no longer a teenager, but a young woman with formidable appeal.

The sudden scream of a woman startled everyone. Raven turned to find one of the guests angrily drenched with water. Balloons filled with water were being strategically launched from somewhere high above. The unseen culprit threw the balloons with startling accuracy, striking staff, residents, and guests. The courtyard was thrown into complete chaos as people scrambled to avoid being struck. Raven tried to focus on where the balloons were coming from. She examined each of the compound buildings and noticed a figure on the roof of the multistory Victorian bulding. It was by far the tallest structure at Oakwood. Yet even at so great a height, the figure was unmistakable. It was the black one. She glared down at the crowd and wailed triumphantly. All eyes were directed upward toward her.

Her identity now revealed, the black one then took her act to a higher level of madness. She stepped out onto the roof's narrow ledge and danced. The crowd gathered below watched, frozen with horror. Acting without thought, Raven raced over to the building, rushed up the stone walkway, and headed for the oaken entrance door. Ignoring shouts from staff members to stay put, she burst into the building, sprinting across the lobby and up the marble staircase.

The crowd in the courtyard maintained its fearful focus on the black one high above. She was well aware of the confusion she had caused below and she reveled in it. She added manic leaps and spins to her dance routine in order to maximize the terror. Clearly, there was a disaster unfolding before everyone's eyes.

The black one performed a series of acrobatic cartwheels along the ledge. She landed on her feet with graceful confidence, laughing at the petrified crowd below. A sound from behind startled her and she turned to find Raven now on the roof and slowly approaching. The black one smiled as if pleased to see her. Raven reached out, her eyes pleading for an end to the madness. Perhaps it was the sincerity in those eyes that impacted the black one. Her raving demeanor suddenly changed. She calmed completely, even lowering her eyes as if truly ashamed of her actions.

"I'm sorry", she said softly.

The transformation was astonishing. It was also the first time Raven had ever heard her speak. Though this subdued, peaceful personality was completely out of character, the apology seemed genuine. The black one looked up with eyes that reinforced the sincerity of her apology. She had long been Raven's crazed tormentor, yet now there was no trace of that monster. A very different old woman stood on that ledge. She looked more like a mother than a monster. And she radiated a strange glow that hovered about her. Raven stared at her as if seeing her for the first time. The eyes of both women *locked*. The black one then dutifully extended her hand for assistance, even managing a naughty smile. Raven took firm hold of the hand and the black one stepped down from the ledge. But her heel slipped on a patch of bird droppings, causing her to lose her footing and stumble backwards, toppling from the roof. Raven maintained her grip and quickly managed to pull her to safety, only to lose her own balance in the process. It was now Raven who toppled. She fell first on the ledge, knocking the wind out of her, then tumbled over the side. The crowd shrieked as she began her descent. Raven's doom was unavoidable and many people covered their eyes to avert witnessing the tragedy. But the black one had lightning-quick reflexes. She reached down and snatched hold of Raven's wrist. For a few moments, Raven literally dangled from the grip as the throng below watched with dread. Then the black one hoisted Raven up and onto the roof. Effortlessly. Raven collapsed into a heap, and momentarily lost consciousness. When she opened her eyes again, she found the black one kneeling beside her. Raven stared into her eyes and saw something astonishing. Raven saw *love*. The black one gently caressed Raven's brow and smiled sweetly. Then suddnely, she stuck out her long tongue and burst into laughter, reverting back to her typical, crazed demeanor, barely able to contain herself. Raven shook her head in weary confusion, unaware that she now wore the black woman's red medallion.

* * *

The next morning, Raven lay in her bed staring at the ceiling, still very much traumatized by the events of the previous day. She climbed out of bed and went to the window. As she peered out, she was surprised to see several police officers, staff members, and Mr. Freeman gathered by the fountain in the courtyard, talking with distressed faces. Something was wrong. Raven dressed and hurried out of her room.

The courtyard was still festively decorated from the day before. But except for the cops and staff members, the wide space was deserted. Mr. Freeman was surprised to see Raven approaching. He embraced her warmly and held onto her. She buried her face in his chest as he caressed her head.

"What are you doing here?" he said with fatherly concern. "Get back to bed."

"What's going on?" Raven asked.

Mr. Freeman took a deep breath. "It's your friend again. Only, this time, she's gone. We don't know where she is. There's a search underway."

A county sheriff's Jeep cruised into the courtyard and came to a stop beside the group. A deputy climbed out, his face somber. He opened the back hatch and pulled out a wheelchair—the black one's wheelchair.

"I found this a few miles from here," said the officer. "No sign of her, though."

As the rest of the deputies headed back to their vehicles to continue the search, the remaining staff members looked to Mr. Freeman for answers. Dolly, the activities director, was particularly distraught.

"What are we going to do?" she asked fearfully. "She's still out there somewhere."

"All we can do for now is wait," said Mr. Freeman. "We'll let the authorities handle this." He turned to Raven, who remained by his side. "As for you, young lady, you get back to your room. And stay there. You've got the day off. Tomorrow, too, if I've got anything to say about it."

Raven didn't argue. She went back to her room.

* * *

Raven's room had undergone a considerable transformation from when she first arrived at Oakwood. Mr. Freeman had promised her free rein in its decoration and she had taken him up on the offer. Large pillows lay scattered around a low round table. The bed was replaced by a simple futon. The walls were covered with large theatrical posters of famous magicians, though there was one poster of *The Flamenco Kid*. There was also a large illustration of the human body displaying the various acupuncture points. A small bookcase held only a few books. With the Oakwood library so close at hand, Raven saw little need to transform her room into a library as well. A portable stereo played exotic music.

It was late evening. Raven sat crosslegged at the round table practicing card manipulations. She had spent the entire day in her room, something she *never* did. But today, she needed healing solitude. All day, Raven relived the madness of the previous day, particularly the moment on the roof when she tumbled and fell. She had never felt such fear before. Raven knew she was dead at that precise moment. She had always heard that at such moments, one's entire life quickly passed before them like a movie on fast forward, but that didn't happen to her. There hadn't been time, because at that precise moment of certain extinction, she had been miraculously, and literally, snatched from the grip of death and given life. A new life?

There was a light knock at her door.

"Come in."

Mr. Freeman entered carrying a long object wrapped in red fabric. He placed the item on the table in front of Raven and took a seat on the floor beside her.

"What's this?" asked Raven curiously.

"I believe it's meant for you," he said.

"From whom?"

"Earlier today, I was in the room of your dark friend, searching for clues, for anything that might explain her sudden decision to leave. I found nothing, but I did find this. And this was attached to it."

Mr. Freeman took a piece of paper from his jacket and handed it to Raven. On one side of the paper was the crude drawing of a fierce face with evil eyes and a long, protruding tongue. There was something unsettling about the drawing, something frightening.

"Turn it over," said Mr. Freeman.

Raven was afraid. Her radar told her that some revelation was about to take place. She hesitated.

"Go on," insisted Mr. Freeman. "Turn it over."

Raven took a deep breath and turned the paper over. There was a name scrawled on the other side. "Ravendiablo."

"I don't know what it means. But there's only one Raven around here, and that's you. Whatever this is, it's meant for you."

"I don't understand."

"Neither do I. I don't understand why she's had it in for you all this time. I don't understand that whole episode on the roof yesterday. I don't understand any of it. All I know is that she left this behind for you. *You*. So you take it. You try and make sense of it. I can't."

"She's still missing?"

"She's gone. And you know something else? I don't think we'll ever find her, either."

Mr. Freeman kissed Raven's cheek, then stood and walked to the door. "Take a few more days off, Raven, you certainly need it. We'll be okay without you for a while." Mr. Freeman opened the door.

"Who was she anyway?" asked Raven.

"Who was she?" Mr. Freeman laughed. "This time, you tell me."

Mr. Freeman walked out and closed the door behind him. Raven stared at the mysterious, long object, and her radar told her that whatever it was, it was both wondrous and frightening. She slowly peeled away the fabric to uncover a large sword sheathed within a black leather scabbard. The sight of it made her heart race with excitement. As she gazed at it, she gently caressed the red medallion around her neck. Raven grasped the sword handle and stood, drawing the blade out from the scabbard. The weapon was unlike anything she had ever seen, with a deadly blade that curved at an odd angle. Raven could sense that this was a weapon specifically designed for maximum damage. Seeing the sword completely exposed ... *naked* ... she felt a hot, molten rush of energy surge through her veins. She lunged into a fighting stance and swung the weapon several times forcefully and expertly, as if she'd handled the blade before. The sword felt strangely familiar and at home in her hands. Imaginary demons lay at her feet, hacked to pieces.

And she smiled *diabolically*.

10

Masterpiece

The Oakwood theater was filled to capacity. Every eye was excitedly focused on the stage bathed in bright light. There was a master magician on stage that night, performing ingenious card tricks, daring escapes, and thrilling illusions. The magician performed with skill and confidence, and each trick was more astonishing than the last. Guy Dupont was not the featured performer, but a spectator like the others, and he watched with tear-filled eyes. Because the magician on stage was Raven, or rather, *Ravendiablo*. Others in the audience shared Dupont's joy. Mao Ying and Loona sat huddled together. Red Knife, Beasley, and Swanigan were in attendance as well. And, of course, Mr. Freeman. All of Raven's master sculptors watched her with great, gushing pride. They had all played a significant role in her creation, and the fruit of their efforts stood before them in full ripeness.

As Raven performed, the bright lights blinded her from seeing her mentors sitting out in the audience, but she knew they were there. She could feel their loving, supportive energy urging her on. When Raven first arrived at Oakwood, she could never have imagined that her ten-year punishment would become the home she never had, the school she never knew existed, and the happiness she never dreamed possible. Far from a punishment, Oakwood was a *reward*, but for what, Raven didn't know. Before her arrival at Oakwood, Raven had never seriously pondered the concept of destiny. It had always seemed like a silly notion, the stuff of myth and fairy tales. And yet, she now felt a sense of purpose that she had never known before. She knew in her heart that she belonged at Oakwood—doing her work, interacting with the residents, learning from the elders, and most of all, reinventing herself. Oakwood was more than a compound comprised of surreal *buildings* on acres of land. Oakwood was a *wellspring*, and the more Raven drank from that wellspring, the more fortified she became.

When Raven concluded her performance, the audience erupted into wild applause and everyone stood to honor her. The entire theater swelled with love for her. As she stood center stage, bathed in the spotlight, the audience loudly chanted her name. All her mentors were weeping now, and Raven was unable to hold back her own tears. This was her moment, her defining, *magical* moment. Over time, nurtured by the loving guidance of her mentors, Raven had developed talents, discovered truths, and solved mysteries. She had found the career that she would pursue into adulthood as a performance magician. And she had become a *real* magician as well, a miracle worker. Her most accomplished miracle was transforming herself from Raven Chandler into Ravendiablo.

11

Ravendiablo, Outlaw

Fifteen years later …

The audience slowly filed into a dimly lit theater for the afternoon show. They were tourists, dressed in jeans, T-shirts, shorts, and worse. Clutching gigantic drinks and tacky Las Vegas memorabilia, most of them seemed indifferent and even a bit confused. They hadn't really come for the show anyway. The tickets came with the hotel package. The show merely provided the opportunity to sit and digest the buffet food in their bloated bellies. The only entertainment they were really interested in was the slot machines and blackjack tables. In the back of the theater sat a very different audience. Exquisitely dressed in black leather and lace, a contingent of pale-faced Goths watched the arriving tourists with contemptuous eyes. Once everyone was seated, the theater darkened.

Moments later, a mysterious female voice was heard over the loudspeakers.

"Ladies and gentlemen, if you are of a delicate nature, the producers of the show take this opportunity to warn you. Please leave the theater now. It's not too late … to save yourselves."

The tourists traded befuddled looks, but the Goths grinned knowingly.

"Very well," the voice continued. "You have been warned."

Howling wind, baying wolves, maniacal laughter, and other unsettling sounds filled the theater. The sudden sound of earsplitting thunder startled everyone. The tourists nervously realized that this was not a typical Las Vegas afternoon magic show. The blood-red curtain lifted and revealed a candlelit set that looked like a cross between a New Orleans cemetery and a medieval torture chamber. There were children in the audience who began to cry, and their parents were genuinely frightened as well. A thick purple fog enveloped the stage as a coffin rose up from the floor and came to an upright position. There was a deafening explosion as the coffin lid blew off and splintered into pieces that flew out into the audience.

"Will you now welcome to the stage ... Ravendiablo!"

Raven stepped out of the coffin dressed in black leather that lovingly hugged her curvaceous form. Her face was adorned with elaborate Day of the Dead makeup.

And she smiled *diabolically*.

Ravendiablo was an unsettling presence, and several of the tourists hurried out of the theater. Those who bravely remained were treated to a remarkable magic show. Raven was a master performer, effortlessly moving from traditional sleight of hand magic to dangerous escape tricks to larger illusions that utilized her many torture chamber props. Her martial arts and gymnastic abilities were on clear display as well. Raven controlled the stage with the authority of a well-seasoned professional. But the tone and presentation of her show were chilling in the extreme. Her assistants looked like cadavers dressed in formal attire.

As the show progressed, the illusions increasingly involved horrible death and disfigurement. Blood flowed freely. The pipe organ music that accompanied the show only served to darken the atmosphere and keep the audience in a perpetual state of dread. A Ravendiablo magic show was absolutely *not* for the squeamish.

When the lights finally went up, most of the tourists were gone and the ones who remained looked shaken. Relieved that the show had finally ended, they fled the theater. The Goth crowd gave Raven a rousing standing ovation and she returned to the stage to take a bow. The Goths approached the stage where Raven happily signed autographs and posed for pictures. Two important looking well dressed men stood by the exit doors watching as the last of tourists departed. The men appeared to be involved with the theater. Watching Raven hold court with the adoring Goths, the men traded disappointed glances, and left the theater.

* * *

Raven's nest was an immense loft apartment with a gigantic window that overlooked downtown Fremont Street. There was far more space than actual furniture. Naturally, much of the wall space was lined with huge shelves laden with books. The remaining wall space was decorated with numerous awards, plaques, trophies, and other items testifying to Raven's long and successful career as a magician. She was particularly well-known in Europe and Asia as a result of many years of international touring. She was well respected within the close-knit magic community as well. The walls displayed other images, pictures of Raven's personal heroes. There were posters of Muhammad Ali, Bruce Lee, Steve McQueen, the Man with No Name, and the Flamenco Kid.

One area of the loft was entirely devoted to her wardrobe. Several long racks lined with clothes stood near a sewing table covered with fabric waiting to be cut and assembled. Another area had been painstakingly converted into a weapons museum where various instruments of death and destruction were carefully and lovingly displayed. Rifles, handguns, swords, knives, whips, chains, and other exotic weaponry from around the world hung on the walls, sat in display cases, and rested on pedestals.

In the very middle of the loft space sat a low, round wooden table surrounded by large, comfortable pillows. Ornate rugs covered the floors. Only one item was strangely out of place in Raven's lair. A huge, flat-screen television was mounted to a wall. Shanice and Sophia would have been absolutely shocked to have seen it. Raven loathed television, even as an adult. Still, she had long referred to it, among other terms, as *the delivery system*, so she kept one on hand just to stay aware of exactly what was being delivered. It remained on at all times.

It was late evening and Raven was wired. She stood in her workout area facing a large mirror and focused on her own image. She was dressed in black workout attire with her hair pulled back and piled high. She took a deep breath, then launched into a martial-arts workout routine, kicking and punching with ferocious intensity. The television was loud enough to be heard, but Raven paid no attention to it. Onscreen, the handsome host was seated next to a beautiful blonde airhead.

"Welcome back to 'Celebrity Rimjob' with my next guest, the lovely and talented Miss Jenna Thalia. Thanks for being with us tonight, Jenna. It's a real honor to have you here."

"Thanks for having me!" she said. "It's great to be back in Vegas! I love this town!"

"Jenna, you've done so much with your career. You're an acclaimed actress, a bikini spokesmodel, an international ambassador for world peace. You've truly done it all. And now I understand you're moving into an entirely new area, isn't that correct?"

"Yes, that's correct. I want to show my fans a side of me that they've never seen before. So I've chosen Las Vegas to unveil my first ever magic show!"

Raven immediately stopped in midkick and walked over to the television.

"So, tell us, Jenna, what made you decide to pursue a career in magic? And why Las Vegas?"

"Well, I've always loved magic. And as everyone knows, Las Vegas is the magic capital of the world."

"That's right."

"So, it was a perfect fit. Besides, to be honest, I think the so-called art of magic has really gotten stale."

Raven glared at the screen stone-faced but with growing irritation.

"Everybody has been doing the same thing, the same way, for so long, they just don't seem to know any better," Jenna continued. "I just felt it was time for a change. It's time someone came in, shook things up, and took magic to a whole new level. I decided that I'm just the person to do that."

"And how long have you been studying magic?"

"For about three weeks now. I've been studying with Criss Angel, and I've learned a whole lot, too. It's going to be a great show."

"And what's the show called Jenna?"

"G-String Divas of Magic."

Raven snarled. The sudden sound of door chimes rang throughout the loft. Raven picked up a remote from the round table and aimed it at the television. Jenna Thalia's image was replaced by that of Raven's manager, Manny, who could be seen onscreen standing at the entrance door to Raven's loft. Raven pressed another button on the remote and Manny could then be heard opening the entrance door far across the loft.

Raven placed the remote back on the table and returned to her workout area. Her mood had darkened considerably. To calm herself, she took several deep breaths and practiced the slow, soothing Tai Chi form.

Manny entered the main area of the loft. Raven could see him reflected in the mirror as he approached, but she didn't acknowledge him and kept her back to him. Theirs was a contentious relationship on the best of days. She was certainly in no mood to see him now. Manny was a middle-aged, eternally tanned dreamer with a bad toupee, a gift for gab, and naturally nervous energy. Before the coke took its toll, he had been relatively good-looking. Now, he was just looking, for that dream act that could propel him to the big time. His idol was Elvis's manager, Colonel Tom Parker. Manny grabbed one of the few pieces of furniture, a wooden bar stool, and seated himself a few feet from Raven's workout area. He watched her perform the Tai Chi form but said nothing. Raven said nothing, and on it went for several excruciating moments. Finally, Manny spoke.

"Can't you speak?"

"I *am* speaking. Maybe you don't understand body language." Raven was still seething about Jenna Thalia and the G-String Divas of Magic.

Manny moved on. "How did the show go this afternoon?"

"I'm always good, it's the audience that needs improving."

Manny shook his head and rolled his eyes in exasperation. Raven always made him uncomfortable. Tonight, for some reason, more uncomfortable than usual. Manny had something important to say but his courage was lacking. He chose his words carefully. "Maybe the audience isn't the problem, Raven. Maybe it's you. Your whole way of doing ..."

Raven abruptly stopped Tai Chi and turned to glare at Manny face to face. She felt like a fight. "What's wrong with *my* way of doing things? I made a name for myself with my way of doing things. I made money with my way of doing things. When I was performing for royalty in the south of France, you were managing puppet shows. You just came on board two years ago. What do you know about my way of doing things? What do you know about anything?"

Manny could tell that Raven was in a bad mood—far worse than her normal, everyday bad mood. However, he was determined to make his point and say what he had come to say. "Your show is changing for the worse and so are the numbers."

Raven stared at Manny defiantly. "What about the numbers?"

"I'm all about the numbers, Raven," he said defensively. "You know me. The numbers are down. Way down."

"They're down all over town. So what else is new?"

"Yeah, well I think your numbers are down for a whole different reason. I think the time has come for you to realize that. You're a magician. You do a magic show. But there's something you don't seem to understand, Raven. Magic is suppose to *entertain* people, not *traumatize* them. An audience isn't supposed to need counseling after they leave a show."

Raven smiled *diabolically*.

"You think it's funny," he continued with more courage. "But the only person laughing is you. And if you don't listen up, you won't be laughing for long."

"I ain't Copperfield."

"Yeah, well the show is getting a little *too* dark ... even for you. I think you need to – "

"There's only a handful of people in this world who can touch *my magic*!" Raven took her magic very seriously. It was an ancient and respected art form and she had learned from the best. "What do you know about magic anyway? Maybe you need to go back to the sock puppets, something you understand," Raven sneered.

"The problem isn't your talent, Raven. We all know how incredibly talented you are, and lest we forget, you're always there to remind us." Manny felt more courageous and he liked the feeling. "When it comes to blowing your own horn, you're a virtuoso. The problem is you and your whole approach. Your act is just plain wrong, especially for an afternoon magic show." Manny sighed wearily. "You don't need to be in Vegas, you need to be in Transylvania working the lounge in Vlad's castle."

"I've got plenty of fans!" she exclaimed, almost in desperation.

"Yeah, I know all about your fans," Manny said with supreme sarcasm. "Orphans from the Addams Family. The only thing scarier than your show *are* your fans. And I'll tell you something else. The casino has never been particularly thrilled about your fans."

"The casino better be glad for anybody who shows up to their sorry ass, overpriced, watered-down excuse for a —"

"The casino writes the check!" Manny interrupted with a triumphant smirk. "Little Miss Know-It-All always seems to forget that. So do me a favor and chill with the rebel routine. I know the tune. I've heard it before, thousands of times, and quite frankly, I'm bored with — "

"So what's up, Manny?" Raven shot back. Her radar was fully activated. "Every time you've got something to say but lack the testicular fortitude to say it, you give me the Manny punkass floor show, and quite frankly, I'm bored with ... "

"We've come to the end of our relationship, Raven. It's been a blast and I mean that sincerely, but I'm out. As of right now. As of ten minutes ago. I'm through representing you. I'm through dealing with you—or *trying* to. I'm out."

Raven was surprised by his words. They had certainly fought in the past, but Manny had always remembered who the star of the show was and crawled back to his proper place.

"I'm not a young man anymore," he said somewhat wistfully. "I've got my own future to think about. You want to keep working the cemetery circuit, scaring the shit out of normal people, playing for vampires, werewolves, zombies, and cenobites, be my guest. But I'm moving on." Manny paused for a moment and took a deep breath as he summoned what little testicular fortitude he had available. "The casino is moving on. They don't want you anymore. They've decided that you're bad for business."

Raven was livid. "Say what?" she exclaimed. "I'm bad for business? The casino can kiss my black ass! If they care so much about business, tell those bean-counting MBAs to loosen the slots, lower the prices, and start being Vegas again instead of trying to be Monte Carlo! It's the casinos that are bad for business! What do they know? What do you know?"

"I'll tell you what I know. I know everything is always a confrontation with you. You might want to try a little less fighting and a little more listening."

"My contract runs until the end of the year. Listen to that!" Raven smiled victoriously, convinced she had her usual upper hand.

"Yeah, well, if the casino decides that for whatever reason you're bad for business, that contract is null and void. And they've decided." Manny giggled. "Ravendiablo has just left the cemetery."

Raven felt as if she'd been kicked in the stomach. "As of when?" she asked softly.

"You've already done your last show."

Raven exploded in anger. "What?" she screamed. "This is bullshit!"

"It is what it is." Manny felt cocky now. "You're a tough chick, the bad bitch of magic. Deal with it."

Raven tried to control her emotions. "You seem to be taking this pretty well," she said sarcastically. "You being my representative and all."

"It's like I said, I've got to move on, Raven. And it's just that simple. Besides, I've got other projects I'm working on anyway. I do happen to like and appreciate magic in spite of what you may think. Vegas is a magic town." Manny looked at the floor as he continued. "But I want to produce a different kind of magic show. The casino wants a different kind of magic show. Something a little less ... traumatic."

Suddenly, it all crystallized in Raven's mind and she understood completely. "G-String Divas of Magic! *You*? You no good, lousy, back-stabbin', punkass, prick mother ..."

"Now hold on!" he said defensively. "I didn't stab you in the back."

Raven screamed as her eyes filled with tears. "No, you stabbed me in the front! Jenna Thalia? You dumped me for some *porn star*?"

"She's an actress!"

"Actress? *Wacktress*! That dumb bitch! She can't even spell magic, let alone perform it! She needs to go back to the money shots and leave the magic alone! What do you take magic for, anyway, some kind of *joke*?" Raven wept.

Manny had said what he'd come to say. At that moment his only concern was getting out of Raven's loft as quickly as possible. He did his best imitation of sincerity. "I'm really sorry, Raven."

"You got that right! The sorriest piece of shit manager I've ever had in a town full of sorry-piece-of-shit managers! I just emptied my bank account for this gig and you *know* it! How could you do this to me?" Raven was hysterical.

"You need to calm down and understand something. This is business, not personal. You always take everything so personally."

Suddenly Raven rushed at Manny. "I'm gonna personally kick your ass out of this world, Manny!"

With a wide, circular sweep of her leg to maximize the force, Raven violently kicked the wooden stool out from under Manny and it broke into pieces. Manny spun in midair before landing on his head with the wind knocked out of him. He was momentarily dazed. He looked up at Raven as his vision slowly cleared, and the look in her eyes chilled him. He had seen that look before. He had seen her slap hecklers and kick drunks off the stage. Times when she went from just being pissed to *possessed*. This was one of those times. Manny frantically tried to scramble away on his hands and knees as Raven advanced toward him menacingly. She was no longer crying.

And she smiled *diabolically*.

"Don't you crawl away from me when I'm talking to you!" she ordered.

"Violence isn't going to solve anything!"

Raven laughed wickedly. "If it makes me feel good, it's solving something. And I'm feeling pretty damn good right about now."

Raven lunged at Manny, grabbed him by the collar and hoisted him to his feet. He shook in fear and his knees threatened to buckle.

"G-String Divas of Magic!" she screamed. Raven punched Manny in the mouth and the stomach. He doubled over as his legs turned to noodles, but Raven maintained her grip on his collar and held him upright.

"Calm down, Raven," he gasped, bleeding from the mouth. "You've got enough problems right now."

Raven seemed almost giddy. "Yeah, and I'm getting rid of them right now, starting with you!"

Raven punched Manny in the mouth again, effortlessly hoisted him high into the air, and slammed him to the floor. Manny moaned in pain and when he drooled, Raven giggled.

"You'd better cool it or you're going to need a lawyer," Manny managed to say as he struggled to a kneeling position.

Raven laughed. "Yeah? Well you're going to need a dentist, an orthopedist, and a proctologist!"

Raven kicked Manny's ass ... literally ... and the force sent him rolling head over feet. Suddenly, as if realizing that his life was truly in danger, Manny jumped to his feet and made a frantic dash for the entrance door. Raven was tempted to run after him, but she restrained herself, afraid that she might hurl him through the window if she laid hands on him again. She allowed him to escape her lair and possible death. Raven sat down on one of the large pillows beside the round table. She looked like a sad little girl with tears streaming down her face.

A commercial came on the television. "Come to Las Vegas!" said the hyped announcer. "It's the entertainment capital of the world!"

Raven shook her head sadly and wept.

* * *

Raven hated Las Vegas and she always had. So she particularly hated the Strip with a passion because the Strip *was* Vegas—a neon nightmare. Those four miles of electric idiocy were an accurate representation of the city as a whole: big of tit, small of brain, undercultured, oversexed, and hopelessly tacky. But well illuminated, or rather, *lit up.* Raven never drove on the Strip, it made her too uncomfortable. Walking on the Strip was completely out of the question. Yet, there she was—walking on the Strip, surrounded by the casinos she loathed and the tourists she laughed at. It was nauseating. No wonder she needed to puke. And puke she did, right on the corner of Las Vegas Boulevard and Tropicana Avenue, violently vomiting up her guts in front of the fake Lady Liberty and a small crowd of well-wishers. Wiping her mouth, she felt emptied but hardly relieved. So she kept walking. Raven on the Strip. No one who knew her would have ever believed it.

Tonight, Raven wanted to feel pain. Subjecting herself to Las Vegas Boulevard, on foot no less, maximized the pain she already felt. Raven wanted to get in touch with her inner masochist and wallowing in the sights and sounds that made Vegas world famous was a first-class ticket. Raven had never understood the fascination with the Strip, a street that looked like an idiot architect's bad acid trip. Every building, casino or otherwise, was more gaudy and tacky and hideous than the one before. As a magician, she had traveled the world many times and seen real wonders. Raven had seen the real Pyramids, the real Sphinx, the real Eiffel Tower, and the real Lady Liberty, too. She had stood on the Great Wall of China. When the Chinese tour guide found out she was from Las Vegas, he excitedly wanted to know if she'd ever seen the Strip. Or if she knew Criss Angel.

After walking a few blocks, Raven was ready to puke again and wondered what was left to come up.

"Well, what do we have here?" the man asked. "A *devotchka* out for a stroll?"

Raven turned to find four young men leaning against the wall of some architectural monstrosity. They were dressed in white, wore black bowler hats and combat boots, and carried walking sticks. Just like the *droogs* from

Stanley Kubrick's film, *A Clockwork Orange*. It was then that Raven remembered that this was Halloween night. Oozing with attitude and ballsy bravado, the four young men weren't just dressed like droogs, they truly fancied themselves to *be* droogs. They were looking for sex and ultraviolence and they eyed Raven's leather-clad figure in a way they shouldn't have. Raven had always hated *A Clockwork Orange* with a passion. It turned rampaging thugs into romantic heroes and cultural icons, when in fact, droogs were nothing more than terrorists. Seeing those hateful characters standing before her, *leering* at her, caused the masochistic tendencies she had been nourishing to subside. Her nausea vanished, replaced by a sudden surge of electricity that rushed through her body. Raven could barely believe her good fortune.

The musical group, The Police, often performed a song called "One World" with the chorus, "One world is enough for all of us." The droog leader was aware of the melody but changed the lyrics, singing instead, "One *girl* is enough for all of us." He arrogantly stepped forward and two accomplices followed, all singing with him. Raven could tell they were drunk, high, stupid, and otherwise impaired. Too impaired to understand or avoid the mistake they were about to make. The fourth droog stayed back. Perhaps smarter and less impaired than the others, he clearly saw something in Raven's icy eyes and bold body language that suggested that she might be a *devotchka* to avoid.

"Come and get one in the *yarbles*," Raven said.

Raven rushed the leader. She snatched his walking stick, snapped it over her knee, and tossed the pieces like broken twigs. The crazed look in her eyes startled them all and they quickly sobered up, but it was too late. Raven flowed into them, attacking them all simultaneously with a blindingly fast succession of slaps, punches, and kicks. Two of the droogs fell to the ground bloodied and broken. The leader wobbled on rubbery legs ready to collapse. Raven kicked him in the groin and he did collapse, dropping to his knees as he howled in agony.

"I wasn't kidding," she said looking down at him.

Raven turned and walked away. She was feeling a bit better and had worked up an appetite.

* * *

The small restaurant was unusually noisy, particularly considering there were far more empty chairs than clientele. Loud classic rock blared from a jukebox, mixed with sounds coming from a dozen different televisions that hung suspended from the ceiling, scattered throughout the room. Every screen displayed some sports activity. The restaurant area was deserted, but the bar was jampacked with patrons dressed in outlandish Halloween costumes. They were in a lively mood and a jovial bartender kept the drinks flowing.

Raven entered, and every eye gradually turned in her direction. She ignored the stares as she surveyed the restaurant. There were several choice tables to pick from, but a booth in a back corner looked the most inviting and she coolly walked over to it. Curious eyes followed her. As Raven settled into her booth, she immediately realized to her extreme displeasure that there was a television directly above her head. The volume was turned up full blast. She liked the booth but the television absolutely had to go.

"Hey, Mr. Bartender!" she yelled out while pointing up toward the television. "You wanna turn this thing down? Or better yet, just turn it off! I can't hear myself think!"

The reaction at the bar to Raven's forceful request was mixed. The incessant chatter died down as patrons looked to the bartender to gauge his reaction. A clearheaded waitress stood nearby and reminded the bartender that it was good business to make customers comfortable, particularly when there were so few on hand to begin with. He complied, somewhat begrudgingly, and turned off the television above Raven. The other televisions remained on at full blast. The bar went back to normal except for one idiot dressed like Batman who was nursing his third consecutive shot. He was a large idiot with a distinct air of hostility, mostly the result of the money he had just donated to the video poker machine in front of him. A man dressed as Superman sat beside him.

"You really gonna take that shit?" Batman asked the bartender in a voice loud enough to be heard over the noise and throughout the restaurant. "If the bitch doesn't like the environment, then maybe the bitch needs to move to a different environment."

The chatter immediately died down again. Most of the patrons seemed to know one another; it was a neighborhood establishment and they were regulars. But Batman was a stranger to them so no one knew just what to make of him. He was clearly in a foul mood and looking for trouble. Batman drained his glass and slid it forward for an unneeded refill. The waitress watched him uneasily as she tried to appear busy.

"Don't sweat it," said the bartender addressing Batman. He knew potential trouble when he saw it and wanted to diffuse a possible scene. "It's cool, really, it's cool." He reluctantly filled the glass and watched with mounting nervousness as Batman drained it and slid the glass forward for another refill.

"I don't think it's cool at all," Batman continued with more volume and more hostility. "Bitches think the world revolves around them and their needs, especially these modern day bitches. A bitch used to know her place ... before Oprah."

Realizing that his glass remained unfilled, Batman looked up at the bartender for an explanation. The bartender wasn't looking at him, but rather over his shoulder. Batman turned around to find Raven standing behind him.

"You've got a big mouth," she said.

Batman smirked and turned back to face the bartender. "So do you, and if you don't get out of my face, I'm going to put something in it." He laughed.

Raven snatched Batman's cape and jerked him off the bar stool. Batman was drunk, but not physically impaired. He quickly spun around with a loaded fist and fired it full force at Raven's face. Raven calmly leaned back and allowed the punch to sail past her, slightly deflecting it with the palm of her hand. Batman's wild punch had thrown him off balance and left him wide open to her attack. Now it was Raven's turn and she looked at the exposed parts of his body like food selections at a buffet. First she chose legs, kicking his shin, knee, and thigh in rapid succession. Then, she chose ribs, punching him hard enough to double him over with the wind completely knocked out of him. Finally, she grabbed him by the head and with a vicious twist, sent him airborne and spinning before slamming to the floor. Raven stood over him with her hands on her hips and glared down at him. She wanted Batman to get back up. He didn't.

"That mouth of yours is going to get you in trouble," she said, barely out of breath. "Next time, it's going to get you in the hospital." Raven glanced over at Superman who sat frozen. "If you're a friend of his," she said pointing down at Batman, "then you'd better be one and keep him out of my face."

Raven turned and walked away as the eyes of stunned patrons followed her. She returned to her booth and settled back in her seat. Moments later she was joined by the waitress.

"Miss, your order is on the house tonight," said the waitress excitedly. "Whatever you want to eat or drink, all night long, you got it, free of charge. Right now, there's a bunch of people fighting over who is going to pick up the check."

Raven shrugged. "I'm down. Let's start with a pitcher of sangria."

"Comin' up!"

The waitress hurried off. Batman was carried from the restaurant, and all chatter was now centered on the badass in the booth in the back. One patron dressed as a Parisian street hooker, in a tight, lowcut satin dress with a slit up the side and a red feather boa, sat quietly. The costume she wore was quite fitting indeed. She wasn't French, but she really was a hooker, albeit a very high-priced one. She stared at Raven from across the restaurant. Raven's forceful persona was more than compelling; it was *familiar*. The hooker finished her drink and left the bar. Slowly, she made her way through the restaurant. As she approached the back booth, her heartbeat quickened. Raven shuffled a deck of cards absentmindedly. Her radar detected a presence and she glanced up. When the hooker saw Raven's distinctive facial scar, her eyes filled with tears. Raven immediately recognized the hooker as well, even after fifteen years. It was Shanice. For a moment, they were both stunned and unable to move. Then Raven leaped up and they embraced desperately.

* * *

The bar had long since emptied of patrons. Only the bartender remained, keeping himself occupied by shining glasses and watching television. The restaurant area was pitch black except for the booth where Raven and Shanice sat. Raven continued shuffling cards, occasionally stopping to take a sip of sangria. Shanice hungrily gnawed a rib bone. Beside her sat a tall stack of dirty dishes. Raven hadn't eaten at all but she did feast her eyes on the sight of her old friend. Whenever their eyes met, they locked. Their bond remained intact, even after so many years.

Shanice was unrepentant about her chosen profession. "You know, contrary to what they say, everybody's *not* created equal," she said tossing her final rib bone. "Beauty, brains, talent, and all the other stuff you take for granted, some of us didn't get as much of that. Some of us had to do the best we could with what we had." Shanice laughed. "Besides, just because I was born to money doesn't mean I got any of it. I never got shit. So, I do what I've got to do."

"Baby, I don't care what you do. A gig's a gig." Raven momentarily stopped shuffling. "So where's Sophia?"

Shanice sighed. "After we got busted, she ended up in European boarding-school purgatory. We kept in touch for a minute, but then we just lost contact after a while. Besides, with you gone, nothing was ever the same anymore. Everything changed. The magic was gone."

Raven and Shanice exchanged bittersweet glances.

Shanice changed the subject. "You've done all right for yourself. You're famous." She laughed. "You're Ravendiablo, the bad bitch of magic."

"Think I ain't?" Raven smiled *diabolically*.

"I cracked up when I first heard that. I've followed your career a little. I know you're an international bitch. You never play Vegas."

"I've slipped in every now and then for a convention or corporate party, if the money was right. But an extended gig? Never. Until now." Raven shook her head and smiled sadly. "I must have been out of my mind to even think about doing my thing for a bunch of afternoon knuckleheads. And what happens? My magic show pulled a vanishing act. I should've known better than to try and do anything here. I should've just kept moving. I'm a nomad anyway."

"You're just mad."

Raven laughed. "This is true, especially now. Mad and broke. Broke as a joke."

"The broke bitch of magic?"

"I spent my last dime on my new show." Raven continued. "My Vegas show. Elaborate set designs, costumes, grand illusions, the whole nine. I had this idea, this ridiculously *stupid* idea, of trying to do *Ravendiablo* in Vegas. Something dark and dangerous and unique. And that was my mistake, trying to do unique in Vegas. Vegas doesn't want different, Vegas wants dicked to death." Raven laughed bitterly. "Vegas wants Jenna Thalia and the G-String Divas of Magic. I hate this town. Las Vegas can kiss my ass. Please, feel free to quote me."

Shanice lit a cigarette and poured herself a glass of sangria. "If Vegas were any more square, it would be a box. Corny and horny. It's always been that way, you know that. But as good as you look, you sure don't have to be broke. You'd put me out of business in a heartbeat. Money is tight everywhere. Vegas ain't what it used to be, that's for damn sure. I work twice as hard for half as much. And if that weren't bad enough, the level of appreciation is never in proportion to the level of expertise." Shanice laughed. "I got skills, too. Think I ain't?"

Raven laughed. "No doubt. If I don't solve my money problems pretty quick, I'll be game for just about anything."

Shanice took a long drag from her cigarette. As she exhaled, her somewhat dizzy demeanor changed. The sly smile vanished from her face as wheels turned in her head. She no longer looked at Raven but rather, looked *through* her while focused on the thoughts in her mind. Shanice was constructing a highly involved plan, slowly and deliberately. Raven could tell. She knew the look. They had once been successful partners in crime. After a few moments, Shanice seemed illuminated and the sly smile returned. But her eyes burned with a predatory intensity.

Shanice focused back upon Raven. "Around midnight, I meet my last date for the night. Some Eurotrash high roller from Vulgaria or wherever. I've been hired as part of the hotel entertainment package. Lita, my connect at the agency, says Euro is seriously loaded. And I believe it. I'm booked at three times my going rate and that's just to be his arm candy. He's flying in for some elite private baccarat tournament. Lita said that the last time he was in Vegas, he traveled with suitcases of cash."

Raven stopped shuffling, set the cards off to the side, and listened closely.

"This chump is being handed to us on a platter," Shanice continued with a ruthless smile. "I don't know what kind of business this Dmitri Kaviani is in. I didn't ask. I never ask. But for him to be slinging that much jack, and all in *cash*? Whatever his business is, it sure ain't Save the Children, that's for damn sure. Mr. Kaviani has been screwing somebody, somewhere, somehow. It only stands to reason. Which means that whatever we do to him, he's got it coming."

Raven's eyes locked with Shanice's. Raven was already on board.

Shanice lit another cigarette and smiled innocently. "Besides, whatever we do to him, we do for *Mama* ... Mother Nature. This is what they refer to as *divine intervention*. Surely you see that."

Raven smiled but her eyes were deadly serious. Wheels were now turning in her head as well.

Shanice laughed. "If anything, it would be wrong for us *not* do this! You don't want to do anything wrong, do you?"

Raven laughed at the absurdity of the question.

"I didn't think so," Shanice said. "There's nothing wrong with taking from people who take. All that jack he's slingin' ... he took that from somebody and you know it. Now Mama wants us to take it back. If there was some way to return that money to the rightful owners, we'd do it in a heartbeat. You know we would. But, unfortunately, we can't, so we have to do the next best thing. We have to keep it because it's the right thing to do. And we have to do the right thing. Mama wants us to have that money. You know why? Because we're good people and we need it. Mama needs something, too. She needs her righteous revenge and she can have it *through* us. We're her instruments of goodness and righteousness. Don't you see? She's using us to restore harmony and justice in this cruel, evil world."

Raven shook her head as she pondered the wicked wisdom of Shanice's words. "I never realized you were such a philosopher. I'm impressed."

"There's a lot about me you don't know. You've been gone a long time. But there's one thing you must remember. I'm a hustling bitch. What I lack in other areas, I compensate for with my hustle. And we're gonna hustle this Eurotrash chump tonight."

Raven and Shanice stared at one another and the booth crackled with energy.

"You think it's a coincidence that after all these years of being separated, we reconnect *tonight*? On Halloween night? On the very night I'm supposed to entertain some chump coming in with cases of cash, money he got from ganking somebody? This is no mere coincidence, Raven. This is straight up, Biblical style destiny. Mama wants this to go down, *tonight*. This is meant to be. And it's gonna be."

Shanice was ridiculously right, and Raven knew it.

Shanice laughed. "Everything will be totally different after tonight. I can just feel it. Our lives will be forever changed by what happens tonight. Besides, with Mama in the driver's seat, it's all good."

Shanice raised her glass in a toast, "To bitches and riches."

Raven raised her glass, "Bitches and riches."

The old friends tapped their glasses.

* * *

As she sexily strolled through the hotel lobby, Shanice turned many heads, both male and female. She was no longer dressed in hooker costume. Now she was dressed for work. With a fashion style both understated and sophisticated, she looked more like an executive than a prostitute, and she was stunning. Shanice stepped into an elevator packed with well-dressed men who all eyed her flirtatiously. She was oblivious to them. She was absorbed in thought, focused on the plan that would separate Dmitri Kaviani from his money and put her and Raven on easy street.

The other occupants departed one by one, leaving Shanice to continue her ascent to the top floor alone. When the elevator door slid open, Shanice smiled with confidence and showed no trace of nervousness. She stepped out and walked briskly down the hall until she reached the door of destiny. She popped a mint into her mouth and knocked on the door.

There was no answer. Shanice waited a moment then knocked again, a bit harder. Still no answer. She was about to knock once more when the door slowly opened. Shanice was instantly terrified.

Dmitri Kaviani was middle-aged, expensively dressed, and bedecked with jeweled accessories. Clearly, a man of great wealth. He also wore a considerable amount of makeup, even more than Shanice. But he was no cross-dresser. Dmitri Kaviani wasn't made up to appear feminine, but rather, to appear *human*. He was certainly alive, a sentient being to be sure, but he radiated nothing that could be called humanity. His ghastly face, pale and accented with heavy black eyeliner and dark lipstick, was a Halloween mask *for real*. The garish, overabundance of makeup only maximized his monstrousness. A toothy gargoyle smile took up the entire lower half of his face. His eyes sparkled mischievously.

"Hello, my dear," he said with a strange, thick accent. "I've been expecting you and it was well worth the wait. Please come in."

Shanice's fear fused her feet to the floor and Dmitri smiled knowingly. He took her by the arm and pulled her inside—at least it felt that way to Shanice. The enormous suite was lavishly decorated and looked like a movie set. Dmitri closed the door, and the sudden sound of the turning lock startled Shanice. When she jumped, Dmitri smiled. He enjoyed her fear. He released her and strolled over to an ornate bar where he busied himself. Shanice felt trapped and nauseated. She was still unable to move and remained standing by the door. Dmitri had his back to her as he stood behind the bar, searching for the right ingredients.

"Come over here," he said firmly. It sounded like a command. "Have a seat. Relax."

Shanice tried to breathe normally as she slowly made her way across the mammoth room to the bar. She seated herself on one of the two stools, holding onto the bar to keep herself from shaking. Dmitri still had his back to her.

"What can I make for you?" he asked pleasantly.

"Maybe a little wine," Shanice answered, wondering if the fear in her voice was obvious. It was.

Dmitri laughed. "Unfortunately, there doesn't seem to be any wine here. I'll make you something else. Something special."

The faint chimes from Dmitri's cell phone made Shanice jump, and she was glad he was still turned away from her.

Dmitri removed his phone from his pocket. "Hello? Yes, that will be fine, do as you wish. I'll be down a bit later. I'm going to entertain my guest up here for a while."

As Dmitri continued his conversation, Shanice noticed the prize. A small black leather suitcase sat on top of the bar in plain view. It was laying open and filled with neat stacks of cash. On the floor beside the bar were three more such suitcases. But rather than excite her, the sight of the money only amplified her terror. She wanted to vomit.

Dmitri laughed wickedly. Yes, that sounds like a very good idea. I like the way you think. I'll see you later." He ended the call and turned to face Shanice once again. He seemed more animated. "Now, where were we?" he asked with a sinister smile. 'Ah, yes, the refreshments."

Dmitri reached for the drinks that he had prepared. "I hope you like it." He walked from behind the bar and seated himself on the stool beside Shanice. He handed her a glass as he took a sip from his own, watching her, molesting her with his eyes.

"Drink," he said, and it was an order.

Shanice could barely keep her hand from shaking as she brought the glass to her mouth. She tried to smell the contents.

"Go ahead," he insisted, watching her closely. "You seem tense. You need to relax. You're in good hands, so drink."

Shanice had no choice. She obeyed, took two large sips and he seemed satisfied, for the moment.

"Are you a dancer?" he asked eyeing her up and down.

"No," she managed to answer.

"Really?" Dmitri seemed surprised. "Well, you'll be dancing tonight. You were hired to entertain me, no?"

Shanice was too frozen with fear to answer. She nodded affirmatively.

"Take your shoes off," he said, and his voice seemed colder. "We're not going anywhere."

"I have to go to the bathroom," Shanice stammered.

Dmitri didn't answer right away and he continued to stare at her. He knew he was frightening her. Now, he wanted *her* to know that he knew. Finally, he pointed to a door across the suite.

"In there," he said.

Shanice placed her drink on the bar and climbed down from her stool, afraid her legs might fail her. As she walked across the room, she could feel Dmitri's eyes upon her. She opened the door and found a huge bedroom. Across the room was another door leading to the bathroom. Shanice entered the bedroom, closed the door behind her and sprinted into the bathroom. Quickly locking the door behind her, she removed a cell phone from her pocket and frantically entered digits. Staring at her reflection in the bathroom mirror, she was startled by the terror in her eyes. She was in deep trouble and the knock at the bathroom door confirmed it. She slipped the phone apprehensively into her pocket.

"Just a minute!" she said nervously.

Shanice flushed the toilet and ran water in the sink to buy time. She splashed her face, adjusted her clothing, and took one last look in the mirror. She was petrified and looked it. She took a deep breath, opened the door, and tried to look as relaxed as possible, but when she saw Dmitri standing before her and holding her drink, she panicked. Dmitri's eyes were no longer sparkling, and the gargoyle smile was replaced by a gruesome grimace. All pretense of humanity was now terrifyingly gone. He was sweating profusely and his makeup had begun to run, particularly the thick black eyeliner, making him appear corpselike. He glared at Shanice suspicously and she forced an innocent smile. Suddenly, Dmitri seized her in his arms and poured the drink into her mouth. Shanice reflexively vomited as she struggled against him, but Dmitri was strong and held her tightly in his grasp. And he laughed, an eerie, high-pitched feminine sounding laughter that filled the bedroom. A long, reptilian tongue darted out of his mouth and flicked at her face and neck hungrily. Shanice began to lose consciousness. Her knees buckled completely, and she collapsed, but Dmitri quickly snatched her by the hair. She dangled in his grip. Dmitri Kaviani had claimed his prize.

* * *

The penthouse elevator doors slid back, and Raven stepped out, dressed in black leather. As the doors closed behind her, she paused momentarily, staring down the long hallway. Raven's radar was fully activated. Something was wrong. She continued into the hallway at an anxious pace, her eyes reflecting her growing apprehension. She arrived at Dmitri's door, pressed her ear firmly against it, and listened closely. She heard nothing. Raven used a small tool to gingerly pick the lock. She turned the knob and slowly eased the door open, just enough to peek inside the suite. The living rooom area of the suite was empty, and Raven stepped inside, closing the door behind her. She immediately spotted Shanice's purse on the bar, and the sight of it compounded her dread. As Raven approached the bar, she also noticed the suitcase of cash resting nearby. She was now indifferent to the money. She picked up the purse and stared at it nervously, then glanced across the room at the closed bedroom door. Raven rested the purse on the bar, walked over to the bedroom door, and pressed her ear against it. She turned the knob and gently opened the door. When she peeked into the room, she saw Dmitri on the bed with Shanice, who appeared to be unconscious. He was tying her to the bed.

Raven stepped into the bedroom, closed the door and locked it. Dmitri looked up, startled by her sudden appearance. He was also startled by the look on Raven's face. Her eyes were rolled back into her head and her tongue dangled from her mouth. She was horrifying, even to a monster like Dmitri. Stripped down to his underwear, Dmitri leaped off the bed and charged at Raven, his eyes filled with rage. Raven casually stepped aside to avoid his attack, then grabbed hold of his wrist with one hand. Her grip was viselike, and she sadistically twisted the wrist to the audible breaking point, causing him to howl in pain. Then Raven erupted with a shriek. She savagely kicked Dmitri off his feet and sent him sailing against the locked bedroom door. The door splintered as it slammed open, and Dmitri tumbled into the living room where he landed in a crumpled heap.

As Dmitri struggled to stand, he looked up. Through blurred eyes, he saw Raven approaching, moving as if in slow motion, calmly loosening her fingers, wrists, arms, shoulders, and neck like a fighter about to begin a match. The look in her eyes was unnerving. Dmitri lunged at her, but Raven kicked him in the face, and he dropped to his knees cradling his broken, blood-spewing nose. Raven loosened and stretched her entire body slowly, *elegantly*, like an accomplished dancer. She was in no hurry whatsoever. She kicked Dmitri in the face again, shattering his jaw completely. The force of the kick lifted him up into the air and when he fell back to the floor, several teeth spilled from his bloody gaping mouth. He lay spread-eagled at her feet, wide open for more punishment. Raven continued the punishment by strategically stomping his most tender areas with sadistic, surgical precision. She wanted to toy with him before hurting him for real.

Raven reached down, grabbed Dmitri by the throat, and effortlessly jerked him to a standing position. He stood on wobbling legs, gurgling incoherently. While holding his throat with one hand, Raven forcefully slammed the palm of her free hand up into his groin, grabbed hold of his balls, and crushed them mercilessly. The pain sent Dmitri into hysterical convulsions and he performed a frantic dance as he struggled to break free from her grip. Raven continued squeezing, twisting and turning his testicles with delight, savoring his agonized cries. Raven finally released him and kicked him in the chest, sending him airborne and flying into a wall several feet away. Dmitri bounced off the wall and collapsed to the floor unconscious. Raven moved toward him again. She was just getting started.

Suddenly, three large and dangerous-looking men burst into the suite. They were Dmitri's personal body-guards, startled by the sight of their beaten boss on the floor and by the woman standing before them, totally fearless.

"Who the hell is this bitch?" the leader of the three yelled out to no one in particular.

"I'm the entertainment!" Raven answered.

One of the men immediately rushed ahead of the others, convinced that he could easily put Raven down on his own. An experienced martial artist, he fired well-aimed kicks and punches at Raven, but she coolly and easily deflected them all. Then she moved in on him, pep-pering him with slaps, elbow strikes, and punches. A kick to the shin dropped him to his knees. A blow to the temple knocked him out completely.

The other two men attacked, delivering the kicks and blows of well-trained, seasoned fighters. Raven dodged all their attacks with an effortless grace and style. The men were astonished by her advanced abilities and her auda-cious attitude. It was clear that she enjoyed the conflict, and the more violent, the better. Raven delivered a spin-ning kick into the face of one man and he fell at her feet unconscious. The remaining bodyguard leaped on her and dragged her to the floor where they struggled and traded blows. Raven maneuvered herself on top of him and head-butted him into unconsciousness.

Raven jumped back to her feet and was attacked from behind by the newly revived Dmitri. He grabbed her in a bear hug, momentarily gaining the upper hand. But Raven slithered out of his grasp and threw him over her shoulder, sending him flying several feet and into the bar. He slammed into it, toppling it completely. Raven ran over to Dmitri, straddled him, and pinned him to the carpet. Screaming with rage, she viciously pummeled him with fists, elbows, and head butts. Raven noticed one of the money suitcases laying nearby and snatched it up. Grabbing a handful of his hair, Raven jerked Dmitri to his feet and clubbed him with the suitcase, sending him stumbling backwards toward an immense floor-to-ceiling window. He teetered back and forth as he struggled to remain on his feet. Raven threw the suitcase at him and he reflexively caught it as he stumbled ever closer to the window. With a shriek, Raven leapt feet first into Dmitri's chest. The force knocked him off his feet and sent him hurtling through the window with a clanging crash as shards of glass rained to the floor and outwards into the air. Raven rushed over to the open window and watched as Dmitri tumbled screaming to his death past floor after floor. The suitcase sprang open in midair and greenbacks blanketed the sky like snowflakes. Remembering Shanice, Raven rushed across the room and peered into the bedroom. Shanice was slowly regaining consciousness, as were the bodyguards. Raven sprinted out of the suite like a panther.

One of the now fully conscious bodyguards made an animated emergency call on his cell phone, and moments later, several men rushed into the suite. One of them was

Gaspar Kaviani, Dmitri's brother. Like Dmitri, Gaspar wore an abundance of facial makeup, an attempt at normality that was as useless as his brother's. He was younger than Dmitri but he reeked of the same fiendishness. Gaspar surveyed the suite, which was in shambles, then looked to the fallen bodyguards for explanations. The men quickly struggled to their feet as Gaspar eyed them angrily.

"What's happened here?" demanded Gaspar.

"It was some crazy chick," one of the bodyguards exclaimed excitedly. "She was here when we got here. We tried to —"

"Some chick? Some *woman* did this?" Gaspar interrupted with astonishment, speaking in his strange, thick accent. "Are you insane?"

"I've never seen anything like it," offered another bodyguard. "She blew through here like a hurricane. We tried to stop her, Mr. Kaviani, I swear we did!"

The other bodyguards nervously corroborated the story told by their comrade. They watched Gaspar closely to gauge his reaction but were unable to read him. Gaspar turned away from the men and walked over to the open window. Far below he could see a crowd gathered around a black spot, the spot where his brother Dmitri lay burst open by the concrete. The crowd was far more interested in the money that continued to fall freely from the sky. Gaspar looked down at the scene as his eyes filled with tears.

"A woman?" he said, barely able to contain his fury. "A woman defeated the three of you, and killed my brother?"

The three bodyguards stood in silent fear and they made no attempt to explain themselves further. Suddenly, two police officers rushed into the suite.

"What's going on up here?" one of the cops demanded breathlessly while glancing around the demolished suite.

Gaspar was still standing at the window with his back to the others. He removed a pistol from a shoulder holster and calmly attached a silencer to it. "There have been some murders," he said. "My brother, and the both of you."

Gaspar turned and calmly shot both officers, one shot to each head, and they dropped to the floor. The bodyguards looked fearfully at Gaspar and wondered if they, too, would die next. But Gaspar holstered the pistol and turned back to stare at the scene below.

* * *

Raven rushed out of a rear exit of the hotel, knocking down two kitchen workers in the process. Her car was waiting nearby, a 1968 Highland-green Ford Mustang, specifically the Mustang Steve McQueen drove in the classic film, *Bullitt*. Even the license plate read "Bullitt". Raven leaped in through an open window, revved the engine, and sped off into the night. The normally supercool Raven was panicked now. She took several deep breaths to calm herself as she turned the car onto the Strip. Raven slammed the accelerator and the Mustang burned rubber, taking off like a missile down the boulevard. She weaved the car in and out of traffic at breakneck speed like an experienced racer, passing petrified drivers who barely had the chance to clear the way. She ran a red light and nearly collided with a taxicab.

Raven gripped the steering wheel as the Mustang screeched around a corner. Now a police siren could be heard. Raven checked the rearview mirror and saw a Metro squad car approaching from behind. She had no intention of pulling over, and it was at that moment that she officially became Ravendiablo, *outlaw*. The squad car pulled up beside her and the two officers inside were shocked to see a woman behind the wheel. Raven glared at them defiantly, then snapped the steering wheel to the left. The Mustang slammed into the squad car, sending it out of control and crashing into the side of a parked car.

Raven turned onto another street and within moments, more sirens could be heard. She looked in the rearview mirror and saw another squad car approaching. She turned the Mustang onto a oneway street, floored the accelerator, and sped directly into the oncoming traffic. Cars frantically cleared the way for her, narrowly avoiding collision as she roared past them. The squad car behind her continued its dogged pursuit. Raven sneered as she glanced up into the mirror. She stomped the accelerator and the Mustang burned rubber around another corner— directly into the path of an old woman crossing the street in a motorized wheelchair. Raven screamed and jerked the steering wheel, avoiding certain collision by inches. But she lost control of the Mustang.

The car jumped the curb and rocketed into the entrance of a convenience store, crashing through the glass and steel and narrowly missing several store patrons. The Mustang slammed into glass-fronted refrig- erators that lined a backwall, causing an earsplitting explosion of shattered glass. The salesclerk stood frozen at the counter and watched in wide-eyed shock as Raven kicked open the door and spilled out of the car onto the floor. She was badly injured. The sound of more sirens signaled the impending arrival of more cops. Raven managed to stagger to her feet, suppressing her pain by sheer force of will. She spotted a rear exit door several feet away and took off running. Bursting through the door, she emerged into an alley and sprinted off into the night.

Raven raced up one alleyway and down another, occasionally stumbling, but never stopping. She was exhausted, but she kept moving. Far behind her, she could hear the cops in pursuit, filling the air with the sound of sirens. Weakened and dazed, Raven could run no longer. Her legs finally gave out and she collapsed into a bunch of trash cans. Lying face down on a bed of garbage, she desperately tried to crawl under a nearby Dumpster. But several hands reached out from the darkness and seized her. Unable to fight back, Raven passed out.

12

Xandra

When Raven regained consciousness, she was bandaged and lying in a bed in a dimly lit room. Two young women stood at the foot of the bed watching her closely. A black woman crowned with dreadlocks and dressed in purple entered. She looked at Raven with caring eyes. She asked the two women to leave and they complied. The woman in purple pulled up a chair beside Raven's bed. Raven tried to sit up but was barely able to move. The woman smiled and stroked Raven's brow.

"You need to just relax, girlfriend," she said in a sooth-ing, reassuring tone. "You're not going anywhere. The show's over."

Raven trusted the woman immediately.

The woman took Raven's hand. "I'm Xandra. You're safe now," she insisted. "Rest, we've got plenty of time to talk."

Xandra stood, smiled down at Raven, then turned and left the room. She walked down a long hallway and up a winding staircase, eventually entering her private office. Several women were huddled around her desk waiting for her. They were all visibly nervous. Xandra sat behind her desk and exchanged glances with each of the women. Then she picked up a remote and activated a television across the room. The nightly news had already begun.

"Las Vegas magician Raven Chandler, who performs under the name Ravendiablo, is wanted for questioning for the murders of European businessman Dmitri Kaviani and two Metro police officers. According to witnesses questioned at the scene, Kaviani was murdered during a robbery attempt. The two Metro officers were killed as they attempted to apprehend the suspect. A high-speed chase through the streets of Las — "

Xandra turned off the television and sat back in her chair. The newscast made the collective mood even more fearful, but Xandra seemed relaxed.

"Well?" she asked.

The women looked at one another uneasily but no one answered. Finally, all eyes focused on Xandra. Everyone was obviously waiting for her response. Like a noble ruler, Xandra sat with an air of authority and dignity. Then, suddenly, her calm and refined demeanor morphed into something more aggressive.

"Does anybody in here actuallly believe that bullshit?" she asked cynically. Her eyes were blazing. "We all know who Dmitri Kaviani was, what he was up to, and what he was into. As far as I'm concerned, anyone who took him out deserves the Medal of Honor, the Nobel Prize, and lunch on me!" Xandra's face beamed as she thought of her new guest in the basement. "And the way she took him out!" Xandra gushed excitedly. "Damn! This bitch is fierce!"

"But what about the those police officers?" asked one woman anxiously. "The newscaster said ... "

"The newscaster said?" interrupted Xandra mockingly. "Said what? That she killed two Metro cops?" Xandra sneered. "Newscasters say a lot of things. Newscasters say what they're told to say." Xandra pointed at the silenced television. "We all know what that box is for." She picked up a newspaper laying on her desk. Raven was on the cover. "And we all know what this rag is for. I don't know about you, but I don't have time for manufactured reality. I'm only interested in the truth."

The room was silent. No one wanted to confront Xandra. It was clear that her position was passionately inflexible.

"So let me remind everybody of something," Xandra continued, "just in case you've forgotten. There's a war going on out there. And we're fighting it! Our enemy is Dmitri Kaviani and reptiles just like him. I don't know what happened up in that hotel." Xandra pointed at the television again. "And neither does Mr. Smiley Face over there. But I'm telling you something right here tonight. This ain't nothing but a setup! Ravendiablo stays here!"

Xandra abruptly stood and exited the office, leaving the women in stunned silence.

* * *

Dmitri Kaviani's three beaten bodyguards were ushered into a room by a man considerably larger and more dangerous looking than they. He closed the door behind them and locked it. The room was near dark, the only source of light being a low-watt bulb suspended over a conference table. At one end of the table sat three empty chairs. At the far end of the table, obscured by shadows, sat Gaspar

Kaviani. Though they were unseen, the presence of others in the room could be felt as they stood in the darkness just beyond the illuminated conference table. The three bodyguards still wore the cuts and bruises of their encounter with Raven, and one of them was on crutches. As they stood waiting for the next chapter to unfold, their faces reflected their collective dread.

"Be seated," ordered Gaspar.

The bodyguards hobbled over to the three empty chairs and seated themselves.

"A man is dead," said Gaspar calmly. "and not just any man, but my brother. A great fortune was lost as well. Two great losses. One simple reason. Incompetence."

The bodyguards looked at one another apprehensively.

"It can't be tolerated. It won't be tolerated." Two large men emerged from the shadows holding several thick leather straps. They bound two of the bodyguards to their chairs. They seized the third man and literally ripped his clothes off, stripping him down to his briefs. They violently slammed him on his back to the conference table, strapped him down spread-eagled, and stepped back into the darkness.

"Ravendiablo took my brother's life," said Gaspar. "She will be found and dealt with. It was your job to protect my brother. You failed. Now you must be dealt with."

A straw basket was placed on the table near Gaspar by hands that disappeared back into the darkness. Gaspar stood. With one hand resting on the basket, he slowly made his way down the length of the table, sliding the basket along as he went. Reaching the end of the table,

Gaspar positioned the basket between the legs of the spread-eagled man.

"What is your name?" Gaspar asked the man strapped to the table.

"Devlin," stammered the man as he eyed the straw basket with mounting terror.

Gaspar's demeanor became strangely lighthearted and he smiled. "Well, Devlin, I'd like for you to meet some friends of mine."

Gaspar opened the lid of the basket, reached inside, and removed two black, squirming, worm-like creatures. Each one was about eight inches in length and as thick as a sausage, with bulging eyes and a serpentine tongue that darted out from between piranha sharp teeth. When Devlin saw the creatures, he screamed in horror and struggled against his restraints. The seated bodyguards had a clear view of the creatures and they, too, struggled against their bonds.

Gaspar placed two of the creatures on the table where they squirmed excitedly. He removed a dagger from his jacket and plunged the blade deep into each of Devlin's ankles causing him to scream even more. Gaspar positioned each of the creatures close to the fresh bleeding wounds. The creatures hungrily attacked the gaping wounds, and quickly burrowed themselves into each ankle. Devlin became hysterical and thrashed wildly against the bonds that held him. The thick, bulbous outlines of the creatures were visible through Devlin's flesh as they slowly wormed their way up into his calves and along his inner thighs, literally eating through muscle and tendons. Gaspar removed two more creatures from the basket and directed them into the gaping wounds. Devlin's agonized screams filled the room as he struggled in vain against the restraints. The two bodyguards sat strapped to their chairs, their eyes filled with terror as they watched the nightmare unfold before them.

The creatures were clearly heading north. Three of them worked their way up from the thighs and into the stomach region, eating through intestines and vital organs as Devlin thrashed against the restraints. He vomited blood that spewed up and out of his mouth like a fountain. One of the creatures lingered in the groin area. Then, suddenly, it chewed its way up through flesh and underwear and poked its head and body out into view. Devlin looked as though he had sprung an erection and Gaspar wailed in maniacal laughter at the freakishly macabre sight. The unseen others in the darkness roared with laughter as well. The creature then burrowed itself back down into Devlin's crotch. Devlin passed out, but his body twitched and convulsed as the feasting taking place inside of him continued unabated. With a fiendish smile, Gaspar turned to face the bound bodyguards. His eyes sparkled mischievously.

"By the way, this is a dinner party," he said, "and you're the dinner."

* * *

Xandra's House was a modern-day oasis in the desert. Located in a small strip mall on the west side of the city, it was a combination free clinic and soup kitchen that ministered to the needs of the poor, the elderly, and the abused. Business was always booming. On this particular afternoon, the large lobby was bustling with people. The small staff, which included both medical professionals and volunteers, seemed overwhelmed by the crowd. For all its good intentions, Xandra's House resembled a kind of organized chaos. Hidden away in the basement, Raven lay alone in her room staring at the ceiling, deep in thought. Still badly bruised, she was healing and in far better shape than when she had first arrived. There was knock at the door.

"Come in," said Raven.

Xandra entered with a tray of food that she placed on a small table beside the bed. "You need to eat something, girlfriend," she said with motherly concern.

"I'm not hungry," Raven said wearily. "Maybe later."

"I don't want to hear it," snapped Xandra. "Besides, I made this myself, especially for you."

"Yeah?" Raven sat up and glanced over at the covered food. "What is it?"

Xandra removed the cover with a flourish. "Collard greens!" she answered excitedly.

Raven smiled. "I think I just found my appetite."

Xandra placed the tray on Raven's lap, pulled up a chair and seated herself. She watched anxiously as Raven sampled the food. "Is it okay?" she asked.

"Delicious, and a nice surprise, too. I haven't had greens in years." Raven was momentaily transported to the past. "My friend Swannie used to make them for me."

Xandra seemed relieved. "Good. I'm glad you like it."

Xandra continued to watch Raven as she ate. She was fond of Raven and loved having her around, in spite of the circumstances. Raven's energy was powerfully magnetic, and Xandra was a moth to Raven's flame. Raven was aware of her effect on Xandra, but pretended not to notice.

"Okay, let's talk," said Raven as she finished her last bite and placed the tray back on the table.

"I agree. Let's get to it." Xandra sat back in her chair.

"I would imagine you know who I am by now."

"Xandra smiled proudly. "Sure, I know exactly who you are. You're Ravendiablo, the bad bitch of magic."

"The dead bitch of magic," Raven said cynically.

"You're safe," Xandra said with warm reassurance. "No one knows you're here except my trusted staff. So, tell me, what happened?"

Ravens seemed surprised by the question. "What happened? I must be a reality star by now."

"You are, but what's your version of reality?"

Raven smiled. "I took out the trash."

Xandra laughed heartily. "Sure did! Tossed it right out the window, too!" Xandra became serious again. "Did you know the trash you took out?"

"We were never formally introduced, if that's what you mean." Raven's mood darkened. "There was a girl there that night. What happened to her?"

"The TV and newspapers never mentioned anything about a girl being there. Just three witnesses."

"Yeah, there were three guys who got in my way." Raven sneered. "Tried to."

"Two Metro cops were shot to death in the suite."

Raven was surprised. "Well, I didn't do 'em. I never saw cops till I hit the street." Raven sighed wearily and shook her head in disbelief. "So now I'm a cop killer, too, huh? Ain't *that* a bitch?"

Xandra smiled. "The trash you took out. Do you know anything at all about him?"

"My friend had a date with him that night. She said he was traveling with big bank, so we decided to make a withdrawal. I was going to snatch the jack while she kept him occupied." Raven took a deep breath as images from that night flooded her brain. "But everything got turned around. When I got there, I saw him, and her … " Raven fell silent.

"Then what?"

"Then what?" Raven sneered again. "I took out the trash."

"The trash was named Dmitri Kaviani. He was a very wealthy businessman. But his primary business was women and children. You took out some very bad trash, indeed."

"No one dies who's not supposed to."

Xandra adored Raven's attitude. "You're so *bad*," she said with fangirl admiration. "But you're in serious trouble. For one thing, there's a price on your head now. A big price. The Kavianis are an international crime family. They're powerful, well-connected, and extremely dangerous. Pissing them off is bad enough, but killing one means a fate worse than death. And if that weren't bad enough, you've been framed for the murder of two Metro cops. You're in deep shit, girlfriend. I can't even see the top of your head."

Raven sighed, seemingly unconcerned. "It *is* complicated, isn't it?"

Xandra laughed. "It doesn't matter. No one is going to lay a hand on you. I'll make sure of that."

Raven looked at Xandra curiously. "Why are you doing this? You don't even know me."

"That's not entirely true. Sure, I know Ravendiablo, the bad bitch of magic. But I know somebody else, too." Xandra paused for a moment as she carefully chose her words. "I know a little girl. An extraordinary little girl with a brain as big as her heart. Always running away from bad homes. Always dreaming about a real home. She finally found one as a teenager. She and her two friends were a family. A somewhat devious family, but a family just the same." Xandra laughed. "Teenage cat burglars! Unbelievable."

Raven stared at Xandra suspiciously.

"They had a good run, too," Xandra continued. "But eventually they got busted, and the only reason they got busted was because that same little girl was trying to help somebody else. Some other little girl."

Raven abruptly looked away.

"She took the fall for the family and got sent away. But not to the joint. Because somebody special saw something special in her and arranged for her to be sent to a special place. And that place turned out to be a *real* home. The very thing she'd always dreamed of."

Raven looked back at Xandra again.

"Her new home was very unusual to say the least. Because it was a home filled with ... *sculptors*. Master sculptors. She arrived at that home a raw block of marble, but these master sculptors carved her into a masterpiece. A living work of art.”

Raven became agitated. “Okay, I’m convinced, you’re well-informed. So who are you?”

“Who I am isn’t nearly as important as who you are,” answered Xandra. “And *what* you are. You really think you ended up here by accident, Raven? You think this is some kind of coincidence? This is no coincidence. You’re here because this is your destiny,” said Xandra. “And to whom much is given, much is required.”

“What’s that supposed to mean?”

“Reality is comprised of two worlds. The world we see and the world we don’t. And the world we don’t see controls the world we do. Most people will live their entire lives and never know that. You probably figured it out as a child. But there’s a problem. This world we don’t see, this *shadow world*, is for the most part an evil place filled with evil people like Dmitri Kaviani, his family and their associates. They come in all shapes, sizes, colors, and ethnicities. And these shadow people are predators, merciless predators who feed on the poor, the weak, and the defenseless. They deal in exploitation, violence, and death. And their primary weapon is fear.”

Xandra’s words were profound and the message penetrated and resonated with Raven.

“Ancient prophets foretold a time, an age, when evil would reach its epitome. A time when the predators would seem to be invincible and the world would stand on the brink of destruction. I believe that time is now.”

Raven's heart raced as she looked deep into Xandra's eyes.

"But the prophets also foretold of brave warriors who would rise and defeat this evil," Xandra said confidently. "You ain't no coincidence, girlfriend."

Xandra stood, walked to the far corner of the room, and pressed a hidden button. Suddenly, the entire wall beside Raven's bed slid back revealing a much larger room. This room appeared to be the base of operations for an elite secret organization. One entire wall was lined with a variety of elaborate, high-tech consoles that sparkled with flashing lights. Mounted on the opposite wall were several flat-screen monitors. The middle of the room was a maze of desks, tables, and cubicles, apparently the hub of the headquarters. Images flickered and data scrolled down dozens of laptop screens. The room was filled with women and men of all ages and races, all of whom appeared to be actively involved in various tasks. They all stopped what they were doing and looked at Raven with curious and hopeful eyes. It was as if Raven had been expected. Raven immediately sat up in amazement. Beaming brightly with tear-filled eyes, Xandra approached the bed and extended her hand. Raven took hold of it and slowly climbed out of bed. Xandra slipped an arm around Raven's waist to support her as they walked into the headquarters.

"We are the warriors," said Xandra proudly.

13

No One Dies
Who's Not Supposed To

They were a gathering of *predators*.

The private casino was filled with them, all male, of various ethnicities. While they certainly apeared human ... dressed in expensive suits and adorned with fine jewelry, their cold, malevolent eyes revealed the truth. These men were *reptiles*. They were international serpents at the top of the global food chain. Many different languages were spoken, making the exact geographical location of the casino a mystery. It could have been anywhere in the world. Most of the patrons were focused on the games of baccarat, blackjack, and poker. Others sipped drinks at a bar. Music played softly in the background from unseen speakers. The lighting was low, and it was best that way. These were shadow creatures.

In the far corner of the casino, a muscular man in a tight-fitting three-piece suit stood guard beside a wooden door with a large, sliding lock. He stared at the patrons with jealous eyes. He was only muscle, not power, and he knew his place in the food chain, to be sure. But even muscle has delusions of grandeur, and his eyes were filled with desire ... to be one of *them*.

A knock at the door returned him to harsh reality and he peered through a peephole to investigate. Slightly confused, he slid back the lock and opened the door. Raven brazenly brushed past him and entered like a panther. She wore a purple floor-length coat and a long yellow scarf. The doorman firmly placed his hand on her shoulder to prevent her from going any farther. Raven stopped, glanced first at his hand, and then turned to stare directly into his eyes. The fierce look in her eyes both startled and chilled him. Raven was fearless. The doorman removed his hand.

"Who are you?" he asked forcefully in an effort to reassert his masculinity. The look in her eyes had unnerved him.

"I'm the entertainment," Raven answered.

Raven turned and continued into the casino with every eye glued to her fascinating frame. She walked boldly, trading glances with the curious patrons who stared her down.

Who is this bitch? they wondered collectively.

Raven paused momentarily and scrutinized the casino carefully. Studiously. One entrance. No exits. No windows. There were about a hundred men in the casino, a third of them muscle. Most of the patrons were probably armed. A group of men sat in a booth a few feet away. They watched Raven curiously. Raven watched them right back.

She decided to investigate them more closely and walked over to their booth. These men reeked of power and position. There was a laptop computer on their table beside a stack of photographs. Raven reached out and positioned the computer so she could view the screen. She saw a teenage girl dressed in a nightgown sitting on a bed.

 RAVENDIABLO

Her eyes were listless, and she appeared to be drugged. A leering, middle-aged man sat beside her, stroking her hair lovingly. Raven looked away from the screen and picked up several photographs. Looking through them, she saw more young women and they all had the same vacant, hopeless eyes.

Raven tossed the photos back onto the table, and glared at the men contemptuously. They only smiled back at her, seemingly amused by her reaction. Raven turned away and walked over to the bar. As she moved closer, the space she wanted for herself was currently occupied by two men. She paused a few feet away and stared them down. They looked at one another, then moved aside. Raven took her place at the bar. A bartender stood nearby watching her. He wasn't occupied with customers, yet he made no effort to serve Raven. He only stood and stared. Raven removed her coat and scarf and placed them on the bar. She was dressed in black leather and boots.

Raven noticed an elaborate stereo system behind the bar. She strolled around the bar as if she owned it, and examined the stereo closer. An iPod connected to a receiver by a cable was the source of the music. Raven disconnected the iPod, plunging the casino into a sudden silence that was jarring. Every eye was aimed in her direction. She removed a domino-sized MP3 player from her pocket and connected it to the stereo receiver. Soon the casino was filled with her music ... flamenco music. Raven spotted a deserted table a few feet away. She walked from behind the bar over to the table and effortlessly leaped on top of it. Raven danced with her eyes closed. Enraptured by the exotic rhythm, she was dancing for herself, not for others. Her sexy self-expression was riveting, and most of the patrons were quite entertained. One burly, black brute watching her from across the room was not entertained. He drained his glass and angrily walked over to Raven's table for a closer inspection. With hands on his hips, he glared up at her.

"Come down from there!" he ordered. Raven heard him but ignored him. "I said, come down from there!"

Raven continued to ignore him, which brought his anger to the boiling point. "I said bring your ass down here right now!" he shouted.

Many of the patrons laughed in anticipation of some scene that was sure to follow. Raven stopped dancing and looked down at Burly, then demurely offered her hand to him. He begrudgingly accepted the hand and helped her down from the table. But he was still angry. Facing one another, he towered over her. Raven stared up into his eyes fearlessly.

"Just who do you think you are?" he asked.

"Kiss my ass," Raven answered.

Burly slapped Raven, hurling her backward. She bounced off the wall and fell at his feet. He grabbed her by the hair and stood her upright on wobbly legs. She seemed dazed by the blow.

"Didn't quite catch that," he said through clenched teeth.

"You heard me. I said kiss my ... "

Burly slapped her again and the blow sent her sailing back once more, bouncing off the wall and landing in a heap before him. The patrons were entertained by the violence and many of them moved closer to watch the show unfold. Burly looked down at Raven as she struggled to a kneeling position. Finally, he snatched her hair and jerked her head up, allowing him to stare down into her eyes.

"You got something else to say?" he asked with a cruel smile.

Raven reached behind with her right hand and jerked a revolver from the waistband of her pants as with her left hand she unzipped Burly's fly. She jammed the gun barrel into the gaping opening, causing Burly to go wide-eyed with terror. The surrounding patrons were shocked by the sudden and dramatic turn of events.

"Yeah, I've got something to say. Are you circumcised?" Raven asked calmly. She cocked the hammer and the deadly sound reverberated throughout the entire room. "'Cause if you're not ... you're about to be."

Burly immediately began singing the classic Jewish folk song, "Havah Nagilah". Before he could finish four bars, Raven sprung up and head-butted him in the face, lifting him off his feet and high into the air. He hovered in midair momentarily before slamming down to the floor onto his back, dazed. Raven stomped her heel down into Burly's groin and he jerked into an upright position, howling in agony. She kicked him in the face and the force sent him rolling backwards into a table of patrons. They collapsed on top of him like bowling pins. Raven slipped the gun back into her waistband and rushed over to the entrance door. She slid the lock firmly into place and the sound echoed throughout the casino. With eyes ablaze,

Raven turned to face the roomful of reptiles. Every evil eye was nervously focused on her.

"I'm the entertainment!" she screamed. "Showtime!"

Two men seated at a table several feet away reached for concealed weapons, but Raven was ready. She quickly drew her pistol and fired off several shots, blasting the men out of their chairs. Simultaneously, several patrons reached for their own weapons as well. Raven sprinted toward the bar. As the gunmen opened fire in her direction, she gracefully dived, snatched up her coat, and rolled over the bar, landing safely behind it. The patrons continued firing, spraying the bar with a barrage of bullets. Bottles and glasses exploded and shattered, turning the casino into an indoor fireworks display. Calmly crouched down behind the bar and completely unfazed by the deafening commotion, Raven reached into hidden folds within her coat. First, she removed a small makeup kit and applied her signature war paint ... Day of the Dead. Then, she removed a long, Old-West-style holster. Finally, she removed several pieces of black metal that she quickly assembled into an automatic shotgun.

The patrons finally stopped shooting and the casino was plunged back into silence.

Long moments passed as nervous glances were exchanged. "Is the bitch dead?" the reptiles wondered.

Raven answered the question by leaping up onto the bar with shotgun in hand. She assumed a squatting position and opened fire, hitting targets with marksman skill. Blasted bodies were bloodily blown in all directions, slamming into tables, walls, and each other. With a dancer's grace, Raven jumped down from the bar and landed lightly on her toes. Several men suddenly rushed her at once, knocking the shotgun from her hands. One of them grabbed her from behind in a bear hug. Raven remained calm. She slapped his ears and stomped his shin, and he quickly released her. She unleashed a fast and ferocious combination of slaps, kicks, elbows, and punches against the multiple attackers, leaving them all beaten and broken on the floor.

Another man armed with a knife lunged at her. Raven dodged his attack with ease and stepped back. The long holster strapped to her thigh didn't contain a pistol but a weapon far worse. Raven drew the strange object from the holster. It was made of glistening steel and appeared to be folded. With a flick of her wrist, the object extended to its full length and snapped into place.

It was a sword; long, curved, and clearly designed for butchery. Raven hacked off the attacker's arm at the elbow with one clean stroke. Her attack was so fast her victim didn't realize what had happened until he saw his arm fall to the floor with the fingers still moving. Then he screamed as blood spurted from the wound. The worst for him was yet to come.

Using a wide, circular motion for maximum acceleration, Raven forcefully spun her arm and brought the blade up into his groin. The force of the blow lifted him off his feet and he screamed in agony. There was a collective gasp throughout the room. With the sword still embeddded in his groin, Raven released her grip from the handle and adjusted each of her gloves. Then she grasped the weapon once more and jerked the blade upward toward the man's navel. She mercilessly twisted the blade and tore it out of his flesh, ripping his abdomen completely open. Blood and flesh sprayed walls and patrons. Her victim's legs buckled, and he dropped to his knees. The force of the landing caused his entrails to spill out of the gaping wound and onto the floor. As he continued to shriek, the disemboweled man instinctively tried to cover the enormous wound and contain the intestinal spillage—in vain. Looking down at him, Raven seemed amused by the futility of his actions. But she grew weary of his screaming and beheaded him with one graceful blow that sent his head rolling like a soccer ball past patrons who watched in horror. Finally, Raven kicked what remained of her headless victim back to the floor where he violently convulsed.

And she smiled *diabolically*.

The remaining crowd was stunned by the savagery they had just witnessed. At that moment many of them slowly backed away from Raven, because it was now terrifyingly clear that they were not in the presence of a woman, but a beast. Several patrons turned and rushed for the entrance door, but Raven drew her pistol and shot them all in the legs and they fell to the floor. She had no intention of killing them just yet, she only wished to prevent their escape. Because now was the time of the judgment and she would judge not with firearm, but with blade. Her eyes rolled back, her tongue protruded, she threw back her head, and *wailed*

Raven unleashed herself.

With sword firmly in hand, Raven erupted and blew through the casino like a homicidal whirlwind, chasing her terrified victims who ran before her like helpless rats. She kicked and tossed aside tables and chairs as she butchered her way throughout the room, splitting heads and severing limbs. Her victims fell, and when they did, she viciously hacked them to death. Some of them attempted to hide—quivering in corners, in booths, and beneath fallen debris. Raven swept aside all obstructions and furiously rained lethal blows down upon them as they screamed for mercy. But Raven was merciless, and the more she killed, the more possessed she became. She was feeding on the violence. Soon, most of the patrons were dead or near dead, lying in pools of blood and gasping for breath. A pink mist hung thick in the air. Raven had single-handedly transformed the casino into a slaughterhouse. The judgment was finished.

Raven danced.

Leaping and spinning wildly with flailing arms, Raven was in ecstasy, intoxicated by the mayhem and the music. A sudden sound from across the room jolted her from Nirvana. Burly, her nemesis from earlier, was back on his feet and frantically struggling with the sliding lock on the entrance door. He managed to slide the lock back, but he wasn't going anywhere. Raven hurled the blade full force and it whistled a lethal tune as it spun in his direction. The sword tore through his back, out his chest and into the door, literally nailing him to it face first. Raven walked toward the bar, carefully scrutinizing the fallen bodies around her. A handful of patrons were still alive, and

Raven shot them dead. She walked behind the bar, retrieved her coat and scarf, and slipped into them. Checking her reflection in a wall mirror, she wiped away the war paint and adjusted her hair.

Nailed to the door as blood and life slowly drained out of him, Burly watched fearfully as Raven advanced toward him. Even now, there was still murder in her eyes. Burly's eyes begged for mercy, but Raven's eyes were cold. When she reached him, she grasped the sword handle that protruded from his back. She jerked the blade out of the door, out of his body, and he collapsed at her feet. She finished him with a shot in the head. Raven took one last look around the casino, surveying her grisly handiwork. She had literally painted the room red. Not one reptile had been left alive. She reached down and dipped her fingers into the pool of bood that was forming at her feet. She drew an image on the door, a face with angry eyes and a protruding tongue—the face of Kali. Raven exited the casino, softly closing the door behind her.

14

The Fall of Babylon

A small private jet cruised high above the clouds. Raven was the only passenger on board, and she was fast asleep. An attractive female attendant came over and gently awakened her by tenderly stroking her forehead.

"We'll be landing soon," said the attendant with a shy smile before walking away.

Raven brought her seat to an upright position and glanced out the window. The city of Las Vegas glowed below in the darkness. She had been away on assignment for many months, but now she was back home. And the sight of the neon nauseated her. Raven sighed and rubbed her eyes wearily. The plane soon landed on a long stretch of deserted airstrip. Dressed in a long black cape that flowed behind her, Raven stepped out of the plane and walked down the steps to where a limo awaited. A female driver climbed out of the car and rushed over to open the passenger door for her. As Raven climbed inside, she glanced back at the plane and noticed the attentive stewardess still standing in the doorway watching her. The driver hurried back into the limo and drove away into the night.

As the limousine cruised past the gaudy landmarks that dotted the Strip, Raven's heart sank. Seeing Vegas from the clouds was difficult enough, but cruising the Strip was only a more painful reminder that she was back in Sin City. As much as Raven despised Las Vegas, she would never be able to escape the fact that it was her home.

Strangely, the Strip felt somehow less illuminated, at least it seemed that way. Raven could sense a distinct difference in the air. The familiar sights and sounds of the neon nightmare remained, but something had changed. Raven could feel it, and her radar was rarely wrong. When the limo moved off the Strip and into the more normal neighborhoods, Raven's astonished eyes confirmed her intuition. Scores of businesses were closed. Chain stores, local stores, mom and pop stores, supermarkets, banks, resaurants, nightclubs, and bookstores had vanished. The buildings remained, like skeleton bones, but the flesh was gone, and the sight was eerie and unsettling. Raven lowered the limo window and stared in shock at this completely transformed environment. Seemingly overnight, Las Vegas had become a neon nightmare for real. Sin City was a ghost town.

* * *

In a dimly lit conference room, Xandra sat at the head of a long table, examining various documents. There was soft knock at the door, and Xandra smiled.

"Come in," she said.

Raven entered, dressed in black leather.

Xandra stood and rushed over to her, and the two women warmly embraced.

"You look so good, baby," Xandra said as she took Raven by the hand. "I've missed you so much."

"It's good to see you, too," Raven answered. She still looked weary.

Xandra returned to her seat at the head of the table, and Raven sat to her right.

"You're looking tired, girlfriend," Xandra said as she eyed Raven closely. "Let me get some food in here. What do you want?"

"I'm okay ... maybe later."

"I appreciate your coming in so soon after just getting back. But there's something going down and I need my best girl, right now."

Raven smiled. "I'm all right. Really."

Xandra pressed a button on a remote laying on the table and dimmed the lights completely. Another button activated an immense flat-screen television mounted to the wall at the far end of the room. Images of Las Vegas filled the screen, images of abandoned construction projects, foreclosed homes, bankrupt businesses, laid-off workers, and people living on the street.

"A lot has changed since you've been away," Xandra said. "I've never seen anything like it."

"I got a taste of it coming in. I always knew it would happen, but I never thought I'd see it in my lifetime." Raven's eyes were riveted to the screen.

"Lately, the most popular game in Vegas has been dominoes. The collapse of the housing market was the first domino. Then the construction industry went belly up. Now even the casinos are facing bankruptcy, and I'm talking major casinos, too. Businesses are dropping like flies. Unemployment numbers are through the roof. It's unbelievable."

"Babylon has fallen."

"It sure looks that way. You can imagine the damage control going down. The political machine, gaming, and big business interests, they're all working overtime to paint a less bleak picture. Naturally, the media co-signs all their bullshit. But the truth is right there. It's as obvious as a bad toupee. You're looking at it." Xandra sighed. "If Babylon hasn't fallen, at the very least it's a broke hooker on life support."

"I'll send flowers," said Raven.

Xandra rolled her eyes as she fought a smile.

"Las Vegas was just a mirage anyway, right from the jump," Raven said as she watched the images on the screen. "There's no way it could ever last. It's a wonder it lasted as long as it did, the whole illusion of an emerald city at the end of the rainbow. Maybe what's happenijng now is what Zappa used to talk about. He said if the illusion ever got too expensive to maintain, they'd just dismantle the theater altogether."

"One thing is for sure. The current economic conditions have enabled a few enterprising entrepreneurs to slip in and prosper from the crisis."

"No doubt," Raven said cynically. "Let me guess, international *bad boys*?"

"You got it."

There was a knock at the door.

"Ah, just in time," Xandra said with a smile. "That's probably Kim Desmond from the London office. Come in!"

The conference room door opened and a figure could be seen in silhouette. With the name Kim Desmond, Raven was obviously expecting a female. She was mistaken. As Kim entered and closed the door behind him, Xandra brought up the lights a bit. Like Raven, Kim was dressed in black leather, but his fashion style was out of another era altogether. His formfittng tunic, belt, and boots, combined with his rippling muscularity, made him look like warrior from ancient times. His dark skin and sculpted features reinforced his rugged, old-world masculinity. Kim's eyes were his most compelling feature. They were green with unusually long eyelashes. As he approached the conference table, Raven pretended not to be fascinated and looked at him blankly. Kim was fascinated with Raven and made no attempt to pretend otherwise.

Xandra stood and extended her hand. "Welcome to Las Vegas," she said cordially.

"Thank you," Kim said as he took her hand.

"And this is Raven," Xandra said, watching Kim closely.

Kim extended his long, muscular arm across the table and looked down into Raven's eyes. "It's an honor," he said.

Raven remained seated but shook Kim's hand with a grip much firmer than his own. Xandra sat down and Kim took the seat on her left side.

"Kim is here to brief us about a few of our new neighbors."

Kim rested his thick forearms on the table. "The economic meltdown of Las Vegas is a dream come true for the international criminal elite. Over the last few months, they've been moving in like well-dresed vultures, buying casinos, hotels, strip clubs, and other properties at bargain prices. For them, it's the opportunity of a lifetime."

"They're going to revive this broke hooker and put her ass back to work," Raven said sarcastically.

"That's certainly part of it," Kim continued. "It's important to remember, Las Vegas has long been a source of fascination for many of these people. It's their favorite American city."

"No doubt," said Raven. "Vegas was created by people with mentalities just like theirs."

Kim smiled. "You're absolutely right. They feel a strong connection and kinship to the city. And for what it's worth, most of these people genuinely love Las Vegas. Bugsy Siegel is like a Christ figure to them. These international players believe that what's happening in Vegas right now is nothing more than a reflection of what's happening in America as a whole—unchecked greed, gross mismanagement, and sheer incompetence. They're convinced they can do a better job than Americans."

"They might be right," deadpanned Raven. "They couldn't do much worse."

Kim laughed. "They see Vegas as a great idea that got derailed by self-serving politicians and the new corporate casino owners who took over from the Mob. They believe Vegas was a better town when the Mob ran it, so they intend to come in and run it the same way."

"Back to basics," said Xandra.

"Back to basics," agreed Kim. "Rejuvenating Vegas is only part of the agenda. It's my belief that Las Vegas is set to become the American headquarters for transnational organized crime."

"Makes sense," said Xandra.

"Over the past few months, the more obvious players have been surveying the situation and determining their strategies. There's the Russian, Balkan, Israeli, and South American mob elements. There's also the yakuza and some of the triad factions as well. But there are some newer, less familiar faces on the scene, too. Like the Kaviani family."

"Minus one," said Raven.

"Minus one," repeated Kim. "But that still leaves two, Gaspar, and his sister, Sholeh. And they're far more dangerous than Dmitri, particularly Sholeh, who is considered to be the driving force of the operation and the head of the family. The Kavianis are one of the most notorious crime families on the planet. Well-known and well-feared. In addition to being one of the world's richest families, they're also one of the oldest, supposedly descended from ancient royalty. They maintain bases of operation all over the world, but since the death of their brother, they've remained in Las Vegas."

"We're aware of them," said Xandra.

"There's another family on the scene as well, though we're less sure of their motivations. They're the Zavada brothers, Marek and Gregor. They're from the Czech Republic. They're like the Kavianis, genuine bluebloods, descended from a very old and wealthy family. Their new presence in Las Vegas probably stems from an unusual hobby they're known to have. They enjoy rebuilding and rejuvenating hopelessly distressed neighborhoods and communities from behind the scenes. For example, though it was never reported, the Zavada brothers were heavily involved in the rebuilding of various New Orleans neighborhoods following Hurricane Katrina."

"Are they known to be involved in any criminal activities?" asked Xandra.

"We can only speculate."

"It's difficult to imagine anyone coming to Vegas to do nice things ... without some ulterior motive," Xandra said skeptically. "Sin City doesn't attract philanthropists."

Kim nodded in agreement. "Evil often hides behind good deeds. I suggest we watch the Zavada brothers very closely."

"I agree," said Xandra.

"And, finally, there's the Janus Cartel. It's a relatively new organization, but in a few years, it's grown to challenge some of the more established crime groups. The cartel is led by a man named Simon Janus. He's a criminal mastermind with the intellect of a genius and the vision of a philosopher. He was like a corporate headhunter, stealing the best and brightest from various other criminal organizations from around the world. Then he formed the cartel, which he created to be a kind of super syndicate. With Janus at the helm, the cartel has quickly become a dominant force in all aspects of international crime—arms dealing, drug running, and so forth. Along with his criminal inclinations, Simon Janus is also rumored to be a practicing black magician. I'd describe him as a combination of Bugsy Siegel, Aleister Crowley ... and Steve Jobs."

"Simon Janus and the cartel have just done some very serious shopping, isn't that correct?" asked Xandra.

"That's correct. As you well know, the recent economic meltdown caused several major projects on the Strip to be halted indefinitely. The Crystal Oasis was the largest and most amibitious of these projects. It ran into trouble when some of its Arab investors had a change of heart and pulled out of the deal. The project was even facing possible bankruptcy until the Janus Cartel stepped in and bought it outright. Construction was recently completed, and the project was renamed Sanctum Tartarus. When the cartel took over the project, they poured mega millions into additional construction, primarily underground construction. The cartel clearly has big plans for the revived project, with most of those plans taking shape underground and out of view. It's my belief that Santum Tartarus is meant to be far more than just a hotel and casino. And knowing the Janus Cartel, I can only expect the worst."

"In a few days, Sanctum Tartarus will officially open," said Xandra turning to Raven. "As you can imagine, it's going to be a major event. Completion of this project is about the only good thing that's happened to this city in a long, long time. There's going to be a massive celebration with media, celebrities, and elite guests from all over the world. The distraction of the opening festivities will be a perfect cover for a prevention specialist to slip in and find out what's *really* going on in there."

Raven nodded with complete understanding and confidence.

Xandra had another point to make. "Raven?"

"Yes?"

"The job at hand is reconnaissance, not violence."

"No one dies who's not supposed to." Raven smiled *diabolically*.

Xandra rolled her eyes. When Kim saw Raven's wicked smile, a strange jolt of electricity surged through his body. There was a knock at the door.

"Come in," said Xandra.

A young woman opened the door slightly and peered inside. "I'm sorry to bother you, Xandra. Could I please have a word with you?"

"Yes, of course," said Xandra as she stood. "You two excuse me."

Xandra hurried off and Kim could barely believe his good fortune. When the door closed behind Xandra, he wasted no time getting next to Raven.

"When I said it was an honor to meet you, I wasn't kidding," Kim said sincerely. "I know who you are ... and what you are."

"I believe you," Raven answered flatly as she allowed herself to look directly into his eyes. "So you're from the London office. Funny, I don't hear any accent."

Kim smiled. "I'm not a Brit. I was born on the island of Oahu."

Raven looked away. "You're a long way from paradise." She abruptly stood and prepared to leave. Kim stood as well, hoping he didn't look as anxious as he felt inside.

"Can I walk you out?" he asked.

"That's unnecessary."

Kim offered Raven his hand and when she took it, he held onto her. "I don't know if I'll ever see you again," he said. "But I want to."

"It was nice to meet you, too, Kim. You're very sweet." Her tone was cordial but aloof. She was well aware of her effect on Kim and saw no need to encourage him. Still, Raven allowed herself one last look at him. She had never seen a modern man dress so fearlessly. Kim obviously understood the true meaning of fashion, and Raven respected that.

Kim reluctantly released Raven's hand, and his eyes followed her as she walked to the door.

"Good luck," he said.

"Thanks, I'll be all right," she said as she walked out.

Kim sat back down in his chair and sighed. "I wish I could say the same thing," he said to himself.

15

The Zavada Brothers

A stolen car raced rocket style along a deserted stretch of Vegas freeway. Inside, four men passed around liquor and drugs they did not need. Their eclectic fashion style accurately mirrored their mentality. They embraced all styles with open arms and open legs. Cowboy, buccaneer, storm trooper, rock star, and even beauty queen Careful attention was paid to the accessories and they had lovingly adorned themselves with all manner of baubles, bangles, and beads. They wore women's wigs and makeup that was garish and cartoonish. They looked like hags, but calling them fags would have been a mistake—a *fatal* mistake. They were plenty gay, all right, but no one was ever going to bash or belittle them in any way and live. Because these four unusual men were homosexual homicidal maniacs and they were looking for trouble. They'd come to Vegas specifically to find some, or *make* some. Fleece was both leader and driver and he sat up front alone. The front seat was his throne. He wore a tiara and smoked a fat blunt from a long, gold cigarette holder. In the back seat were his boys, Pete, Link, and Julie. Collectively, they were the Fudge Pack.

Far across town, trouble awaited. About a dozen motorcycles were lined up in front of an establishment affectionately known as the Toe Tag Lounge. The bikes belonged to members of the Cannibal Club, a particularly fearsome motorcycle gang that made the Hell's Angels look like the Muppets. The Toe Tag functioned as their hangout and headquarters. Inside the lounge was a colorful assortment of psychopaths, sociopaths, lunatics, and other miscreants every bit as dangerous as the Fudge Pack. Some mingled at a bar, some played pool and pinball, and others sat at tables playing cards. Everyone was under the influence of *something*. A jukebox in the corner blasted classic rock. When the Fudge Pack boldly swaggered in, it was as if four Martians had just landed. All talking, drinking, and game playing immediately ceased and the Cannibals were collectively frozen in shock.

The typical response to the average stranger entering the Toe Tag would have been an automatic ass kicking. It should have been a fate worse than death for any stranger with a gender presentation as blatantly ambiguous as that of the Fudge Pack. But the Pack's bold entrance and bizarre presence were so utterly preposterous that they completely boggled the minds of the Cannibals and offered genuine entertainment value—like a carnival freakshow. So the bikers stared rather than stomped. But they weren't exactly rolling out the red carpet, either. Laughter mixed with taunts.

"Look! It's the New York Dolls ... in black face."

"Pride Fest was last week, ladies!"

"The bath house is down the street. There's plenty of soap for you to drop."

The Pack was unfazed by the unbridled animosity. The situation was entertaining for them as well. They immediately realized that they had finally found the very thing they were looking for. Pete took control of an unattended pinball machine. Link scrutinized the jukebox for song possibilities. Julie approached the pool table where two Cannibals stood glaring at him. Fleece went to the bar, where he calmly and purposefully positioned himself between two particularly mean-looking dudes. The bartender eyed Fleece up and down and made no effort to hide his contempt.

"We're fresh out of banana daiquiris," the bartender said with a smirk and every patron within earshot roared with laughter.

"No banana daiquiris?" said Fleece in mock disbelief. "What kind of *twink* bar is this, anyway?" The laughter abruptly died and for a few tension-filled moments, everyone maintained their cool. "Well, if you serve beer in this establishment," Fleece continued, "I'll have a Corona— with a lime ... and a smile, if you think you can manage one."

After a moment of hesitation, the bartender finally served Fleece. He even smiled, though it was more a baring of fangs than a genuine smile. "Here you go, honey," he said.

Fleece smiled and placed some money on the bar. "You're a very attractive man, but you need to work on that attitude of yours. After all, you're in the customer service business. So do your job ... and act your *wage*."

Across the room, Julie remained the focus of evil eyes at the pool table as the two burly bikers stared him down. Julie stared right back, unconcerned.

"I feel like a game. Either one of you chumps man enough to take me on?" Julie asked arrogantly.

The bikers were holding cue sticks and they looked as if they wanted to beat Julie with them. Julie placed a twenty-dollar bill on the edge of the pool table.

"Mind if I borrow this?" Julie said as he snatched the cue stick from the hands of one of the bikers. The man was ready to strike, but his associate calmed him.

Julie racked up the billiard balls and sank two difficult shots back to back. He was skilled but cocky. "What's your name?" he asked his beefy opponent after effortlessly sinking a third ball. "I like to know the name of the ass I'm kicking."

The biker took a deep breath before answering. "Larry," he said between clenched teeth.

"Nice to meet you, Larry. Who's your friend here? Moe?" Julie giggled. "Where's Curly?" Julie continued his mocking with the manic sound effects associated with The Three Stooges.

Julie finally missed a shot and Larry took over the table, angrily shoving Julie aside in the process. Larry proved to be a highly skilled opponent as well. He completely dominated the rest of the game and went on to win easily. Finally, he snatched the money off the table and slipped it into his pocket.

"Did you want to lose another game before you get back to the Turkish prison?" Larry said.

Julie smiled innocently. "Great game, baby," he said sweetly. "I want to give you something."

Julie leaped onto Larry, trapping him in a viselike grip using both arms and legs. To the astonishment of everyone, he gave Larry a deep French kiss, tonguing him passionately. It was an unbelievable sight, and there was a collective gasp heard throughout the bar. Larry went berserk and frantically struggled to pry Julie off him, lips and all. It wasn't easy, and Julie held on as if for dear life.

Finally, Larry managed to jerk his head away, and their mouths separated with an audible slurp. Larry threw Julie to the floor while spitting and wiping away any moist remnants of the kiss. Julie leaped back to his feet and landed a spinning kick to Larry's face, knocking him to his knees.

"You call that a kiss?" screamed Julie. "You kiss like a girl."

Julie grabbed a chair, clubbed Larry into unconsciousness, then flung the chair far across the room and into a mirror on the wall, shattering it to pieces.

"I'm not leaving till I get a proper kiss!" Julie insisted. "Come on, somebody!"

The Cannibals all stood simultaneously and there was murder in their eyes. One of them went to the entrance door and bolted it. Pete and Link immediately ran over to join Julie.

"If he's getting a kiss, I want one, too!" shouted Pete.

"Me, too!" echoed Link.

Several Cannibals rushed the three men and the entire lounge soon realized they were no ordinary freaks. The men defended themselves against multiple attackers with ease and skill. Cannibals were punched, kicked, thrown into walls, slammed to the floor, and clubbed with chairs. The freaks easily dispatched the first wave of aggressors and seemed positively rejuvenated by the experience. The next wave of attackers came with brass knuckles, knives, and baseball bats. Pete and Link armed themselves with cue sticks and joyously beat down several men. Julie leaped onto the pool table, grabbed several billiard balls, and fired them into the foreheads of Cannibals with major league accuracy, dropping men to the ground in rapid succession. Giggling as they dished out punishment, the freaks acted as if they were at a party. Violence was just another drug to them, and they were feeling plenty high, too. The Cannibals were astounded by their fighting prowess.

Fleece stood at the bar alone and watched the proceedings with a proud smile. Finally, he pulled a handgun from his pink purse and fired a shot into the ceiling. Everyone in the room froze.

"Okay, everybody, that's enough," he said with mock seriousness. "Recess is over, and church is now in session. But before we begin, we need to take up the collection. I realize we're in the midst of a deep recession, but, please … do the best you can. Dig deep."

The surly bartender remained behind the bar out of view. Suddenly, he snatched a shotgun hidden beneath the bar, but Fleece quickly turned around and fired two shots into his head. As the bartender toppled backwards, the shotgun flew out of his hands and into the air, spinning. Fleece snatched it and tossed it across the room to Julie. Pete and Link now revealed handguns of their own.

"Up against the wall, girlfriends," Fleece said with a smile. "And, please, don't make me ask again."

The beaten Cannibals reluctantly limped over to a wall and lined up facing it.

"Spread out!" Julie screamed. "Crucifixion style!"

The Cannibals complied, and their faces reflected both their anger and their growing dread. As their victims stood helplessly facing the wall, Pete and Link moved from man to man, removing their wallets and emptying them of cash.

Fleece joined his comrades who stood with guns aimed at the Cannibals. "Thank you very much for an entertaining evening. We've had a wonderful time, and I mean that sincerely. And now, in the words of Mr. Alphonse Capone, Happy Valentine's Day!"

The Fudge Pack opened fire on the Cannibals. The roar of the gunfire echoed throughout the room as blasted bodies were hurled in every direction. The floor was strewn with the bloody dead and near-dead. Fleece went behind the bar and kicked open the cash register. He stuffed the money into his purse and joined his associates. As they walked out of the lounge, Fleece noticed the long line of bikes parked in front and kicked the first one in line, causing the rest of the bikes to fall like dominoes. The Fudge Pack climbed back into their car and sped off into the night. The night was young, and they were still looking for trouble.

* * *

A city bus cruised the northern end of the Strip heading toward Fremont Street. On this night, the bus was particularly crowded. Bums, junkies, cheap hookers, intoxicated tourists, and other human refuse filled every seat and jammed the aisle. Every eye was glued to the two unusual passengers seated in the back, Marek and Gregor Zavada. Even in a rolling freakshow like the bus, the Zavada brothers stood out like extraterrestrials. Both brothers were extraordinarily handsome, with the finely chiseled features of Greek statues. Each of them had long hair that hung past their shoulders; Marek was brunet and Gregor was blond. The Zavadas appeared to be outrageously wealthy. They were dressed in luxurious ankle length coats made of ornate brocade that looked like something fit for the royalty of yesteryear. On each finger they wore large, glittering rings of silver and gold. But the most striking thing about them was the radiant aura that surrounded them. The Zavada brothers *sparkled*, making them extremely out of place in this halfway house on wheels. Happily oblivious to the stares of their fellow passengers, the Zavadas peered out the window, gleefully pointing at Vegas landmarks with childlike enthusiasm. Gregor took pictures with a small camera.

The bus finally came to a stop on Fremont Street and the brothers stepped out along with the rest of the rabble. Standing on the corner of Las Vegas Boulevard and Fremont Street, Marek and Gregor were transfixed by the colorful sights and sounds that surrounded them. The Zavada brothers were wide-eyed in Babylon.

"I think I like Fremont Street best of all," said Gregor as he took more pictues.

I agree," said Marek. "It's the real Las Vegas."

"Shall we?" Gregor said motioning in the direction of the famous neon Glitter Gulch. "I want to see this Fremont Street Experience that I've heard so much about."

Marek glanced in the opposite direction. There was far less neon but far more potential for drama. "Let's walk down this way first then venture back. I'm a little curious."

Very well."

The Zavadas continued strolling deeper into the less than inviting area of Fremont Street. Soon, the glow of Glitter Gulch was far behind them and they were surrounded by urban blight. Still, they remained cheerfully fascinated by everything around them and Gregor continued taking pictures. Two ornately dressed Causasians strolling the ghetto in the middle of the night made for a highly unusual sight. Passing pedestrians and drivers stared in bewilderment.

"This part of Fremont Street needs a bit of work, I think," said Marek.

"I agree. Should we buy it?" asked Gregor.

"We'll give it some thought," answered Marek.

The Zavadas paused in front of a pawn shop and were gazing at the treasures in the window when the sound of music caught their ears. They turned to find a well dressed older black man blowing a trumpet. He sat on the hood of a limousine that had seen better days. His name was Ignatius Valentine. With eyes closed, he was oblivious to the world around him and totally absorbed in the music he was creating. The Zavadas approached him. Gregor was particularly impressed with the music. When Ignatius finished the song, the Zavadas clapped enthusiastically. Ignatius was startled but humbled by the appreciation. He eyed the Zavadas curiously from head to toe and surmised that they were from *way* out of town.

"That was wonderful!" exclaimed Gregor.

"Thank you, very much," Ignatius said as he scrutinized the brothers.

I know that song," continued Gregor. "That's 'Round Midnight' by Thelonious Monk."

"That's right. Are you a jazz fan?"

"I like all music. Allow me to introduce ourselves. We are the Zavada brothers. I am Gregor, and this is my brother, Marek."

"Nice to meet you. I'm Ignatius."

The three men exchanged warm handshakes.

Ignatius continued staring at the Zavadas with mounting curiosity. "You know, it's none of my business, but I'm a little surprised to see two such ... affluent gentlemen out and about on foot this time of night."

"We're fresh off the bus," said Gregor with a smile.

"Yeah, I can see that," said Ignatius. "You actually took the bus down to Fremont Street?"

"We love riding the bus," said Marek. "It's the best way to really see a city."

"Well, I don't mean to be nosy or anything," Ignatius continued, "but you two might want to start heading back toward the Strip."

Marek looked at his watch. "It's still a bit early, isn't it?"

"Yeah, well … this part of town is a little less than hospitable 'round midnight." Ignatius said with a chuckle. "You know, I'd be happy to give you a ride to wherever you're going. It's no problem, either. I just so happen to own one of the better limousine services in Las Vegas. And as luck would have it, I'm free and completely at your service."

"That's very kind," said Gegor. "But we're not really going anywhere. We're just out for a stroll. You meet a lot of very interesting people at night."

"I know, and around here, that's the problem."

"Perhaps some other time," said Marek. "Do you have a card?"

"As a matter of fact, I do." Ignatius took a card from his jacket and handed it to Marek.

Marek read the card. "Wack City Limousine Service?"

"What is this Wack City?" asked Gregor curiously.

"Well, it's a nickname for Vegas," said Ignatius. "Vegas is kind of crazy –kind of *wack*. But it's a very dangerous place, too. A lot of people have gotten whacked here over the years—and continue to be, that's for sure."

"Wack City," Gregor said with a smile. "I like that."

"Are you sure I can't convince you to leave the driving to me?"

"It's such a pleasant night for a stroll," said Gregor. "But we will, as you say, take the raincheck!"

Marek could tell that Ignatius was genuinely concerned for their safety and he was touched. "Don't worry, my friend. We'll be just fine, I promise."

The three men shook hands once again, said their goodbyes, and the Zavadas continued on their way. As they walked deeper into the ghetto, the lowlife element they encountered increased dramatically in numbers, but the Zavadas remained unconcerned.

Gregor spotted a grocery store. "This place looks interesting. Let's go in and have a look."

The Zavadas entered the store and found the turbaned owner standing behind the counter. He was shocked by the presence of two such well dressed and obviously wealthy patrons.

"Greetings!" the grocer said excitedly. "Welcome to my store!"

The store was a dump, but the Zavadas were genuinely respectful, acting as though they had entered a high-end establishment. They scanned the store with their typical wide-eyed fascination. "It's a pleasure," said Gregor cheerfully. "May we look around?"

"Please do," said the grocer, barely able to contain his glee.

Gregor selected a battered shopping cart that was missing a wheel, and the brothers casually strolled down an aisle, heading to the rear of the store.

"If you need any help, you just call me," said the grocer, his eyes glued to the Zavadas. Their beauty, regal bearing, and charm were hypnotic. They glowed with a radiance that illuminated the sad little grocery store. The grocer was a wise man. He understood that whoever and whatever they were, the Zavada brothers were clearly *special* beings.

The Fudge Pack suddenly entered the store, and it was obvious that there was nothing special about them, at least not in a good way. They were still looking for trouble, only now they were considerably more wired. The grocer instantly sensed danger and watched them fearfully as they approached the counter.

"Good evening," said Fleece with a smile. "Could you please tell us where you keep the banana daiquiri mix?"

"I'm sorry, sir, but I don't carry banana daiquiri mix," said the grocer nervously.

"That's a shame." Fleece pulled out his gun and aimed it at the grocer. "Then give me all the money instead." Fleece snatched the turban off the grocer's head and spread it over the counter. "You can put it in there."

The terrified grocer opened the cash register and emptied the meager contents. As Fleece focused on the grocer, the other freaks scanned the grocery.

"I'm a little hungry," said Julie.

"Me, too," said Pete, "I just don't know what I'm hungry for."

Pete noticed the Zavadas at the rear of the store and he motioned for the others to look as well. The Zavadas were so absorbed in their shopping that they didn't notice the dangerous patrons. The brothers returned to the front of the store, speaking excitedly in Czech and focused on the treasures stacked in their cart. The Fudge Pack eyed them up and down like ravenous wolves and their sexual intent was glaringly obvious. The Zavadas reached the counter and only then realized that there was a robbery in progress. They were blissfully unafraid.

"*Now* I know what I want," said Pete licking his lips in anticipation. I want a sandwich."

"A sandwich is a sandwich but a *manwich* is a meal," said Julie giggling.

"Can we keep them?" asked Link pleadingly, directing the question to Fleece who, too, was now lustfully mesmerized. "I promise to take care of them. I'll feed them and give them water and—"

"Relax! We're *all* going to take care of them," said Fleece with a horny smile. He turned the gun on the Zavadas. "Shopping is over, scrumptiousness, we're going for a ride."

"No, thank you," said Gregor cheerfully. "We much prefer the bus."

Fleece became annoyed. "You know, I've never busted a cap or a nut on Eurotrash before, but there's a first time for everything."

Marek kicked the pistol from Fleece's hand sending it spinning into the air. Gregor caught the weapon, dislodged the clip, and calmly placed both items on the counter.

"Eurotrash?" repeated Marek softly but with obvious anger. "A most unfortunate choice of word, my friend. Most unfortunate."

Gregor was angry as well. He removed his coat and handed it to Marek who placed it on the counter. Gregor unbuttoned the formfitting silk shirt that clung to his sculpted physique. He pushed the shopping cart off to the side. There was an open space in front of the counter, enough space for fighting, and he calmly walked to the center of it.

"You've come here looking for trouble," Gregor said. "Well, you have found what you seek. Zavada *means* trouble."

Pete rushed at Gregor and slammed into him full force, but it was like running into a tree, and the impact left Pete momentarily dazed. Gregor was completely unfazed by the attack. He grabbed Pete's arm and snapped it like a twig. As Pete howled in agony, Gregor snatched him by the throat and effortlessly hurled him up into the air, sending his head bursting through the ceiling. With his head firmly lodged in the shattered wood, Pete dangled while kicking wildly.

Marek removed his own coat and placed it on the counter. Like his brother, he, too, was powerfully built.

"May I?" Marek asked Gregor as he moved to the center of the store.

"Of course," answered Gregor, stepping aside.

Dumbfounded, the other freaks stared up at the ceiling as Pete helplessly hung there. Then Link charged at Marek and launched a well-executed kick at his head. Marek dodged the kick, grabbed hold of the leg, and twisted it so that Link's calf and foot were at right angles to his thigh. Marek collared the screaming Link, lifted him overhead, and forcefully slammed him *through* the hardwood floor. Link plummeted down into the cellar of the grocery as Julie and Fleece watched in amazement. Before either of them could react, the Zavadas took the offensive. Gregor grabbed Julie by the hair and hurled him like a rag doll across the store. Julie slammed into a glass-fronted refrigerator filled with liquor, shattering it completely. Marek kicked Fleece in the chest, and the force sent him flying and crashing through the front window of the store. He landed in a heap on the concrete outside, startling several people who stood nearby.

A small crowd gathered, watching as Marek grabbed Fleece by the ankle and dragged him back into the store. Gregor now had Julie by the ankle as well, and the Zavadas dragged both freaks over to the hole in the floor. They tossed the freaks in like trash. Suddenly, Pete became dislodged from the ceiling and fell at their feet, and the brothers kicked him into the hole along with the others. The Zavadas peered down into the hole at the Fudge Pack below, piled on top of one another.

"We are *not* Eurotrash," the Zavadas said in unison.

The Zavada brothers walked to the counter where the grocer sadly stood, looking at his demolished store. The brothers assisted one another back into their coats. Gregor reached into an inside pocket and removed a massive wad of cash. He peeled off a couple of bills, which he kept, but handed the rest of the money to the grocer, who immediately brightened at the sight.

"Please, forgive our mess," said Gregor. "By the way, you have a very nice store. It was a pleasure to shop here. We'll be back when we're not so rushed."

The speechless grocer watched as the Zavadas left the store and made their way past the curious crowd that continued to form outside. Approaching sirens could be heard in the near distance and the brothers appeared concerned. Then they noticed a welcome sight. Parked in front of the store with the motor idling sat the Wack City Limousine.

Sitting behind the wheel, Ignatius beckoned the brothers with a smile. The Zavadas hurried over to the limo, climbed inside, and Ignatius sped off into the night.

"It's good to see you, my friend," said Gregor, beaming.

"Yes, indeed," agreed Marek. "Your timing is perfect."

"Naturally, I'm a jazz musician," said Ignatius proudly. "I followed you two just to make sure you didn't get into trouble." He laughed. "But from what I could see, you two *are* trouble."

"That was quite thoughtful of you" said Marek.

"Where can I take you gentlemen? I know you prefer the bus but ... "

"Oh, no, this is perfect" said Gregor. "Much better."

"Let's just cruise for a while. I can give you the night-time tour of the city. I'm a great tour guide. I know everything about Las Vegas."

"That's an excellent idea," said Marek. The Zavadas settled back in their seat as Ignatius steered the limo toward a different part of the city.

"We've read and heard a great many things about Las Vegas," said Gregor. "It would be a pleasure to hear what you have to say, Ignatius."

"Well, you've arrived at an unusual time, that's for sure."

"And why is that?" asked Gregor.

"Because Las Vegas is dead," answered Ignatius.

"Dead? Do you really believe so?" asked Marek.

"Absolutely. They just haven't told the general public and won't for a long time—if they ever tell them at all. This bitch is dead. And you know what killed her? She

 RAVENDIABLO

killed herself. The bitch killed herself with greed. Greed and stupidity. All she ever cared about was shaking that money tree. She was greedy enough and stupid enough to think it would last forever." Ignatius laughed cynically. "Vegas has always been a mirage in the desert. But somewhere along the way, the city itself started to believe the mirage. Believing your own bullshit is always a bad idea."

"Perhaps it was a house of cards right from the beginning," said Gregor.

"A city built on games of chance, vice, and dreams," continued Ignatius. "Not exactly the most solid of foundations, that's for sure. It's a wonder it lasted as long as it did."

"So, what happens now?" asked Marek.

"What happens now? Well, Las Vegas becomes even more famous. Because you have to die to become immortal. Now that Vegas is dead, the city will really become mythic. People will always come to Las Vegas. The very name is magic."

"We certainly came," said Gregor.

"So, where exactly are you two from, anyway?" asked Ignatius. "I'm usually pretty good with accents but I can't quite place yours."

"We are Czech," answered Marek proudly. "We come from the city of Jihlava, a very old and beautiful city. You must see it sometime."

"I'd love to. I spent a lot of time in Europe many years ago, touring with jazz bands. I've lived in France, Germany, and Holland. I love Europe. Europeans always gave me the one thing I usually never got at home."

"And what's that?" asked Gregor.

"Respect. I've been all over the world, but the only place I ever felt like an alien was home." Ignatius laughed.

"It's not easy being an alien," said Gregor.

"So what exactly brought you to Vegas?" asked Ignatius. "My guess is that you could live anywhere in the world you wanted. Why Vegas?"

"We've heard that Las Vegas is the city of second chances. Is this true?" asked Gregor inquistively.

Ignatius thought for a moment. "I suppose it could be. It certainly has been for many people. Looking to start over again?"

Gregor and Marek looked at one another, momentarily unsure of how to answer.

"We came here primarily for our younger brother," said Marek. "We thought that perhaps he might gain some deeper insights into himself and his life by being here."

"Yes," agreed Gregor. "Las Vegas is a highly energized city. It's our hope that the Vegas energy might stimulate his brain."

Ignatius roared with laughter. "Stimulate his *brain*? Vegas stimulates a lot of places, but I don't think the brain is one of them. They don't call it Sin City for nothing."

"Yes, that's no doubt true," said Marek. "But Las Vegas was built in the desert and the desert is holy ground."

Ignatius considered Marek's words carefully, and the more he contemplated them, the more sense they made. "You know, you're right. I never really thought about it before, but you're absolutely right. Ancient cultures all over the world thought of the desert as holy ground. Prophets used to go to the desert for revelations. Most religions were born out of the desert."

"That's quite right," said Gregor. "Las Vegas is a city of sin built on holy ground. As a result, there are two powerful, polar opposite energies converging on one single spot. That's why the city is so highly charged. It's quite remarkable, actually. There's no other city like it in the whole world. That's what makes Las Vegas so ... *magical*."

"And thus capable of causing great transformations," said Marek.

Ignatius glanced in the rearview mirror at the Zavadas and stared at them closely. They were stunningly beautiful with the demeanor of genuine royalty, yet they were completely devoid of ego and arrogance. Instead, they reflected a sweetness that was almost childlike in its sincerity. They possessed amazing superhuman strength. And they also possessed profound spiritual wisdom and understanding. Ignatius remembered Gregor's comment, "It's not easy being an alien." Watching the mysterious Zavada brothers *sparkle* in the back of the limo, that comment now seemed eerily apropos. Ignatius seriously considered the distinct possibility that he was in the presence of *angelic* beings.

"Tell me about your brother," asked Ignatius, genuinely curious.

"His name is Alexander," said Marek, "but we call him Sasha."

"Is he excited about moving to Vegas?" Ignatius wondered.

"Very much so," answered Gregor. "Las Vegas is Sasha's favorite American city."

"Does he like riding the bus and strolling in the ghetto 'round midnight, too?"

"Sasha lives a somewhat cloistered existence," answered Marek.

Gregor and Marek looked at one another, momentarily unsure of how to answer.

"Sasha's physical appearance is somewhat ... unusual," answered Gregor. "So he keeps to himself. It's not an easy life, but it's the only life he has. And he's learned to accept it."

Ignatius glanced into the rearview mirror and he saw sadness reflected on the faces of the Zavada brothers. Their ever-present smiles were now gone, and they stared out the window, absorbed in thought. It was clear that they loved their brother very much and shared his loneliness. The Zavadas were obviously a very close and loving family. The limousine cruised in silence for many blocks until Ignatius made a revelation of his own.

"My baby brother Felix has cerebral palsy," he said. "I'd very much like to meet your brother. Right now, if it's okay. I've got nowhere to go."

Gregor and Marek looked at one another excitedly. They liked Ignatius very much and enjoyed being in his company. Ignatius was unique, especially for Las Vegas. He was intelligent, articulate, considerate, and wise. Unlike most of the people they had encountered since moving to Las Vegas, Ignatius was a truly good man and worthy of great respect. The Zavadas felt that their chance encounter with Ignatius had resulted in a jackpot win for them. Meeting him only reinforced their firm belief that the destiny of the Zavada family lay in Las Vegas. They were convinced that Ignatius was what they would need most in Sin City—a guiding angel. They were more in awe of Ignatius than he was of them.

The Zavadas lived in The Lemurian, a luxurious high-rise condo and one of the more ambitious projects built during the great overbuilding boom. It was originally conceived to be a residence for the ultrarich international players who spent so much time and money in Sin City. But after the crash, The Lemurian was just another domino and it fell like so many others. The new Vegas landscape was littered with them. They were big dreams that had died hard and stood empty, more haunted houses in the new Sin City ghost town. The Zavadas had bought it and turned it into their American headquarters. They and a small staff occupied the upper floors.

Marek, Gregor, and Ignatius stepped out of the penthouse elevator and walked down a long hallway to Sasha's suite. The air was thick with the scent of exotic incense. The carpeting was black, and the walls were covered with black velvet. The hallway was lined on either side with massive doors to other suites. But the door at the very end of the hall stood tallest of all. It was ten feet high and made of intricately carved oak. Marek tapped on the door. After a few moments, the door was opened by a beautiful woman who stepped back and allowed them entrance. They entered an immense room filled with more beautiful women. There were as many as thirty women, some dressed casually in jeans and T-shirts, others dressed in comfortable sleepwear. Many of them sat on huge pillows watching a large flat-screen television. Others relaxed on the massive couches and chairs that were scattered throughout the room; reading, listening to personal stereos, playing portable video games, or talking with each other. There were a wide variety of shapes, sizes, and ethnicities, but they all had one thing in common. Aside from being stunning, the women all possessed a very dark and eerie sensuality. They were breathtakingly beautiful, but somewhat unsettling as well. Clearly, these were the consorts of an unusual individual with unusual tastes. Ignatius smiled. This was Sasha's personal harem.

The reaction of the brothers to the presence of the women was revealing. Gregor appeared to be slightly amused, but Marek seemed ashamed. Ignatius quickly and correctly surmised that Marek was the more serious and conservative of the two. Ignatius followed the brothers down a hallway to another huge door.

Pausing at the door, Marek turned to face Ignatius and looked deep into his eyes. "We are a very close family. We choose to share our private world with only a select and trusted few. And once we do, then they become a part of the family." Marek knocked on the door.

"Come in," said Sasha. His voice was sweet and inviting.

Marek opened the door and the Zavada brothers led Ignatius into Sasha's private quarters. It was a pleasure pit, a combination opium den and orgy chamber, with enormous pillows and cushions scattered about. The lighting was low. Exotic music played in the background. Sasha sat in the middle of the room, and Ignatius saw him immediately. The Zavada brothers had described Sasha's appearance as being unusual, but that description could never have prepared Ignatius for what he saw. Sasha had the head of a normal man and he bore a striking resemblance to his brothers. Like his brothers, he was extremely attractive, with the same chiseled features, twinkling eyes, and warm smile. But there the resemblance dramatically ended.

Sasha didn't have the body of a human being. He had instead the body of a *serpent creature*. He sat with the lower portion of his body curled on a large pillow. The rest of his body extended up about five feet, so his entire length was over ten feet total. Instead of hair, his head bore a mass of long, sectioned appendages that moved independently like a spider's legs. Sasha was certainly not a sight for the faint of heart. But Ignatius moved closer, totally mesmerized by the beautifully bizarre creature who sat before him.

"Unbelievable," Ignatius said as he slowly approached Sasha. "I thought I'd seen everything. Now I've see everything. Sorry to stare. My name is Ignatius. Ignatius Valentine."

One of Sasha's long appendages fully extended itself. "And my name is Sasha," he said with an accent as thick and pleasing as his brothers. "I'm quite pleased to meet you."

Ignatius gently took hold of the appendage. "Nice to meet you, too. Welcome to Las Vegas. I'm sorry to stare."

"It's quite all right."

"No, it's not. It's just—I wasn't expecting to see someone so ... "

"Unusual?" said Sasha.

Ignatius smiled. "Well, you are unusual. But in a good way. You're the most unusual person I've ever met, that's for sure. And I mean that as a compliment, by the way."

"You're very kind. But you're quite unusual as well," said Sasha. "Your name, your clothing, your personality, your … *reaction* to me. All quite unusual, to be sure."

Ignatius sat on a pillow beside Sasha. "I suppose." Ignatius continued to eye Sasha up and down in amazement. Sasha's existence certainly seemed to prove that the Zavada brothers were, in fact, a life form other than human. "You know, in a different time and place, you might have been worshipped as a god."

Sasha laughed cynically. "Or murdered as a monster!"

Ignatius laughed. 'Yeah, you're right about that. You never know how humans are going to react to the unusual. Strange creatures, humans."

"Yes, the most unusual creatures of all."

Marek and Gregor were sufficiently pleased with the obvious chemistry between Sasha and Ignatius, so they quietly exited. And as they did, they mischievously plotted how best to bring Ignatius into the Zavada fold. Ignatius was clearly meant to be a part of their family. Sitting with Sasha, he seemed quite comfortable and right at home. He spoke to Sasha with a playful familiarity, the way a roguish uncle might speak to a precocious nephew.

"So what's up with all the chicks?" asked Ignatius, pointblank. "How do you ever get anything done?"

Sasha laughed. "It is quite difficult. And I've cut back, believe me. At one time, things were somewhat out of hand."

"So how do your brothers feel about all that?"

 RAVENDIABLO

"How do they feel about ... my *garden*?"

Sasha sighed. "They feel that I'm neglecting my studies. They're not entirely wrong. But life is very short, and learning comes in many forms." Sasha smiled wickedly.

"Your garden," repeated Ignatius with a smile. "Well, you've got great taste, I'll say that much. A little on the dark side, but that's cool."

"Thank you, very much. Coming from someone as obviously cultured as yourself, that's quite a compliment. Yes, I love women. Why deny it? I surround myself with women for one simple reason, women are the best of what life has to offer. Women enchant me. Endlessly."

Ignatius was feeling enchanted as well. He felt as though he were under the influence of some powerful narcotic, such was Sasha's effect on him. Sasha had a strange but pleasant aroma, a combination of vanilla, honey, and cedar. His melodious voice was pleasing to the ear, and the thick accent only enhanced its musical quality. Sasha possessed a strange energy, a *vibration*, that was both calming and exhilarating. Like his brothers, he, too, sparkled, particularly when he smiled, which he often did. Of course, it was impossible not to stare at him. Every wonder of the known world paled in comparison to him. Indeed, Sasha was easily the most spectacular life form ever to have existed in all recorded history. Part human, part reptile, part insect, Sasha was truly horrifying, yet gorgeous. He was also in possession of an undeniable sex appeal that was powerfully magnetic. Sasha's facial features were a bit androgynous, but his demeanor was decidedly masculine. He was a living, breathing phallic symbol, like something out of ancient myth or a fairy tale. Sasha's beauty was beyond belief.

"I'm sorry," said Ignatius apologetically. "I keep staring."

"It's quite all right, so do I. You're a very attractive man, Ignatius. I only collect female flowers, but I certainly appreciate beauty in all its forms. So I'm very attracted to you."

Ignatius blushed. "Thanks."

Sasha gazed at Ignatius with an almost scientific curiosity. He had known many humans, but Ignatius seemed radically different. Clearly, Ignatius was an alien life form.

"I would imagine you've had many flowers of your own," Sasha said with a smile.

"Here and there. I've never maintained a garden, if that's what you mean. I suppose my music has always been my mistress."

"But of course. I understand that you're an accomplished jazz musician."

"I'd call myself a lifelong student," Ignatius said humbly. "I understand that you're a fan."

"That's quite true. I like jazz very much. I'm particularly fond of the music of Thelonious Monk."

Ignatius laughed. "You look like the Monk type. I dig him, too. I also understand that you're a scholar of Las Vegas."

"I've long been fascinated by Las Vegas, but I claim no expertise, "Sasha said. "I've read books and seen films. but a city like Las Vegas needs to be experienced firsthand. As I'm sure you well know."

"You're right, Vegas does need to be experienced first-hand. I've been all over the world and I've never seen another city like it."

"So you like Las Vegas?"

Ignatius laughed. "Now I didn't say all that. I just said I've never seen another city like it."

"But you choose to live in Las Vegas. So surely, you have feelings for the city."

Ignatius considered Sasha's words. "Yeah, I've got a lot of feelings for the city, all right. I'm just not quite sure what they are. I don't love it, I'm sure of that. I don't even particularly like it. I've been all over the world, but something always seems to bring me back to Las Vegas." Ignatius seemed perplexed. "I don't know what it is."

"My brothers believe that Las Vegas is far different from the way it appears on the surface. They believe that Las Vegas is *supernatural.* Gregor and Marek also believe that our destiny is here. Perhaps it's that way for you."

"In Las Vegas, *anything is possible.*" As he stared at Sasha, Ignatius was suddenly seized by a thought.

"And what are you thinking, my new friend?" asked Sasha. His perceptive eyes could see that Ignatius was constructing a plot of some kind.

"I'm thinking you need to experience Vegas firsthand."

Sasha smiled sadly. "That would be nice. But, while I believe that I'm ready for Las Vegas, I sincerely doubt that the opposite is true."

Ignatius spotted a purple cloth covering a cushion. He snatched up the cloth and hurried over to Sasha. He covered Sasha's head with the cloth, carefully positioning it over the mass of appendages that continued to move, though now much more excitedly.

"You're going to have to relax if I'm going to make this work," said Ignatius as he struggled to cover Sasha's head.

"Please forgive me," Sasha said beaming. "I'm quite excited."

When Ignatius had successfully covered Sasha's head, the appendages appeared to be dread-locks. Ignatius removed the hoop earring from his own ear and attached it to Sasha's ear. Now Sasha looked like a white Rastaman.

"Now, Vegas is ready for you," said Ignatius with a triumphant smile.

* * *

The Las Vegas Strip was alive again. There was a manic energy in the nighttime air the likes of which hadn't been felt in quite some time. The Strip was packed with strolling pedestrians, and the automobile traffic was bumper to bumper. The recent economic meltdown had been a sobering reminder that even the dreamland of Sin City wasn't immune to reality. But tonight felt like the Vegas of old, and the Strip strutted like a neon peacock. It was the perfect opportunity for Sasha's first official exposure to the city. He sat in the back of the limo peering over the half lowered, tinted window with wide eyes. He was as excited as a child at the circus. None of the many books he had read or the films he had seen prepared him for the electrifying sights and sounds that surrounded him. As the limo cruised, Sasha stared at the outrageous Strip landmarks with awe and even respect. Nothing reflected American mentality and culture more accurately than the Strip. To Sasha, the gaudy hotels and casinos were the wonders of the American world and no less breathtaking than the real Eiffel Tower or the real Great Sphinx.

When the limo paused at a red light, Sasha noticed a very different kind of wonder, his most favorite kind. A beautiful woman stood on the corner surrounded by pedestrians. Dressed provocatively, she was oblivious to the stares of the many men around her. But it was the look of hopelessness in her eyes that caught Sasha's attention. Physically, she stood on the corner, but mentally, she was in some dark and disturbing place. She glanced up and made eye contact with Sasha. When he smiled at her, she was instantly fascinated. The light turned green and the limo sped off in a cloud of exhaust. The woman continued to watch the limo in the distance. She had never seen a face or a smile like Sasha's.

"I can't believe how busy it is tonight," said Ignatius, muttering to himself. "You okay back there?"

"I'm quite fine, thank you very much," answered Sasha. "This was a wonderful idea, by the way. I hope we can do it again sometime."

Ignatius smiled. "We'll do it every night, don't even worry about that. You hungry? You want something to eat?"

"No, thank you." Sasha's thoughts were still on the beautiful, troubled woman with the hopeless eyes.

"I'm gonna stop and grab a bite." Ignatius then turned off the Strip and directed the limo toward the West Side. Sasha continued to stare out the window, fascinated by all that he saw. The bleak scenery of the inner city was dramatically different from the screaming neon of the Strip but just as compelling, if not more so. Sasha remained transfixed.

"Is there a particular name for this area of Las Vegas?" asked Sasha inquisitively. "It's quite different from the Strip."

Ignatius laughed. "This is what is affectionately known as 'the 'hood". How do you like it?"

I like it very much, actually. It has its own unique energy."

"You can say that again."

Sasha settled back in his seat "There's so much to see in Las Vegas. I never dreamed that I would ever have the opportunity to actually see it. And I feel most fortunate to have someone like yourself to act as my guide ... and teacher. I'm very grateful to you, Ignatius."

Ignatius glanced in the rearview mirror at Sasha. Part human, part reptile, part insect, he looked like something out of an outlandish dream ... or a nightmare. Yet in spite of his appearance, Ignatius found him to be irresistibly seductive. And the longer Ignatius spent in Sasha's company, the more seduced he became. Cruising the Vegas streets with Sasha as his travel companion, Ignatius also felt a strange sense of serenity. He had lived in Vegas on and off for many years and never felt any real connection to anyone. The people of Vegas often tended to be as artificial as the architecture, and as a result, Ignatius had never made one true friend. Until tonight. And they had bonded immediately, as if by destiny.

 RAVENDIABLO

"Do you miss the old Las Vegas, Ignatius?" asked Sasha. "I've heard so much about it."

"The old Vegas?" Ignatius repeated with a bit of cynicism. "You mean the good old days when the Mob ran the town? I keep hearing about those good old days. I was here then, and I don't remember it being all that good." Ignatius thought for a moment, then burst out laughing. "But it was a hell of a lot better than now!"

Ignatius drove the limo into the parking lot of Big Mama's, one of his favorite soul food restaurants. He parked in the shadows in the far corner of the lot.

"I'll be right back," said Ignatius as he climbed out and headed over to the restaurant.

A late-model Cadillac SUV drove into the lot and parked several yards away from the limo. Sasha watched curiously as four provocatively dressed women climbed out of the vehicle. They belonged to the pimp who remained inside. His name was Bobbie Bradshaw, but he called himself Trigga. He angrily shouted a variety of instructions to the women, who stood listening like frightened children. Finally, he drove away, burning rubber for maximum dramatic effect. The women walked toward the restaurant, but one of them glanced over and noticed the limo. She recognized it. Even from across the parking lot, Sasha recognized her as well. She was the woman with the hopeless eyes. As her friends continued to the restaurant, she instead walked over to the limo. Sasha eyed her up and down as she approached. She was beautiful, but it wasn't her physical beauty that attracted him. He wasn't exactly sure why he was attracted to her, but he was determined to find out. When she reached the limo, Sasha smiled seductively and began his exploration.

"I've seen your loveliness before," he said sweetly.

She smiled. "Likewise, " she said. It excited her to see him again. She knew it was more than mere coincidence.

My name is Alexander, but my friends call me Sasha."

"Can I be your friend?" she asked.

"That would please me greatly."

"Then I'll call you Sasha. Hello, new friend Sasha. My name is Belita."

"Belita," Sasha whispered. "That's an exquisite name. It means "little beauty". Did you know that?"

"No. My grandmother named me."

"Well, your grandmother named you well. Belita. It's a most appropriate name. Belita. It sounds so ... musical. Belita. It's a lovely name for a flower."

Belita adored the sweet sound of Sasha's voice and his strange accent. She adored the way he said her name. Every time he repeated it, it felt like an intimate caress and aroused her. Belita could feel Sasha's powerful gravitational pull take hold of her and draw her closer to the limo. Her knees weakened and she felt lightheaded. In an effort to relax herself, she took a cigarette from her purse, lit it, and inhaled deeply. "I've never seen you before tonight. I'd remember a face like that."

"I'm new to Las Vegas."

"You live here?" Belita asked excitedly. She prayed the answer was yes.

"Yes."

     RAVENDIABLO

Belita's heart quickened. The more she gazed into Sasha's eyes, the more her flesh *burned*. She felt as if she were melting and she visualized a puddle forming at her feet. "I meet people from all over the world, but I can't quite place your accent."

"I am Czech," he answered proudly.

"I've seen pictures of your country. It's really beautiful, like something out of a fairy tale."

Sasha smiled slyly. "So is Belita."

Belita blushed, then took another long drag from her cigarette. "You need to get out more often."

"I plan on it, believe me. Belita. My little beauty. Belita."

Belita was sure that if Sasha said her name one more time, her legs would betray her completely and she'd fall into the puddle. "I don't know what line of work you're in, but you might want to consider phone sex. You'd be a moneymaker."

Sasha laughed. "The sound of my voice pleases Belita?" Sasha was clearly aware of the effect he was having on her. But he still hadn't figured out why he was so fascinated by her. Further exploration was needed. "So, tell me, Belita, what line of work are you in?"

"Social work," she said straight-faced. "And you?"

"I'm a student. I'm currently studying something that has captured my imagination and aroused me like nothing I've ever known. I'm a diligent student and I'm determined to learn as much as I possibly can."

"Yeah? What are you studying?"

"Belita," Sasha answered. His powerfully seductive gaze bore into her like a laser beam.

Belita felt faint. "You need to cool it, Sasha. I mean it."

Sasha smiled. "I'm just getting started. And I mean it."

Belita redirected the conversation. "You know, Vegas is wack. You can't trust your mama in Las Vegas. You've got to be on your guard at all times. Whatever you do, don't ever forget that. I wouldn't want anything to happen to you."

"That's so sweet. Fortunately, I have friends like Belita who would protect me from bad things. Is that not so?"

"Yes," she answered sincerely. "I'd protect you, Sasha. You're my friend. Remember?"

Suddenly, the Cadillac SUV returned to the parking lot and when Belita saw it, she tossed her cigarette and backed away from the limo. Without saying goodbye, she turned away and hurried toward the restaurant. Trigga parked the SUV a few yards from the restaurant entrance and climbed out. He was a large, powerfully built man dressed in modern attire. His angry demeanor was unchanged from earlier. He saw Belita heading toward the restaurant, but he called out to her and motioned for her to come over to him. She dutifully complied. Sasha nervously watched the drama slowly unfold from a distance. Even from across the parking lot, he could sense Belita's fear and Trigga's rage. With his large index finger pointed threateningly in her face, Trigga screamed curses at Belita and she stood shaking from the verbal onslaught. Ignatius came out of the restaurant carrying a bag of food. He glanced over at the altercation but immediately looked away. Ignatius was no stranger to the violent relationships between pimps and prostitutes. It sickened him, but he certainly didn't intervene. Instead, he continued across the parking lot to the limo and climbed inside. He glanced in the rear-view mirror at Sasha, who appeared to be genuinely horrified by the scene he was witnessing.

Trigga's rage only escalated. He snatched Belita by the hair, slapped her, then slammed her full force against the SUV. She slid down to ground and remained there as Trigga towered over her, continuing his profane verbal attack. When he spat on her, Ignatius quickly started the engine and drove out of the parking lot. He continued to drive for many minutes before he dared look in the rearview mirror again. When he did look, he saw Sasha weeping uncontrollably. Ignatius was both surprised and touched by Sasha's reaction to the cruelty and violence. The perceptive Ignatius correctly surmised that Sasha was a tender soul with the heart of a chivalric knight. As Ignatius watched the sobbing Sasha, tears began to form in his own eyes as well. Ignatius then realized that to know Sasha, to *truly* know him, was to love him.

"You've seen a lot tonight," said Ignatius sadly. "The good, the bad, and now the ugly. I'm sorry you had to see that, but that's part of Vegas, too. A big part. There's one thing about Vegas you'll never read in a book or see in a film. It's a *predatory* city. I've never seen anything like it."

Sasha finally stopped crying. He settled back in his seat and collected his emotions. "Marek and Gregor are convinced that we are here for a reason, that we have some *higher* purpose here. Perhaps they're right after all."

Ignatius glanced in the rearview mirror. He saw that Sasha had removed the purple headscarf, allowing his long, sectioned appendages free reign.

And they moved madly. His sweet face was now contorted into a hideous, demonic mask, complete with bulging eyes and a terrifying, fang-toothed smile. Ignatius was stunned by the startling transformation and he gripped the steering wheel to steady himself. But he well understood the message being conveyed. Sasha was a tender soul with the heart of a chivalric knight, but he was also capable of being a fearsome *monster* ... when he needed to be.

"Do you believe in destiny, Ignatius?"

Ignatius took a deep breath as his eyes kept flicking back to the horrific sight in the rearview mirror.

"I do now."

16

Simon Janus

At the stroke of midnight, the grand opening of Sanctum Tartarus Hotel & Casino proudly announced itself with a massive fireworks display that could be seen and heard all over the city. The air crackled with electric anticipation as hordes of the curious descended on the structure like bugs. Traffic was hopelessly jammed for blocks. The word was out, and the buzz was positive—Sanctum Tartarus was the most exciting thing to happen to Las Vegas in a very long time. In the wake of the recent economic meltdown, the opening of Sanctum Tartarus was indeed cause for major celebration. The completed project seemed to suggest that Vegas had weathered the economic storm and was on the comeback trail.

Sanctum Tartarus looked radically different from the other properties on the Strip. It didn't look like a casino or hotel at all. Instead, it looked like a massive, crystalline *gemstone* made of glass and mirrors, and it sparkled like one.

Sanctum Tartarus was certainly a diamond in the eyes of Simon Janus. Aside from being the new headquarters for the Janus Cartel, Sanctum Tartarus was going to be something else. It was going to be a grand cultural experiment. Simon was more than a crime lord. Simon was a highly educated man with an interest in world cultures, particularly American culture. More than any other American city, Las Vegas was the quintessential representation of American culture. Simon had an unusual theory about Las Vegas. He saw the city as being a dark place that bathed itself in bright light in order to conceal the truth. Simon also understood Vegas well enough to know how schizoid, hypocritical, and stupid it was. Vegas was, after all, the real capital of America, not Washington. For all its boasts of being Sin City, Las Vegas had never really looked in the mirror, acknowledged its true nature, and embraced its darkness. With Sanctum Tartarus, Simon was going to do what Las Vegas was too schizophrenic, hypocritical, and stupid to do. He was going to reveal the real Las Vegas and prosper enormously from the revelation.

The interior of Sanctum Tartarus stood in dramatic, conspicuous contrast to the glimmering, sparkling, heavenly exterior. Unlike the luminous shell that covered it, the interior of Sanctum Tartarus was painstakingly designed to reflect Simon's unique theory.

It was dark.

The hotel had been authentically recreated in the style of the LaLaurie House, the site of several grisly torture slayings and the most famous haunted house in New Orleans. Gigantic framed photos of violent crime scenes covered the walls. The floor space was decorated with splattered bloodstains and the chalk outlines of where bodies had supposedly been. The casino was part Gothic mausoleum and part medieval torture chamber. Gaming tables and slot machines shared space with working

     RAVENDIABLO

instruments of torture. In the middle of the casino was a large area constructed to look like a village square, in the center of which were an authentic guillotine and a gallows for hourly mock executions. The staff were dressed like witches, wizards, vampires, zombies, corpses, cenobites, and other creatures of the night. Sanctum Tartarus was designed to be a place of violence and death.

Simon personally created the unique marketing campaign. Slogans like "Enter the Sanctum, Embrace the Darkness" and "Come Get Your Magic On" appeared in blood-red letters on black billboards weeks before the opening. Simon hit a marketing jackpot with the slogan, "Las Vegas, Where It's Always Halloween." The original slogan was to be "Sanctum Tartarus, Where It's Always Halloween", but Simon wanted to show the city of Las Vegas that his dark concept was the best concept for marketing the *entire* city. And it proved to be so. The slogan represented a radically unique view of the city, a view that was surprisingly embraced. It was immediately heralded as a creative and gutsy departure from the boring and predictable marketing campaigns that normally came from the Las Vegas tourist bureau.

If the reaction on opening night was any indication, Sanctum Tartarus was destined to be a monstrous success. It was unlike anything ever seen in Las Vegas. Even the jaded were totally unprepared for the level of depravity they encountered once they stepped inside. Sanctum Tartarus was truly a Disneyland of the damned. The unrepentant fiendishness struck a powerful chord, a chord that deeply resonated with a modern crowd hungry for heightened experiences and sensations. Sanctum Tartarus unapologetically appealed to twisted obsessions and deviant desires in ways that a traditional Las Vegas Strip property never would. The atmosphere was *literally* intoxicating. As patrons wandered about taking in the grotesque sights and sounds, many of them looked as though they were under the influence of some drug. And they were ... the blood lust. Simon's instincts had been proven correct, and it wouldn't be the last time. Sanctum Tartarus would be the first of many high-profile successes for Simon Janus.

Shortly after 2:00 am, Simon held a special press conference in the Sanctum Tartarus theater. The theater was called simply and appropriately enough, The Pit. It was as macabre as the rest of Sanctum Tartarus, the only items missing being a giant, razor-sharp pendulum suspended from the ceiling and an altar for sacrifices. The Pit was an enormous black cave with a domed ceiling decorated with ornate stained glass. Endless rows of plush, blood-red seats faced a colossal stage bathed in blue light. Large, strategically placed screens ensured that no eye in the house would miss the action onstage. On this opening night, each of the three thousand seats was filled with excited audience members. They were entertained by a spectacular variety show featuring acrobats, magicians, and musical artists from all over the world. Numerous gifts and prizes were awarded including a luxury home, a luxury automobile, and a luxury coffin—filled with $10,000 in cash. The energy in The Pit was overwhelming, and the crowd was wired and ready for the grand finale.

The time had come for Simon Janus to take the stage and make his first public appearance.

The city of Las Vegas first heard the name Simon Janus when it was announced that a group of wealthy European investors called the Janus Cartel had purchased the troubled Crystal Oasis project. Simon Janus was the head of the cartel and its official spokesperson, and while he had given a few short interviews to the local press, his picture had never been taken. The public had never seen Simon Janus. Until now.

"Ladies and gentlemen," a female voice said from unseen speakers, "will you please welcome to the stage and to Las Vegas, Simon Janus."

The loud and sudden ring of a gong startled the crowd and echoed throughout the theater. Moments later, Simon Janus walked onto the stage bathed in the glow of a near blinding spotlight. It made for a dramatically *angelic* entrance and the crowd rose to its feet to welcome him with wild applause. Simon was a black man dressed completely in white. His head was crowned with thick, grey dreadlocks that hung past his shoulders. He was obviously not a young man, but he possessed a youthful demeanor and vigor that made him appear much younger than his true age. He flashed a warm and welcoming smile at the crowd and the bright light that enveloped him paled in comparison. There was no ego or arrogance about him. Indeed, Simon Janus genuinely appeared to be the one thing that most rich and powerful men are not—likable.

As he walked toward the podium, he casually glanced at the local dignitaries that lined the stage to welcome him. There were the mayor, the governer, representatives of the gaming commission, and other members of the Las Vegas political machine. Many of the Strip casinos were represented, along with other major players of the business community. Simon smiled cordially at these local luminaries. He bowed graciously to both welcome and thank them. Then he stepped up to the podium and waited patiently until the applause subsided. After the applause had died down completely, he continued to wait, allowing the growing anticipation to build to an unbearable level. When he finally spoke, the crowd was mesmerized.

"Welcome to Sanctum Tartarus. I humbly thank you all for being with me this evening," he began. Simon's English accent was pleasingly exotic to the ears of the American audience. "Sanctum Tartarus is the fulfillment of a dream and you're sharing that dream with me, right here and now. And I thank you from the bottom of my heart. But I'm not here to talk about Sanctum Tartarus. I believe Sanctum Tartarus speaks for itself. I'm here to talk about another project that hasn't been in the news. A secret project that I'm unveiling for the first time tonight. A project as dear to my heart as Sanctum Tartarus."

The crowd listened closely.

"Las Vegas is currently in the grips of trials and tribulations the likes of which it has never seen. Call it what you will—meltdown, downturn, recession, depression, collapse ... take your pick. What caused this nightmare? Was it the bursting of the real estate bubble? Was it bad loans, easy credit, loose regulations? What caused it, and who is to blame? Do we blame the banks? The mortgage companies? Wall Street? Washington? Surely, there must be an answer."

Simon paused and looked throughout the theater as if he were waiting for someone to provide that answer. The audience was silent as it considered Simon's words.

"There *is* an answer, and it's not as complex as many would have you believe. The answer is actually quite simple. We have all witnessed the implosion of Las Vegas, and that implosion was brought about not by dynamite, but by greed. The greed of the predator class."

The luminaries seated behind Simon listened and squirmed uncomfortably.

"In the city of Las Vegas, the most distinguished citizens tend to be the most predatory. And if you don't believe me, just look behind me!"

The crowd immediately roared with laughter and applauded enthusiastically. Simon turned around and slyly smiled at the many dignitaries who collectively represented the city of Las Vegas. They all glared at him angrily. Simon turned back to his audience, who were comfortably in the palm of his hand.

"And, naturally, half of them are lawyers!" he said, causing the applause to escalate even more. Simon waited until the laughter and applause completely died down and he became serious again.

"Don't believe the myth, ladies and gentlemen, the Mob *never left* Las Vegas. Because the predatory consciousness that the Mob brought with them remained." Simon sneered. "The Mob *mentality*. Greed is not right. Greed is not good. Greed is what has kept this city from rising to its true potential, something it has never done in its entire existence. Of course, the people seated behind me now would probably disagree. They're all experts on Las Vegas. I'm just a foreigner, and a Brit to boot. What could I possibly know? Perhaps one of these distinguished experts can explain to me how a city that has generated so much revenue for so many years can have so little to show for itself." Simon scratched his forehead in mock bewilderment. "What's up with that?"

Simon turned around again to face his esteemed guests, all of whom looked very sorry to be onstage under the glare of the audience and the hot lights. Simon winked at them mischievously, then turned back to his *flock*.

"For over fifty years, Las Vegas has been a money machine. The ultimate money machine. Yet this money machine has never produced anything of value in its entire history. No invention, no technology, no art form, no trend, no original idea ... no nothing. *Nothing*! How can this be?" Again, Simon looked around the theater as if waiting for an answer. "With the kind of money this city has made over the years, Las Vegas should have a little bit more going on, don't you think? So I ask you, where did all the money go? Other than lining the pockets of predators like our esteemed guests behind me, what was the money used for? Better hospitals? Better schools? Better infrastructure? Better culture? Was it used for the betterment of *anything*?" Simon paused and waited for an answer. "You know the answer." He turned around to face the dignitaries. "And so do you!" Simon turned back to his flock. "What happens here stays here, huh?" Simon sneered. "Well, as soon as something happens here, you let me know."

 RAVENDIABLO

The spellbound audience was riveted by Simon's words.

"We can either stand by and watch as Las Vegas continues to be run into the ground by our good friends behind me, or we can stand up and collectively say, '*Game over*'." Simon pointed back at the men seated behind him. "Because I don't know about you, but I've had enough of these guys!"

The audience erupted into applause, and Simon smiled triumphantly.

"Sanctum Tartarus was a crazy dream. I wanted to build a place where people could celebrate my favorite holiday, Halloween, year-round. And now they can. But I've got some other crazy ideas, too. For one thing, regardless of what happens in this unpredictable economy, Sanctum Tartarus will never lay off one worker. I give you my word."

The crowd cheered wildly and stomped its feet.

"It's time to start doing things in a whole new way. And the first thing we need to do is get rid of the old Vegas mentality. That's why this town is in the position it's in today. We don't need it anymore." Simon pointed back at his guests. "We don't need *them* anymore. Enough with greed." He paused for a moment to choose his words carefully. "Of those to whom much is given, much is required. And quite frankly, I've been given a lot. Health, wealth, good fortune ..." Simon paused and smiled like a naughty child. "Reasonably good looks."

The crowd laughed and many women screamed out their agreement.

"I can either follow in the footsteps of the predators behind me and continue that time-honored tradition of skimming for self, or I can do something truly crazy. I can do the *right* thing. I can skim for those who truly need it and give back. And with Bleeding Heart, that's what I intend to do."

On cue, an enormous black heart made of canvas was slowly lowered from the ceiling. It remained suspended high above the curious crowd.

"Bleeding Heart is an organization I've created in order to give back to the city that made my dream come true. Bleeding Heart is my thank you to the city of Las Vegas. And that's why thirty-three percent of every dollar taken in by Sanctum Tartarus will be funneled back to Bleeding Heart. That money will be distributed to a variety of worthy charities. Programs for the poor, the elderly, the homeless ... the hopeless. It's time to give something back to the city of Las Vegas. And now is the time."

Suddenly, an ear-piercing explosion jolted everyone in the theater. The black heart suspended high above burst open and showered long blood red ribbons and cash money into the crowd. The screams, cheers, and applause that erupted were deafening.

"Thank you, Las Vegas," exclaimed Simon as he proudly watched the crowd scramble for the money. He turned and calmly stepped down from the podium. The dignitaries were on their feet, and many of them charged toward Simon with furious faces. The mayor led the pack. He confronted Simon and his face was beet red with rage.

"Why you no-good, black-assed, Limey bastard!" he yelled with eyes ablaze. "You're going to be one sorry son of a bitch for the shit you just pulled here!"

"You're finished," laughed Simon cheerfully. "I'll personally make sure of that. Go slither back to your law practice where you belong. You're like everyone else up here on this stage, past your expiration date. You stink."

The mayor lost control and snatched Simon's arm. "You picked the wrong town to play games in!"

Simon broke free of the mayor's grip, seized him by the throat with one hand, and hoisted him off the ground effortlessly. The other dignitaries watched in stunned amazement as Simon held the mayor suspended with his feet kicking madly. They all stepped back, afraid to intervene. The mayor was terrified.

"Don't be an idiot," Simon said. "This is Las Vegas—game central. There's a new game in town starting right now. It's called 'Simon Says'. And Simon says stay out of my way—or I'll mop the floor with you. With *all* of you."

Simon flung the mayor to the floor, sending him sliding several feet and into a bunch of chairs. The dignitaries rushed over to aid the mayor as Simon turned and walked away. No one in the audience even noticed the altercation. They were all too busy picking up money.

* * *

In a low-lit conference rooom, twelve men sat at a long table, six on either side. They were the members of the Janus Cartel. As they waited for the arrival of the thirteenth and final member, they spoke freely amongst themselves.

"Well, it's official, we're a hit. The place hasn't been open twenty-four hours and the numbers are already unbelievable."

"We're going to be on the front pages of the world."

"It's a money machine, all right."

"But thirty-three percent off the top is a bunch of bull-shit. Nobody told me I was joining the Red Cross."

"Sure, it's a lot, but it buys respectability."

"Simon is right."

"Simon is wrong. We buy cops and politicians for a fraction of that all the time."

"Simon has a big brain, perfect instincts, and the Midas touch. And we all know it. That's why we're sitting at this table. He hasn't been wrong yet—about anything. He's onto something with Sanctum Tartarus. Simon Janus knows what he's doing."

"He never lets us forget it either, and that's the problem."

The meeting room door opened, and Simon entered. He had changed clothes since his speech earlier. He was impeccably dressed, still in all white. Simon Janus always wore white.

"Greetings, gentlemen," Simon said, closing the door behind him. He seated himself at the head of the table, crossed his legs, and settled back in his chair. He glanced around the table at the cartel and his infallible intuition told him that the natives were restless. They needed his guidance, and he was ready to oblige.

"Has anyone in this room ever heard of Goldfield? Or Rhyolite?" he asked. No one responded. "They were once big, booming cities right here in Nevada. In fact, they were the Las Vegases of their day. But they don't exist anymore. Just like Las Vegas won't exist anymore unless we grab it by the throat and rescue it. And that's exactly what we're going to do."

The cartel sat in rapt attention.

"Las Vegas has always been a house of cards just waiting to fall. Quite frankly, I'm surprised it lasted as long as it did." Simon sneered. "*Americans*! He spat the word in disgust. "And their world-famous American Dream they brag so much about. You know why it's called the American Dream? It's because you've got to be asleep to believe in it. Well, the Yanks are slowly waking up to the fact that the dream is *over*. And their capital city of Las Vegas is living proof of it. This town is just a tumbleweed ready to roll. Once upon a time, Las Vegas *was* something ... I'd never use the word 'special' ... Las Vegas was ... unusual. Back when it was the only place in the country with legalized gambling. But it's a far different landscape now. Now you can gamble anywhere. Gary, Indiana, Dahmer, Wisconsin, Lynch Mob, Mississippi, or the Indian *rez* of your choice. You certainly don't need to come to Las Vegas anymore. And right now, all those idiots who shared the stage with me are terrified. Because they know it, too. And, of course, they don't know what to do about it. The problem with them is the problem with all Americans, they're stupid. They don't know what they've got here. But, fortunately for us, I do."

The cartel was under his spell.

"The Janus Cartel is going to do things the Mob never dreamed of. And speaking of the Mob, I'm a little sick and tired of hearing about Bugsy Siegel, Meyer Lansky, and the good old days of the Mob. What the Mob did for Las Vegas is a bit romanticized, if you ask me. Not to mention over-rated." Simon laughed. "Funny how the Mob gets all the credit for building Sin City. They couldn't have done it without the Mormons!"

The cartel laughed.

"And what exactly did they do that was so noteworthy, anyway? They took a money tree and lined their pockets with every dollar that fell. What's so difficult about that? What's so intelligent about that? What's so special about that?" Simon sneered. "The Mob. They were just a bunch of lowlife thugs who took advantage of an easy situation. Leave it to a town as stupid as Las Vegas to idolize the Mob. Las Vegas idolizes the Mob because of what the Mob represents, the very same thing this pathetic city represents, greed. Oh, and by the way, why is Las Vegas in the toilet today? Greed. Perhaps there's a connection there." Simon shook his head in disgust. "This is the most backward modern city I've ever seen, particularly considering all the money that's passed through here. And all because of greed. All greed and no vision. None whatsoever. For years, the Vegas idea of vision was building bigger, more idiotic casinos and developing more sophisticated surveillance systems. Real vision would have been taking some of that skim money and investing in *ideas*. Las Vegas could have, and should have, been much more than just a Sin

City. Las Vegas could have been a Silicon Valley instead of the neon dump it is today. Of course, that would have required vision." Then Simon quickly reconsidered his words and laughed heartily. "You know, on second thought, it would never have worked. Can you imagine Steve Jobs or Bill Gates trying to start the computer revolution in Las Vegas? With no slot on the computer to feed money into, they'd have never found an investor!"

The cartel laughed.

"Las Vegas is a myth," Simon continued. It's the Emerald City at the end of the rainbow where dreams come true. I know all about it. Well, with Sanctum Tartarus, I've taken that myth to a whole new level. I've reinvented it, repackaged it, and darkened it for a whole new generation and a whole new mentality. Because Sanctum Tartarus is more than a hotel and casino. Sanctum Tartarus isn't really a destination at all It's a *state of mind*, and the world is finally ready for it. Sanctum Tartarus represents the new Las Vegas, the Disneyland of the damned. Sanctum Tartarus is only the first step. The first step of a massive, monstrous new makeover. I'm going to recreate this whole town completely. And before I'm done, Las Vegas is going to make Babylon look like Salt Lake City. I'm going to make Las Vegas Sin City ... for real."

The cartel was convinced. Simon smiled.

17

The Kavianis

After the death of their brother Dmitri, Gaspar and Sholeh Kaviani moved their principal base of operations to Las Vegas permanently. It was an ironic move. Dmitri had long been a frequent visitor to Las Vegas and had felt it was a natural spot from which to run the family business. Gaspar and Sholeh had steadfastly refused, feeling that the temptations that Las Vegas offered would be too much for their brother to handle. But while they had been proven correct in that assumption, Dmitri had not been wrong about Las Vegas. For all of his many shortcomings, most of which involved his violent personality and perverted obsessions, Dmitri had been highly intelligent with sound instincts, particularly with regard to business. For years, he had argued that Las Vegas was the most perfect city in the world from which to base a criminal empire. Aside from the fact that it was already completely corrupt to begin with, Dmitri believed that Las Vegas possessed an extremely powerful occult energy—literally, a magical energy that could be tapped, harnessed, and utilized by individuals with knowledge of the dark arts. Plus, the weather was nice, and the people were stupid.

The Kavianis established their new headquarters in a black skyscraper that sat on the Strip just south of Sahara Avenue. Compared to other parts of the Strip, this area looked and felt somewhat deserted. Because there were no casinos and hotels and few businesses in the vicinity, the area was considerably darker than the rest of the Strip, which only added to the desolate atmosphere. There had been grand plans to rejuvenate the area, and during the recent overbuilding boom, several projects had been initiated. But the crash put an end to them all and they stood unfinished; more haunted houses in the new Sin City ghost town. The Kavianis purchased the black skyscraper, which they called the Monolith, and immediately set about the task of completing it in accordance with their own unique specifications and inclinations.

Gaspar occupied a penthouse suite that overlooked the city. Servants, bodyguards, concubines, and various other employees lived in other suites scattered throughout the building. Sholeh's private chambers were located on the lower levels.

As Gaspar rode the elevator down to meet Sholeh, his thoughts were focused on their late brother, Dmitri. Moving the family operation to Vegas had been his dream, a dream he never lived to see. Avenging Dmitri's murder was the top priority. When the elevator came to a stop, Gaspar stepped off and continued down a black corridor. Strange, bestial sounds filled the air, the sounds of beasts unknown in the modern world. Located on lower levels was Sholeh's large collection of pets, bizarre creatures accumulated from a lifetime of world travel in dark, distant, and disturbing places. Sholeh's pets were the stuff of nightmares, and she cherished them deeply. Gaspar reached the door of Sholeh's office and knocked.

"Come in," she said.

Gaspar entered. The lighting was low to the point of near darkness except for the far end of the room where Sholeh sat. A single naked bulb hung suspended above her, bathing her in a soft glow. She sat in a thronelike chair behind a desk designed and built especially for her by the artist H.R. Giger. With her crown of thick, unruly hair, sunken eyes and wicked grin, Sholeh herself looked like something out of Giger's dark and twisted imagination. Unlike Gaspar and their late brother, Dmitri, Sholeh wore almost no makeup. She felt no desire to appear normal. A small pet sat curled in her lap and she caressed it lovingly. Gaspar kissed her cheek, then seated himself in one of the two chairs that sat in front of her desk. The other chair had belonged to Dmitri.

"Have you seen the television reports?" Sholeh asked. She pressed a button on her desk and activated a large, flat-screen television mounted on a nearby wall. Images of the hordes of people descending on Sanctum Tartarus filled the screen. "We absolutely must visit this place!"

As Gaspar watched the activity on the screen, it was obvious that he was far from impressed. In fact, he was annoyed, and jealous. "And exactly why must we visit this place?" he asked.

Sholeh knew her brother well and understood his frustration. "Gaspar," she said sweetly, "Sanctum Tartarus is no threat to us."

"Sanctum Tartarus should *be* us," Gaspar grumbled.

Sholeh turned the television off. "It is a wonderful concept, isn't it? A house of horrors! There's no way it could possibly fail. I very much want to meet this Simon Janus. He's obviously a man of great vision."

"I think you're wrong, Sholeh. Sanctum Tartarus is a threat to us, a major threat. Do you really think that Las Vegas is big enough for both the Janus Cartel and the Kaviani family? I don't think so."

"The Janus Cartel is already here, and they're not going anywhere. So that's a reality we must deal with. *How* we choose to deal with that reality, that's the question."

"And exactly how do you suggest we deal with that reality? That's *my* question."

Sholeh smiled. "At some point, we meet with Simon Janus, talk with him, find out what he really wants, and determine if he's a reasonable man. If he is, we work with him. If he isn't, we kill him."

"You're much too complicated, Sholeh. I say we just kill him and be done with it. And the sooner the better. I don't like Simon Janus."

"You've never met Simon Janus. How do you know you don't like him?"

"He's too smart. I much prefer Americans, particularly Las Vegans."

Sholeh laughed. "We can't expect everyone to be an idiot. Besides, you're far too emotional, Gaspar. Doing business successfully requires a dispassionate head, particularly when dealing with someone as extraordinary as Simon Janus. We'll deal with Simon Janus in due time."

Sholeh activated the television, again, only now the screen was filled with surveillance camera footage of Raven from the night of Dmitri's demise. She could be seen sprinting down a hotel hallway as she made her frantic escape. Sholeh paused the moving images and zoomed in to a static closeup image of Raven's face.

"Of course, Ravendiablo is a completely different matter altogether," Sholeh said with evil eyes fixed to the screen. "Ravendiablo must die ... and very, very slowly. There's still no trace of her after all this time?"

Gaspar's demeanor darkened even more. "We've got a web over the entire city. We'll find her."

"Clearly, she's being hidden."

"We'll find her."

Sholeh glanced at the empty chair beside Gaspar and sighed. "Poor Dmitri," she said. "We always knew that his insatiable appetites would be the death of him. He was a remarkable man with myriad abilities, save one, the ability to control himself."

"Dmitri would have sided with me about how best to deal with Simon Janus."

Sholeh rolled her eyes in exasperation. "Why are you so obsessed with Simon Janus?"

"Perhaps I'm not the dispassionate intellectual that you are, but I have intuition and it's always served me well. And my intuition tells me that Simon Janus is a dangerous man. I know blind ambition when I see it."

"And I know raging jealousy when I see it."

"Better jealousy than admiration," snapped Gaspar.

Sholeh smiled. "Yes, I admire Simon Janus and I don't

deny it. I admire creativity, intellect, and drive, three things you see very little of these days, particularly in this part of the world. Simon Janus possesses all three in great abundance. I think he's extraordinary. So, until he becomes a tangible threat to us, I'll refrain from any hostility." Sholeh laughed. "Gaspar, you were the one who always called Las Vegas a neon wasteland. Now you obsess over someone who may be claiming that wasteland as his own. Why should we care if Simon Janus owns one casino, or the entire Strip for that matter? The Kavianis are international. What do we care about local matters?"

"Because Las Vegas isn't local, Las Vegas *is* international. And it always has been. Dmitri understood the significance of Las Vegas long ago but we never listened. We always thought the wrong head was influencing his opinions. Now, in retrospect, it's clear that Dmitri was a true visionary. For years he spoke of the various crime organizations that came here, played here, conducted business here, laundered money here. Dmitri said it was inevitable that one day in the near future, Las Vegas would be the *hub* of an international crime wheel. Dmitri was right. And I believe that future is now, especially now that the city has collapsed. The vultures are circling and the jackals are closing in, but Simon Janus is different. He's no mere scavenger, and that's why he's so dangerous. He didn't come here to feed on a corpse. Simon Janus intends to bring the city of Las Vegas back to life but in a whole new way. Sanctum Tartarus is far more than just some dark destination. It's something else altogether. I believe that Sanctum Tartarus is phase one of a carefully planned, long-term agenda. It's obvious what Simon Janus really wants. Simon Janus wants to be *king of the hub*. King of the world."

Sholeh listened intently and considered Gaspar's wise words. It was clear that he made sense. "I believe you're correct, Gaspar."

Gaspar was both surprised and pleased by Sholeh's response.

"Really?" he said, barely able to conceal his almost childlike delight at having swayed her opinion.

Sholeh glanced at Dmitri's empty chair. "Yes. Dmitri was right all along. He was right about something else, as well. Dmitri called Las Vegas the most magical city in the world. Do you remember?"

"Yes, I remember. He said the city possessed a powerful energy. An occult energy capable of great transformations."

"Dmitri insisted that the real Las Vegas was occult, hidden from the eyes of the many but well undersood by an enlightened few. He also said Las Vegas was an ideal place for performing *real* magic. I thought it was the most ridiculous thing I'd ever heard, and I laughed at the suggestion. But I'm not laughing now. Since coming here, I very much feel ... *plugged in*, as they say. Like a household appliance plugged into a wall socket. I've never felt more energized in my life. And my personal powers have never been stronger."

"Nor mine."

Sholeh smiled as she reflected on the profound truth she had come to accept. "I never would have believed it, but it's clear to me now. Las Vegas is a *sacred* site. So we will conduct the dark work here."

Gaspar understood the implications of Sholeh's words. He nodded in agreement and smiled knowingly. "Yes."

"We will construct the Portal here, beneath our new home. Now is the time of the Invocation. And Las Vegas is clearly the place."

"Yes."

"Here, we will summon the Dalkhu," Sholeh glanced at Dmitri's chair, "and perhaps they will reward us and *restore* our brother."

Sholeh gently lifted her pet from her lap and gently placed the creature on the table. It was black, covered with fur, and the size of a small dog. While resting in Sholeh's lap, the creature's legs had been comfortably folded beneath itself. Now the eight, long, sectioned legs extended themselves one by one, slowly and gracefully. Then the creature lifted its body up from the table, revealing itself to be a spider. As it strolled across Sholeh's desk, she gazed at it lovingly.

"Udo," she purred affectionately.

18

Kim Desmond

Dressed in a black leather jacket, black scarf, black leather tunic, and black combat boots, Kim Desmond strode through the McCarran airport terminal with a small bag in hand. He was stunningly masculine and turned many heads, the vast majority of those heads being female. Kim was a visually provocative man, and women, both young and old, were clearly enthralled by him. Male reaction was mixed. There were curiosity, envy, and jealousy. There was even some ridicule. After all, to the modern man, Kim was a guy in a dress. But Kim was oblivious to the looks and opinions of the people around him. His mind was elsewhere. When Kim arrived at the security checkpoint, he dutifully removed his jacket and boots and placed them in containers to be scanned. It was then that he really did resemble a guy in a dress. Disruptive laughter and taunting erupted in the aisle across from him.

"Hey, girlfriend, I like that outfit."

"Every girl needs a little black dress!"

"Hope you got the heels to go with it, baby."

Kim turned in the direction of the taunts and saw three young modern men. They obviously wanted his attention, and now that they had it, they glared at him defiantly. The security checkpoint area was jampacked with travelers, all of whom were focused on the developing drama. The air was electric with tension. Kim eyed the three men coldly.

"If your pants were sagging any lower, I'd be looking at your whole ass instead of just most of it," Kim said with a bemused smile. "You're obviously advertising, but I'm not interested."

The surrounding passengers roared with laughter and the young men were momentarily silenced. They were hardly expecting such a response.

"The three of you don't add up to one *real* man," Kim said, shaking his head sadly.

Kim turned and continued through security where he was scanned by a fascinated female attendant who took considerably longer than necessary to inspect him. Passing inspection, he put on his jacket and boots, collected his bag, and headed toward his departure gate. Kim was glad to be leaving Las Vegas. He despised the city. His mind was consumed with thoughts of Raven. Tonight was the grand opening of Sanctum Tartarus, and Raven was somewhere inside, searching for answers. Kim wasn't worried about Raven. She was a highly trained warrior. Kim was worried about Kim because he had fallen in love with Raven. It was love at first sight. As he made his way through the crowded terminal past curious onlookers, he wondered if he would ever see her diabolical smile again.

Kim checked his watch. His flight would be boarding shortly, so he decided to go to the men's room to freshen up a bit. When he entered, he found two other men washing their hands. Kim set down his bag and took a place at a urinal. As he relieved himself, he tried to force Raven out of his mind, but it was useless. Raven was like no woman he had ever met or even imagined. She was highly intelligent and physically capable. She wasn't necessarily beautiful, certainly not in a conventional sense, but she was irresistibly magnetic—and *compelling*. Kim particularly liked the fact that she didn't really need a man, or a woman, or whatever it was she was into. She was a lone wolf. Kim could relate to that because he was a lone wolf, too. He had never thought he needed anybody, until now.

"You've got a big mouth—even for a bitch."

Kim turned to find the three men who had taunted him earlier. The other two bathroom patrons were now gone. Kim stepped away from the urinal and walked to the row of sinks. Above the sinks was a huge mirror that reflected the three men behind him. One of the men remained by the entrance door while the other two approached Kim.

"You were all mouth a minute ago," said the man by the door. He seemed to be the leader, at least he projected himself that way. "Say something now."

Kim calmly washed his hands as he faced the mirror. "I told you already. I'm not interested in what you're offering. I'm into women, not *punks*. You'll have to try elsewhere."

The two men rushed at Kim simultaneously. Kim spun around and delivered a kick into the belly of one attacker. As the man collapsed, Kim grabbed him by the collar and slammed him face first into a sink. He fell to the floor as blood spewed from his broken nose. The second man fired a punch, but Kim deflected it, snatched the arm, and twisted it to the breaking point. The man dropped to his knees, screaming in pain, until Kim silenced him with a kick to the mouth.

The leader sprinted across the room, dived onto Kim's back, and dragged him to the floor. The two men furiously traded punches while rolling over the linoleum until, finally, Kim seized control. Kim grabbed the man's ankle, swung him up off the floor, and hurled him into the mirror on the wall, shattering it completely. Now all three men lay unconscious.

Kim checked his appearance in a small piece of mirror that remained attached to the wall. Then he picked up his bag and exited the rest room. Kim had a plane to catch. He was ready to leave Las Vegas, now more than ever.

19

No Chains Will Ever Hold You

As the opening-night festivities continued, a delivery van arrived at the rear gate of Sanctum Tartarus. Security was a major priority. In addition to the tall fencing that surrounded the perimeter of the property, armed security guards patrolled the area as well. This part of Sanctum Tartarus was reserved for special personnel and delivery vehicles only. Visitors who accidentally found themselves in the area were quickly redirected to the proper parking lots and structures.

A security guard stepped out of a booth that stood beside the gate and approached the van. The female driver presented him with paperwork, and he scrutinized it carefully. Finally, the guard directed the driver to a parking structure especially for delivery vehicles. He returned to the booth, and the gate slowly drew back.

The woman drove the van onto the grounds and cruised over to the parking structure. She drove the van into the structure, and maneuvered it to the lower level, finally backing the vehicle up to a loading dock where a workman stood waiting. The man opened the back door of the van and removed several trunks on wheels. He pushed the trunks into a freight elevator, pressed a button, and the door slammed shut. As the elevator slowly ascended, the workman whistled absentmindedly.

When the desired floor was reached, the elevator door slid back, and the workman pushed the trunks out. He remained inside. The door closed and he went on to some other destination. The trunks sat in what appeared to be the backstage area of a theater. Busy workers walked by carrying all manner of lights, scenery, and other stage equipment. When the backstage bustle finally died down, the lid of one of the newly arrived trunks slowly opened. Raven climbed out, dressed in a worker's jumpsuit and hat, carrying a clipboard. She assumed an air of responsibility by pretending to check the contents of the other trunks. A curious worker spotted her and approached. He was perplexed by the sight of her and eyed her suspiciously. Raven saw him approaching and immediately took charge of the situation.

"Who left these trunks sitting here like this?" she snapped angrily. "Do you know anything about this?"

The worker was completely caught off guard. "No, ma'am, I don't know anything about it," he answered nervously. No longer suspicious, now he was concerned.

Raven sighed in exasperation and shook her head. "Nobody seems to know anything around here and I'm getting sick of it. This isn't going to look good on my report, I can tell you that. I don't know what's going on back here, but somebody better start getting their shit together pretty quick or some heads are going to roll. Are you on break now?"

"No, ma'am. I don't normally break until ..."

"Then get down to the loading dock," Raven interrupted. "I'm expecting some more trunks just like these. When they show up, you bring them back here, leave them with these, and wait here till I get back. When I do, I'll tell you where everything belongs. Do you understand me?"

"Yes, ma'am." He was confused, but he wasn't about to argue with Raven.

"Then get moving."

Raven abruptly turned, walked away and continued her clipboard pretense. The massive backstage equipment enabled Raven to hide herself from the many legitimate workers, and she moved deeper into the shadows. Finally, she took refuge in a particularly dark corner where she waited and watched the movement of the others. She noticed one man pushing a trunk on wheels. There was something odd about his body language that alerted Raven's radar and she followed him, concealed by shadows. She watched as he pushed the trunk to a far corner, left it beside a metallic door, and walked away. Moments later, the metallic door opened. Another man emerged, took hold of the trunk and wheeled it inside.

Raven waited a few moments, then moved along the wall toward the mysterious metallic door. She entered, and discovered an empty room with a service elevator. She pressed the "Down" button and waited. When the elevator arrived, it was empty. Raven stepped inside, pressed the Lower Level button, and the elevator door closed. The elevator descended several levels before coming to a stop at the bottom. The door opened, revealing an immense cavern facility. There was some type of construction underway, evidenced by the presence of parked forklifts and other industrial vehicles. Building materials were scattered about and stacked high. There was no sign of workers, but there was the intermittent sound of machinery grinding somewhere in the complex.

Raven stepped off the elevator and darted behind a large stack of construction materials. Moments later, she emerged dressed in black leather with her blade strapped to her leg. Armed with a tiny camera, she snapped pictures of the complex while keeping herself concealed by shadows and stacks of supplies. Raven entered a tubular passageway and paused momentarily. There was still no sign of life, only that strange mechanical grinding noise. There was light up ahead, and Raven moved toward it on tiptoe. She exited the passageway and emerged into an area resembling the platform of a subway, complete with a huge tunnel that stretched far into the black distance. Like the rest of the complex this area looked to be under construction. There were more piles of materials stacked and scattered, but the subway track was completed and appeared functional. Raven took more pictures. Deep in the tunnel, a bright beam of light signaled the approach of a vehicle. Raven hid behind a forklift, though she maintained a clear view of the platform.

Moments later, a vehicle arrived. It was the size of a city bus and looked like a shiny black bullet. There were windows on the sides but none in front. It was unusually quiet, emitting a strange hum instead of the roar of an engine. Raven snapped more pictures. A door slid back, and several men dressed in worker's uniforms stepped out of the bullet. They talked amongst themselves for a moment before heading into the tubular passageway from which Raven had just emerged. Raven waited for a moment, then ventured out from behind the forklift and over to the bullet car. The door remained open and she peered inside. The car was empty save for rows of seats. Raven stepped inside, and made her way deeper into the vehicle. When she reached the rear, she was startled by the sound of footsteps out on the platform. She peered through a window and saw some of the men returning. Raven darted behind a seat and crouched down out of view. She heard the men enter the vehicle and seat themselves. The door closed and the bullet sped off.

Hidden behind the seat, Raven could only wait as the bullet car moved deeper and deeper into the tunnel. She was trapped and heading to some unknown destination at breakneck speed. Long minutes passed until, finally, the bullet came to a stop. Raven heard the door open and the men exit. She waited. Finally, she moved from behind the seat, raised her head, and peered out the window. She saw another platfom, only this one wasn't deserted. There were several men dressed in black military-style uniforms loading boxes onto a pickup truck. Raven crouched down and darted up to the front of the car. The door remained open and she peered out. The military men continued their loading in a far corner. Raven spotted a door marked "Personnel" several feet away across the platform. Seizing her opportunity to escape, she sprinted over to the door and entered.

         RAVENDIABLO

Raven emerged into the hallway of what appeared to be a hospital, brightly lit, and lined with doors on either side. She made her way down the hallway. Each door had a small window and Raven peered into them. Most of the rooms were for storage. There was a lounge, a kitchen, a dining room, and a laboratory where men in lab coats sat hunched over testing equipment. Raven continued down the hallway. The sudden sound of voices coming from out on the platform area indicated trouble was afoot. Raven rushed into a room and carefully closed the door behind her. When she turned to see exactly where she had sought refuge, she found herself in a room filled with young women. They were dressed in surgical scrubs or hospital gowns, and they all peered at her with dazed, confused looks. Their droopy eyelids and slow, shuffling movements indicated that the women were under the influence of heavy drugs. Some women lay on beds that were lined up in a row. Others were seated in chairs scattered about the room. Still others stood motionless like drooling statues, their feet firmly planted to the floor. Raven walked deeper into the room as tears streamed down her face.

The sudden sound of the doorknob turning startled Raven. She dived into an empty bed and pulled the sheet over her head. A young doctor dressed in white entered the room followed by a muscular man in military garb. The soldier remained by the door leering lecherously as the doctor moved from woman to woman, examining their eyes with a small flashlight. The doctor's demeanor was strangely lighthearted, and he whistled cheerfully as he worked. Sometimes he pretended to make conversation with the women, but none of them responded, at least not in a coherent way. It was clear that the doctor had no real concern about their condition. The women were little more than houseplants. The doctor focused his attention on the women lying down. These women appeared to be considerably more drugged than the others and they barely moved as he examined them. When the doctor reached Raven's bed, he noticed her completely covered by the sheet. He sat beside her and stroked her.

"Sit up, sleeping beauty," he said. "I need to take a look at you."

Raven sprung up and head-butted him, knocking him back on the bed. She leaped on top of him and jammed her thumbs into his eye sockets, riding his wildly struggling body as he screamed beneath her. The soldier rushed over to intervene, and Raven was off the bed in an instant. The soldier snatched her by the collar, but Raven spun out of his grasp and dropped him with a kick to the ribcage. The soldier scrambled back to his feet and assumed a fighting stance, ready for a confrontation. Raven attacked him and they exchanged kicks and blows. The soldier proved to be a formidable fighter, but he was outmatched.

Raven had been seething with rage since first discovering the drugged women. She needed to spill blood, so she tore out the soldier's throat and was rewarded with a red geyser that sprayed her, decorating her face like warpaint. The soldier collapsed at her feet.

Raven turned to flee the room when she noticed a woman sitting in the corner staring at the wall. The woman looked a bit older than the others, and familiar.

Raven moved closer for a better view. It was Shanice. Raven rushed over to her, stood her up and gazed into her vacant eyes. She didn't seem to recognize Raven. Raven grabbed her, hurried across the room and out the door. They were confronted by another soldier, but Raven kicked him out of her way and ran down the hallway with Shanice in tow.

They emerged onto the platform only to find the bullet car gone and three soldiers waiting. Raven carefully sat Shanice on a crate and rushed at them. She sent one man flying with a sternum-crushing kick to the chest. The other two men attacked, and Raven confronted them. She grabbed the arm of one man and broke it in several places before sweeping his legs out from under him. She dodged the punch of the last man, then fired a kick to his face, dropping him to his knees. She snatched his head with both hands and viciously spun his neck well past the breaking point.

Raven spotted a three-wheel sport utility vehicle a few feet away. She grabbed Shanice and helped her into the back of the vehicle. She jumped on board, revved the engine, and drove the vehicle off the platform and into the tunnel. It was an act of mad desperation. Raven drove deeper into the tunnel while increasing her speed, occasionally glancing over at the dazed Shanice. Up ahead, she could see the light of an oncoming bullet car rapidly approaching and there wasn't room enough to maneuver around it. Raven snatched hold of Shanice and they leaped out of the vehicle at the moment of impact. The earsplitting sound of the collision roared throughout the tunnel as the bullet car dragged the demolished vehicle up the track with sparks flying.

Raven helped Shanice to her feet, and they continued running deeper into the tunnel. Up ahead was a familiar and welcome sight, the first platform. Seeing it gave the weary Raven a much needed burst of adrenalin. She quickened the pace and forced Shanice to run harder. Shanice was ready to collapse, but Raven held her tightly and pushed on. She helped Shanice climb up onto the platform, and they continued, running into the tubular passageway, finally emerging into the cavern area. Shanice's legs finally gave out completely and she collapsed at Raven's feet.

Then out from the shadows they ran, a horde of men, coming from all directions. Raven turned to face her new challengers. They weren't workers or soldiers, but an ultra-elite security force. They were armed with blades, dressed in blood red, and wore the masks of *demons*. They were the Red Death, and they circled Raven slowly and menacingly. Raven was relieved to see them.

Now was *her* time.

Raven rolled back her eyes and extended her tongue. She became a vessel and a great and terrible power flooded into her. She became one with the beast. Raven unsheathed the folded sword strapped to her leg. With a flick of her wrist, the weapon fully extended, and the curved blade glistened ominously. The circling Red Death rushed in on her. They were deadly fighters and wielded their weapons with savage proficiency, but they were unprepared for the warrior woman confronting them, this agent of Kali. Raven fearlessly ducked, dodged, and deflected their attacks. She wasn't unscathed, but she was unstoppable. The injuries she sustained only invigorated and intoxicated her.

Raven exploded and unleashed her most barbaric of techniques. Like a magnificent butcher, Raven hacked and slashed her adversaries with ferocity, sending severed limbs and heads flying. Blood spurted and spewed from deep gashes and gaping wounds. Raven's powerful punches and spinning kicks shattered bones, crushed ribs, snapped necks, and sent demons airborne. She blew through them all like a tsunami, filling the cavern with her wicked wailing and the agonized cries of her victims.

Their cries were music and Raven danced.

She danced with drunken abandon, splashing joyfully in the puddles of blood that formed at her feet. Raven was out of her mind, *possessed*, and teetered on the brink of a powerful, volcanic orgasm, when she felt a hand seize her ankle. Raven looked down and found Shanice tightly holding onto her, trying to calm her. Their eyes locked, and Raven's madness slowly subsided until finally, Raven became Raven once more. Raven collected her emotions as she surveyed her bloody handiwork. The carvern was littered with the mutilated bodies of the Red Death. Raven had slaughtered them all.

Raven helped Shanice to her feet, and they kissed and hugged desperately. She slid her arm around Shanice's waist and quickly led her over to the elevator in the far corner of the cavern. Raven pressed the "Up" button, but she wasn't going anywhere. From out of the shadows, a wooden plank was swung down upon her head and she crumpled to the ground, unconscious.

* * *

Xandra sat at her desk studying papers in her office. The phone rang and she answered. As she listened to the voice on the other end of the line, it was clear from her pained expression that the information she was receiving was grave indeed. Finally, she dropped the phone, cradled her head in her hands and wept.

* * *

Kim's plane was finally ready for boarding. He stood in line with the rest of the passengers, anxious to put Las Vegas behind him. He looked at his watch and thought of Raven. He knew that by now, she was somewhere deep in the bowels of Sanctum Tartarus. Kim sighed and tried to force Raven out of his mind. There was a beautiful woman beside him who clearly wanted his attention, and she decided to strike up a conversation.

"Good evening," she said with a flirtatious smile.

Hello," Kim said politely. He barely even looked at her.

"Did you have any luck in Vegas?"

Kim laughed cynically. "Yeah, I hit the jackpot. And that's the problem."

Kim's cell phone rang, and he reluctantly answered it. As Kim listened to the voice on the other end of the line, it was clear from his pained expression that the information he was receiving was grave indeed. When Kim finally ended the call, he looked as though he had swallowed a knife. Now, he stood at the front of the line where an attendant waited for him to produce his boarding pass. Kim removed the pass from his jacket, but instead of handing it to the attendant, he tore it up and tossed the pieces into a nearby trash container. The attendant looked at him in surprise.

"Is there a problem?" the attendant asked curiously.

Kim shook his head. "Nothing I can't deal with," he answered. He stepped out of line and headed back into Las Vegas.

* * *

Ravendiablo was tightly bound in chains and suspended upside down in the corner of a dark room. But she looked more like a dangerous black widow spider than a helpless captive. Because there was no fear in her eyes. Slowly and deliberately, she maneuvered her body with serpentine agility. Her bonds would soon be loosened.

And she smiled *diabolically*.

About the Author

Miko Montgomery is a writer, musician/composer, film-maker, and photographer. He makes his home in Las Vegas.

mikomontgomery.com